A Scarlet Knight

Mickey Copp

Contents

Introduction

Since 1972, Title IX has legally guaranteed fairness, opportunity and the prevention of discrimination and harrasment in athletics. The differnce between the law and the actual implementation of said principles are often very different. This story, <u>A Scarlet Knight</u>, tells of one young woman's travails as she endeavors to participate in one of the last bastions of "male" sports - wrestling. Heather Prince battles through every imaginable obstacle to try and achieve success where few others have tried.

This story is dedicated to every young woman, from the early pioneers to the ones who have reached great heights. None of them achieved their goals without great determination and perseverance. The struggle goes on, and the efforts of those young women are a sight to behold. Strive on!!

About the Author

Mickey Copp is an author and lifelong educator. A supporter of women in athletics, they split their time (along with their partner, three daughters and a fourteen pound dog) between the Green Mountains of Vermont and the Jersey shore. When not reading or writing, Mickey can be found enjoying the outdoors that make America great.

Chapter 1

Nothing changes as quickly as a high school hallway. One moment, the only sound is the echo of staccato heels clicking quickly, hurrying to get ahead of the student throng. The next is barely controlled bedlam.

As the annoying buzz (that is called a bell) sounded the alert, doors swung open. Some doors had an initial burst, others a burgeoning swell. Both groups flowed into a 'walking dead' stroll as the mob congealed together. They quickly picked up the pace, just like rush-hour traffic after a merge.

And like said traffic, the slower students kept near the shoulder (in this case, the lockers) while the high-fliers buzzed along in the middle. A young blonde—5'2", extremely fit and attractive in a wholesome way—moved gracefully along with the crowd. Her name was Heather Prince, and like most, she was musing random thoughts when something caught the corner of her eye.

Like the screech of a needle across an old vinyl LP, her sudden stop disturbed the flow of traffic. She was nearly rear-ended by a cell phone-gazing freshman. The bodies swelled behind them and started to surge around—annoyed. She quickly pulled back against the lockers, pressing herself against them like a breakdown on the shoulder, as the mob thinned and finally dissipated with the ringing of the bell to start the next period.

"ARE YOU MAN ENOUGH?" the poster on the wall opposite her screamed. A burly, exaggeratedly muscled wrestler crouched in caricature below the question. The body of the poster read:

"If you're up to the challenge, join us for tryouts. See if you've got what it takes to be a Scarlet Knight.

See Coach Wolf in E-21 or Coach Boxwood in Guidance for a wrestling packet today."

Heather stared at the poster for several seconds, shaking her head. You would think, she mused to herself, that coaches such as they would not stoop to such clichés—the overmuscled Neanderthal filled with enough testosterone to take down a mastodon. Anyone who'd truly been around it knew that wrestling was an art form, a graceful yet powerful dance filled with strength, skill, and wily craft.

Disgusted, she turned to head toward the cafeteria for lunch. She muttered to herself, "Man enough?!" She stopped, turned on her heel, and headed in the other direction—toward the guidance office.

Chapter 2

The swivel chair creaked beneath him as he turned to toss a file onto the cabinet behind him. He sighed as he felt his dress shirt strain at the buttons while his body twisted. It just wasn't easy to keep the weight off once you hit fifty—even though he worked out three times a week. That, along with the need to move the part in his hair further and further down the side to accommodate the thinning of his salt-and-pepper hair. He made a mental note that it was time to get serious about cutting out the carbs.

George Boxwood was the perfect assistant to a program. As a guidance counselor, he could adjust his schedule to accommodate any and all issues. He had been a fine wrestler in his day, albeit never a state champ (his one nagging regret). Coaching twenty-seven champs and counting, though, was a tremendous source of pride and accomplishment. Like Wolf, he was sure that the three young men they needed were about to walk through that door.

With that thought, his phone rang. The sixth period flew by, and he was just about to buzz Anne Marie to say he was grabbing lunch when a silent figure stopped in front of his door.

"Heather," he said, priding himself on remembering all of his students' names. "How can I help you this afternoon? Is everything all right?"

She looked a little nervous, and Boxwood silently wished he'd slipped out to lunch already. He hated "girl drama." And although Heather Prince had never been in trouble, he braced himself for tears, a story of mean girls, horrible internet nonsense, and an absolute need to change her schedule. He sighed inwardly, steeling his resolve. "No schedule changes unless we're going to get sued" was Principal Dale's mantra, and Boxwood tried to follow it.

"Sit down," he offered, checking the tissue box on his desk for easy access. "Is everything all right?"

"Fine," she replied.

He ran what he remembered of her through his head. Top student. Great soccer player. Both parents were alumni. Her dad had been a great wrestler (he also just fell short of being a state champ) and ran the junior youth wrestling program for years. She was also quite attractive, just like her mother, he thought.

Then she surprised him.

"I just wanted to pick up a wrestling packet," she said with a smile.

He was taken aback.

"Well…" he dragged out. "Your boyfriend is going to have to come and pick them up himself. I have a few questions I like to ask, and I like to go over it to make sure they understand what's involved." He said this as pleasantly as he could, thinking that it didn't bode well that a boy didn't even have the guts to pick up his own packet. Probably not one of the boys we need.

"Oh, well, that's fine. They're actually for me, and I have time. This is my lunch period."

He blinked several times, uncomprehending.

"Oh."

A silent, pregnant pause followed as neither seemed to know what to say.

Finally, Boxwood stuttered.

"Look, I know you are a great athlete. I've seen several of your soccer games— the best we've had here in years. But you, more than most kids, should know that this is one sport where guys and girls simply can't compete. It's just not physically plausible—I mean, the risk of injury is catastrophic. I understand how you'd want to be part of the program," he gathered his thoughts. "Being a team manager is just as important—heck, maybe more important—than individual wrestlers and the boy we had graduated, so this would be perfect. After all, you've been around wrestling your whole life."

He remembered her as a little girl, following her dad around like a hyper puppy at all the junior league matches and practices.

"I don't want to be a manager. I want to wrestle," she responded evenly.

"I'm sorry, Heather. It's just not a realistic possibility. Soccer? Absolutely. Wrestling? I'm sorry, it would be irresponsible of me even to encourage it."

"But Coach Wolf said 'anyone' who wanted to wrestle…"

"Obviously, he intended it for the young men. But think about it, we really need a manager, and the job is every bit as—"

"But I want to wrestle, not manage," she interrupted.

Boxwood sighed audibly. "I'm sorry, Heather, it's just not possible."

The stare-down was broken when he reached for one of his cards. "Look, Heather, have your dad give me a call, okay? We'll talk about it, and he'll explain it to you. It's just not something a young lady wants to be involved in. I'm just looking out for you." His face approximated a smile.

Her brows knit as she looked at the card in her hand. She got up and turned to leave, books in hand.

"I'm sorry," he reiterated as he began to rub his temples. The girls always seemed to leave him with a headache.

Chapter 3

The intercom buzzed. "He's here."

"Send him in," barked harried Principal Jim Dale, trying to sit up taller in his chair as he felt dwarfed by the ramrod-straight ex-Marine sitting easily in the chair across from his desk. He glanced over at Coach Wolf, who still looked like he could drop and pump out fifty push-ups without even breaking a sweat, and shook his head.

"George," he smiled. "C'mon in, have a seat," he invited.

"Coach Wolf and I were just having a little chat. We were wondering—have you ever heard of a little thing called Title IX?"

"You gotta be fucking kidding me," he replied incredulously. "You're not seriously going along with this, are you, Walt?"

"Hey. Let's watch the language, George," Principal Dale added.

George rolled his eyes and went on. "Letting a girl wrestle is just flat-out insane. I can't believe you'd even consider it."

"I agree; it's not even a remote possibility," Coach Wolf replied. "But… we need to be smart about how we handle it. We wrestle against some of the best programs in the state. Letting a girl out there against some of them could get her paralyzed or even killed."

"Exactly." George leaned back in his chair.

"But we are also about to field the best team we've had in years. We have three, maybe four, state champs on our roster. We have the potential to win a team state title. The absolute last thing we need is a distraction just before we start on this journey."

"So, it's done. We say no and stick to our guns."

"And have every feminazi in the state protesting in front of the school? Hell, half the female teachers will be in this office tomorrow. We need to handle this in a quiet, sensible way."

"The last thing we need around here is another lawsuit," the principal added. "And if a reporter gets wind of this…"

"Send a CAP student to tell her to come to my classroom next period. I'll have all the papers in a nice file. I'll even put her name right on top."

"C'mon, Walt. This is crazy." George smacked the arms of his chair.

"You remember who her dad is, don't you?"

"Yes, and that's probably who put this in her head, dragging her around to all those practices. Hell, he even used to let her wrestle against the lighter weights!"

"And she used to win, too," Wolf added. "But when was the last time you saw her there?"

"I don't know. Three, four years, I guess."

"Exactly—about the time she hit puberty and started to 'blossom.' And right around the time the boys her age started to grow hair on their balls. Believe me, the last thing Paul Prince wants is his little princess getting groped and mauled by a bunch of horny gorillas. The second she shows him the papers, he'll squash this, and we won't have to be the bad guys."

Principal Dale nodded as he rocked back and forth in his leather chair. Boxwood tilted his head and nodded.

"All right. I guess I should have thought it through and talked to you. But it caught me totally by surprise. I would never have expected this in a million years."

Wolf laughed. "Welcome to the twenty-first century. My jaw dropped, too. Fortunately, I had a few minutes to think it through. It's just our first challenge of the year. You know a state championship isn't coming easy—we can take this as our first battle. It'll help us stay on our toes."

"I guess. You're sure Paul will shut this down?"

"If it was your daughter?" Wolf smiled. "But I think I'll call Paul and check on my insurance tonight. Wanna make sure my personal liability is high enough with the season coming up."

Coach Wolf stood up and leaned over to knock on Principal Dale's desk.

"Don't worry, Jimbo. We'll straighten this out, and you'll never hear about it again."

He turned and headed for the door, giving Boxwood a mocking smirk. As he passed, he glanced back toward Dale and made an upside-down triangle just below his belt with his thumbs and forefingers. Boxwood almost burst out laughing but covered it with a cough.

Boxwood jumped up and added, "Hey, sorry, Jim. This thing just caught me by surprise. Won't happen again, I promise."

"Okay then, just handle it. The last thing I need is gender crap. Just make it go away."

Chapter 4

"No." He simply stated as he tossed the packet onto the middle of the breakfast table.

Heather and her mother stared at him, incredulous. He glanced up from his plate and added after a pause, "And that's my final word on the matter."

"Excuse me," Mom responded. "But this warrants further discussion. You can't simply make pronouncements when she's obviously serious about this."

"So you're saying that you actually want her to be groped and pawed by hormone-filled young men in front of hundreds of people?"

"I'm merely saying that we need to talk about this and come to a decision after considering everything."

"All right, it's pretty simple. I don't want my only daughter becoming a joke and being physically abused as part of some feminist point being proved."

As Heather opened her mouth to respond, her mother beat her to the punch.

"But for the first ten years of her life, it was okay? Do you not see how ridiculous that sounds? You were the one who took her to practices, taught her all the basics, and had her wrestle your boys—frequently beating them, as I recall. Yet now it's 'out of the question'? Please explain this logic to me."

She leaned back in her chair and waited for a response.

Buttering his toast with a sigh, he attempted to reason with the unreasonable.

"That was an entirely different situation." Pointing with the butter knife for emphasis, he expounded, "Number one—I was fully in control of that situation. I never had my eye off any of them for one second, so it stayed completely under control. Number two—this was before puberty hit any of them, her included, and their bodies weren't developed in any sexual way at that point. You'll agree I haven't brought her since she was ten."

"You stopped coaching altogether."

"Primarily for that reason," he responded. "You're just being contentious for the sake of proving you won't be bossed around. And most of the time, I'm fine with that. This, however, is a no-argument situation. It's not happening. I'm not signing that, and I'm done talking about it."

He pushed away from the table, marched down the hallway to his office, and slammed the door behind him.

Heather, still in shock, her mouth open, looked at her mother. Mom shook her head in exasperation, picked up the permission packet, and signed it.

Chapter 5

The intercom buzzed.

"Brian Finnerty to see you." After a pause: "He doesn't have an appointment."

Principal Dale silently mouthed an obscenity and grimaced. Then he screwed his face back into a smile and hit the respond button.

"No problem. Send him right in."

He inwardly girded his loins as Brian Finnerty, Esq., basically squeezed into his doorway. At six feet seven and well over three hundred pounds (though he carried it well in smoothly tailored suits), his face beamed with the friendliest of smiles, as florid as any Irishman could be.

"James!" he fairly shouted in his smooth baritone. "Great to see you."

He strode over to the desk and offered his beefy paw.

"How's Monica? The kids?"

Principal Dale half rose from his chair to shake the proffered hand.

"Great. All doing well. Thanks."

Finnerty gave a strong squeeze and didn't wait to be offered a seat. Instead, he pulled up one of the chairs and plopped down in it. Dale winced, fairly certain he could hear the chair legs groaning under the strain.

"Your youngest just started at Princeton, right? How's she doing?"

"Good, off to a good start, anyway," Dale replied, surprised that Finnerty was being so friendly and conversational.

"She always was your smartest… must take after her mom." He grinned. "I'm kiddin', just busting your balls. Seriously, though, even with the grades, that's gotta set you back a pretty penny, right?"

He still had that "I'm your best friend" smile on his face… What was he getting at?

"Good thing you made it to the principal, huh? Without that salary…" He let it hang in the air, still smiling away.

Dale almost shivered at the ease with which Finnerty dropped a casual threat. The principal tried to recover.

"True, but we planned for it, so it's pretty much covered already."

"Of course, of course. Obviously, she actually got the smarts from dear old Dad. You never were one to miss the important details."

Finnerty leaned back in the chair, and the big smile settled into a more neutral expression.

"That's actually why I stopped by. Just a casual visit to check something. I hate to have folks go off half-cocked about things that can sometimes be resolved with just a little clarification. In my years, I'd say ninety percent of the problems people come to me with are simply misunderstandings that can be solved with a little communication."

"Brian, with all due respect, I'm starting to feel like I should have the board attorney present."

"Not at all, not at all. I wouldn't try to blindside you. Just wanted to check on something."

"Does this involve me or the school?" Dale asked, against his better judgment, half thinking he should stop this right now and call the superintendent.

"Probably neither. I think it's just a little snafu, and we can clear it up without anyone having any problems."

"Okay." Dale waited.

"I was just wondering… do your athletic permission forms require the signatures of both parents?"

Alarms went off in Dale's brain—*Don't answer. Don't answer.* But something about Finnerty's conversational tone brought it out of him.

"No, not usually. Of course, if there are custody issues, we may take a slightly different approach. But generally, one custodial parent's signature is sufficient."

"Yeah, that's what I thought. When I played football here, back in the Stone Age, I'm sure there was only one line for a signature."

Dale braced himself for the knockout punch he knew was coming.

"Must have just confused your coaches. Just a little slip-up. After all, it's probably the first time your wrestling coach got a permission slip from a female. Probably never had to deal with Title IX issues before. At least, I thought so… Could you maybe check for me? See if any of the boys were told to get both signatures?" Finnerty asked with total innocence.

I'm going to fucking kill them. I couldn't have been clearer, Dale thought, rage growing in his head. But on the surface, he smiled and told Finnerty:

"Really? I didn't know we had a girl going out for wrestling. I'll get right on that. If a parent signed a slip, barring a court order, it's valid. Like you said, I'm sure they just never ran into it before."

Dale rose from his chair and offered Finnerty his hand.

"I'll have this straightened out before your car's out of the parking lot."

"Great, great. That's what I figured."

Finnerty gave Dale his hardest handshake and a huge cuff on the shoulder.

"That's why I stopped by. I knew you'd never let something like this happen. Oh, and maybe you better warn those boys. They may have been great wrestlers…"

Every hint of a smile was gone from Finnerty's face.

"But they absolutely don't wanna fuck with me."

Dale shivered inwardly but kept his smile and composure.

"Don't worry. I'll make sure it never comes to that."

Finnerty gave a slight nod and wave as he turned and ducked through the doorway.

Dale waited until he was sure Finnerty had left the outer office, then hit the intercom button.

"They're already on the way up…" a voice intoned.

"Thanks."

I am going to fucking kill them, he thought again.

Chapter 6

She rounded the corner and turned up the slight slope of the school's curving entry. Striding smoothly and easily, she added a slight kick as she headed up the wide lane, even though no other runner was near her. Coach Boxwood was waiting at the top of the hill with a stopwatch and clipboard, looking as if he had swallowed something sour, while Coach Wolf casually strolled around with his arms folded across his chest. He stopped pacing, planted his feet widely, and watched as Heather approached.

"Good job, Prince. Walk it off to the front doors and back." He kept watching the bottom of the incline for more wrestlers—none were yet in sight.

"Did you run the whole course?" Boxwood asked as she ran past.

She circled back around, running in place. "Yeah, the cross-country course—right? The 2.2?" she quizzed, barely breathing hard.

"Yes, just checking."

Wolf interrupted, "Excellent job—now go, walk it off. We don't need any cramps or pulled muscles on the first day," he barked at her.

"Don't fuckin' start, George," he said softly as she jogged, then strode off. "Just deal with it."

"C'mon, that was nearly a full minute better than anyone we've ever timed." Boxwood shook his head and smirked.

"And right about where her soccer coach said she would be. They run it three times a week, and he said if she ran cross country instead of soccer, she'd probably be a state champ. She's a great athlete, period. And we need to just let her be for a while. So just don't start with her," he said just above a whisper.

"Finally," he added as he saw a scrawny little freshman named Willy turn the corner and start up the hill.

Boxwood shook his head, wrote Prince's time down, and reset his stopwatch as the first of the boys puffed and chugged up the hill.

Chapter 7

Coach Wolf handed her two singlets, both extra small—one silver, one scarlet—a small headgear and a plastic package.

Heather looked at the package and couldn't control a chuckle.

"I'm pretty sure I won't be needing this," she said, trying to hand it back.

"Unfortunately, it is required. The state rule book says clearly: *'No wrestler shall practice, participate in any scrimmage, or meet without a state wrestling commission-approved jockstrap or cup.'* I figured this would be less cumbersome."

"You're not just kinda, you know…" She hesitated. "Jerking my chain?"

"No. Believe me, I called the state commission, and they were adamant about it. No exceptions. And there's one other thing."

Now, he hesitated.

"The same rules say wrestlers may wear the singlet only or with a school-color T-shirt underneath. And believe me, I'm not trying to be inappropriate in any way here, but they said I couldn't have a waiver for any other items. They'd have to vote on it during the next rules committee meeting—which, unfortunately, is in the offseason."

She made no response and just waited.

He stalled but finally added, "So… that means no sports bra. I, uhh, am not sure if a T-shirt is gonna be enough to, uuuhh, make you feel comfortable."

"Oh. I see. Well, during soccer, most of us just wear an Under Armour body-fit shirt—can that work?"

"The rule doesn't specify any type or brand—only that it be tight enough so that it can't be grabbed and that the bottom of the sleeves cannot be more than six inches from the shoulder seam. So, if it looks like a regular T-shirt, it should be fine. Also, it has to be white or in team colors."

"I have both silver and scarlet. Should I wear matching or contrasting?"

"Hmm. I never thought about it. I suppose matching, I guess. You know what—either way, I'll find out before the meets start. Okay, wrestling room in five."

"Wait." She paused. "Do I change with everyone else?"

"Right. No, of course not. Ms. Dykstra is in the girls' locker room. Check with her—she's supposed to be setting something up for you. You know her, right?"

"Yes, she's my pre-calc teacher."

"I thought you were a sophomore?"

"I am."

"In pre-calc? Wow. How are your grades?"

"All A's so far, but pre-calc is pretty tough. Especially with Ms. D."

"Well, good job. You're gonna have to put in some extra time to keep it up with wrestling, you know."

"I will, I promise."

"Good. Oh, and you actually *have* to wear that." He nodded at the package in her hand. "So, you may as well start getting used to it."

"Okay." And she headed for the girls' locker room.

Wolf inwardly sighed. *She seems like such a good kid. Why does she have to do this? I don't want to have to crush her and force her to quit. And there'll be crying.*

He hated crying.

Chapter 8

Heather tapped lightly on the large window next to the office door. An attractive, fortyish woman with a very 1980s haircut framing her face looked up and smiled. She beckoned Heather to come in.

"Hey, I've been waiting for you. How's it going so far?"

"Good." She nodded down at the collection in her arms. "Got all my stuff, anyway."

"Wow, wrestling, huh? I never would have guessed that."

Heather braced herself for the *Are you sure...* lecture she thought was coming, but it never did.

"So, what weight class are you shooting for?" Ms. Dykstra asked enthusiastically as she rose from her chair and started walking into the locker room. Heather assumed she should follow.

"106 or 113. Those are the two lighter spots up for grabs. I could probably make weight for 113 by Friday, but 106 might be a little tougher."

She inwardly winced, realizing she had just opened herself up to another lecture—this one about the dangers of cutting weight. *Watch out for bulimia—blah, blah, blah...*

Again, it never came.

"Hah, no problem. Us girls know all about dieting and dropping weight. Those boys have no idea who they're dealing with. You'll run circles around them—and look good doing it."

Ms. Dykstra lightly placed a hand on Heather's shoulder and steered her past the showers toward a room at the far end of the locker room.

"This is the gymnastics team room during the fall. I just finished cleaning it all out," Dykstra chatted as they approached a door that Heather had thought was just a closet. "It's smaller than the other two—there's usually only a half dozen or so girls on gymnastics. It's a shame; it's such a great sport, but with so few girls participating, we may lose it." She turned and smiled. "But that's exactly what the wrestling coaches are whining about with wrestling. Maybe you'll start a new trend and re-energize their sport."

For a second, Heather thought she might be mocking her, but she had been around Ms. Dykstra enough to see from her face that she was actually serious.

Dykstra opened the door with one of her many keys. "I'll have it open right after school every day. You can put a lock on anyone you want. You'll have it all to yourself, but I'd lock it up anyway—you never know. It has access right to the showers."

She gestured through a large window that looked directly into the showers and to the other side, where a matching window faced the coaches' office.

"And if you turn right out of here, the locker room exit goes directly into the lobby and right to the wrestling room, so you won't have to go through the gym and around."

"Thanks, it's perfect." Heather smiled as she looked at the dozen lockers—six on each side with a bench in the middle, sitting at a right angle to the shower window. "But I better get going. The coach said to be out in five."

"All right, I'll leave you to it."

She turned to leave, then paused. "If you need anything—anything at all—I'm right there." She pointed through the Plexiglas picture window to the offices across the way. "Every day."

She lightly tapped Heather's shoulder with an open palm.

"Go get 'em, Heather. You're going to be great."

"Thanks."

Chapter 9

The whistle shrieked, and the murmur of talking stopped.

"On the line," Coach Wolf barked, and wrestlers moved quickly toward the silver boundary of the scarlet mats.

Heather felt the large hands of senior captain Juwann Davies grab her shoulders and pull her back.

"Off the mat when you're not wrestling!" he barked, pulling her back a step.

She instinctively backed up, and he seemed to be right on top of her. Then she flinched a little—was that…? No, it couldn't be. Then he leaned his pelvis forward just a bit. She heard him chuckle as he held that closeness and seemed to slide across her as he passed. She knew she was turning a bit red but then steeled herself and toed the line.

Wolf paced around and looked at the waiting group. They were fit, fired up, and ready to get in that circle and wrestle, but there would be no wrestling for at least the first week, maybe more. Nope, it was time for good old-fashioned torture. He shook the tree hard—nothing but exhausting drills and repetition, and the losers would be shaken out.

His eyes touched on Heather Prince for a second and kept going. He glanced at his senior tri-captains. Each one should be a state champ this year. This year, the tree would be shaken to its roots, and only the real fruit would remain.

"Captains," he barked again. "Inside the circle. Let's show our newbies some warm-ups."

They burst in and put their toes right on the inner line of the wrestling circle.

"Arms width."

They hopped, widening their arms out, fingertips nearly touching.

"In, out."

They began a toe hop from inside to outside the line, quick, in unison, effortless yet intense for these champions.

"You will follow their pace. These are champions, and you will keep up, or you won't be here. We only want champions. Nothing less."

At the end of 30 seconds, he blew the whistle.

Heather smiled to herself. She had run all these drills for years when her father coached the youth wrestling program. There was no doubt in her mind that she would be able to keep up with his so-called champions.

She moved in an easy, smooth motion as others struggled to find the right timing. Not even breathing hard, Heather switched easily as the whistle shrilled again, and Coach Wolf barked out, "Alternate."

As a group, they began to fall into a rhythm as the coaches strolled around the circle, arms crossed, watching progress.

Heather had settled quickly and easily into the movement, but as the coaches turned away, the wrestler in front of her, Marco Castaglia, stopped short and then quickly double-hopped back into the rhythmic line.

Heather was caught completely off guard, stopped short, and found herself slammed into by the freshman behind her. She went down in a tangle.

The whistle screeched.

"Well, aren't we lucky today?" Coach Wolf smiled. "Prince here just got us all some bonus work. This is a team, what one Scarlet Knight does, all Scarlet Knights do. So, as a team, we're going to start this over, and this time, we're going to get it perfect. How many times around, Box?" he casually asked Coach Boxwood.

"Let's see if they can handle three without any screw-ups."

"Three it is. Five if they make another mistake. Then seven. I'll stand right here and wait for you, Prince. If by the time I see you for the fourth time, you can stay upright, maybe we'll be able to move on to something else."

Heather gritted her teeth and focused on staying in rhythm. She glared at Marco in front of her, but he smiled obliviously. She felt sure that Coach Boxwood had been looking their way when it happened, but she must have been wrong.

So that's how it's going to be, she thought to herself. Hell no, Marco. You guys aren't going to run me off that easy.

She was still seething when the whistle broke her thoughts.

"All right, good job. Stop. Way to stay on your feet this time, Prince."

Wolf strolled around for a second, giving them a short moment to catch their breath.

"Three lines, one behind each captain."

Heather moved to the closest line, which happened to be mostly returning varsity wrestlers. She was third in Jake Alder's line, right behind Marco still. He turned and gestured magnanimously.

"Ladies first," he said with a slight bow.

She moved forward, ignoring him.

"Time for leapfrog."

Heather blew out a breath and tried to relax. Again, she was familiar with the drill and readied herself. She was determined to avoid any attention coming her way this time.

The captains dropped to their knees in the starting position. Wolf summarized for the newbies.

"You will go back and forth across your opponent, two times on each side, as fast as you can. Each time, you will try to collapse the other wrestler's far arm. They will not let you collapse their arm. Then you will assume the position and the next wrestler will go over you, then the next—each assuming the position as they finish. We will continue until the captains finish the line. They will then stand, and the line will continue until everyone is standing.

"In the event that you are weak enough to let your arm collapse, the wrestler will move on, and you will reassume the position."

Wolf slowed his stroll.

"In case you were wondering, me seeing your face hit the mat is not going to help you make this team—so be strong. First wrestlers up."

He waited for a second.

Heather locked her hand around Jake's rock-hard near arm.

Whoa, she thought. He is strong.

Her other arm wrapped around his powerful torso. Before another thought came, the whistle blew, and she went as fast as she could. No chance of collapsing his arm as she flew back and forth over him.

She hopped quickly into position as she watched Marco fly across Jake, also with little effect. She braced herself as he pounced across and tried to crush her arm, but she held her ground.

The second pass almost did her in. Marco missed her arm and went directly onto her right breast, squeezing hard. It was no mistake.

Her surprise almost caused her to pull her arm in, and his weight would have buckled her. She steeled herself just in time as he finished his pass and hopped away.

There was no time to react as the next wrestler pounced on her. Fortunately, he was one of the lighter weights, and she held on, regaining her composure.

"Let's go. Faster," Wolf and Boxwood both screamed as they walked around, watching.

"I shouldn't see any space at all between you and your opponent's ass… as close as you can get to them. The closer you are, the faster you can control them."

That was close, Wolf thought. I'm going to have to watch it.

He looked over at Boxwood and wanted to give him the finger as Box smiled and shook his head.

The lines moved quickly and efficiently, with very few collapsing.

After several more wrestlers passed over her, Heather felt like she had everything under control. Then, a wrestler she didn't know seemed to go a bit slower, and he stopped ever so slightly on top of her.

She was sure of it this time.

He was definitely partially excited and quickly pressed himself into the cleft of her buttocks as he passed over.

After two passes and thrusts, with no attempt to collapse her arm, he hopped away with a barely audible chuckle.

She was distracted when the next wrestler, 260-pound heavyweight Jon Martin, landed on her.

Literally landed.

She wasn't fully braced when he jumped on her, and the contact against her recently violated hindquarters caused her to instinctively tuck and roll away from her assailant.

Martin rolled right over her and into the next wrestler, who dominoed into the pair next to him. The line came to a halt, and the whistles screeched.

"Jesus Christ, Prince," Wolf barked. "Is this going to happen at every drill?"

He noticed that a lot of people were just barely controlling their laughter, and he decided to roll with it.

"Although, I suppose we should have warned you there are elephants in the room."

She brushed Jon's hand away as he tried to help her up. The tension was broken, and the room roared with laughter.

Everyone assumed that the bright red color on Heather's face was from the laughter, but it was not.

"Assholes," she said quietly and went back to position.

"All right, that's enough. Everyone back to where they were. Let's pick up the pace."

The whistles shrieked, and they continued.

The drill commenced without further incident. Heather waited in line a few steps back after her last pass over her opponent. She couldn't help but notice Marco whispering something to Jake as soon as he finished while looking right at her. Marco had a big, leering smile on his face, while Jake had a slight grin as he looked away.

"Don't let them get to you," she said to herself as she got in line, ignoring Marco.

As she waited, she watched the boy who had kind of molested her, and she was surprised to see he still seemed to have a partial erection. He seemed to pass just as slowly and hesitate above the guys, too.

"What a perv," she thought.

As he finished, she noticed he was sweating profusely and breathing much harder than anyone else. To her chagrin, she also noticed he was one of the few actually wearing a cup. She reddened again upon realizing her overreaction, glad that no one else really knew her thoughts.

The last line finished. A number of wrestlers bent over with hands on their knees, catching their breath. Others, like Heather, simply waited with hands on their hips, ready for the next drill.

"On the line. Line up by weight class," Boxwood yelled in his deep baritone. "If there is an odd number, one of you shifts up or down so every line has an even number of wrestlers. Let's go, move your asses!"

They were going to do the lifting drill, Heather thought. Fairly simple. Lock your hands around your opponent's waist and run, carrying him to the far wall. Easy peasy.

"Again, if there is more than one pair in your weight class, step to the side and go with the next group."

Giving them ten seconds to organize, the scrawny redhead next to Heather stuck out his hand.

"Willy," he said with a smile of crooked teeth.

"Heather." She squeezed it. "I'll go first."

"Cool." He stepped in front just as the whistle shrieked.

He was surprised by how firm her grip was and how quickly she ran, carrying him nearly as fast as the seniors. No sooner had they reached the wall than the whistle shrieked again.

"Back on the line," Boxwood called resignedly, and they all jogged back across.

"Get your shit together," Juwann Davies snarled as he passed a pair of sophomores who were running back with their heads down.

"Ready, ladies?" Boxwood asked and blew the whistle.

Wolf thought he and Box would need to talk about changing a few things they had been saying for years, but he just strolled and watched as the entire group made it this time. They returned across without incident.

After each group went three times, with several more restarts, Wolf saw enough wrestlers leaning over, ready to puke, that it was time for a break. His whistle shrilled.

"Five minutes. Small sips over the whole break, no big gulps. If you puke, you're cleaning it. SMALL SIPS!"

They walked off for five. Some were laughing and back-slapping, while others looked like they wanted to die.

A few of the tryouts were still breathing hard, hands on their knees, when the whistle shrieked.

"No way that was five," they thought, but the returnees were already lining up, anticipating what came next.

"Back with your partners. Let's go, move it!" Boxwood yelled, whistle still in hand. "Front wrestler in a push-up position." He paused. "Rear wrestler, pick up his ankles and hold his legs at your waist. Hold them steady as they do their push-ups. After fifty, switch roles."

"Davies," he yelled to one of the captains, "count them out."

"And stop," Boxwood called after fifty grueling reps.

Suddenly, he turned on a slightly flabby heavyweight and got right up in his face, screaming.

"DID I SAY DROP? PICK THOSE LEGS UP!"

The wrestler immediately obeyed, as did the pairs behind him who had also let go.

"This is not a free-for-all, gentlemen. And lady. You do what you're told when you're told and nothing else. Or you will not be here."

He looked around as they all stood ramrod straight, holding the ankles of the planked wrestlers.

"Gabiche?" he asked rhetorically.

The answer was clear as they all waited. He let the pause extend for a moment.

"Drop," he barked. "Switch."

The wrestlers scrambled, immediately grabbing ankles and locking into plank positions.

"Oooooonnnnnnnnneeeeeeeeeee..."

"And drop," he said after fifty reps without incident. "Switchback."

They all scrambled again.

"Don't pick up yet. Front, get in a push-up position. Now slide your hands in so they're right under your shoulders. Then, creep them forward so they are even with your face. Back wrestlers, pick up, but get your hands on the bottom of their ankles and bring them up to your shoulders as if you were preparing to do a military press with free weights."

As they readied, Wolf had a moment of internal panic. *Shit, we should have dropped this,* he thought. Too late. Stopping it now would look like a change of routine for the girl, the exact opposite of what they needed. He put the whistle down and walked around as Boxwood continued.

"Fronts will roll back as far as their arms will let them, and backs will squat, holding those ankles up—not resting them on their shoulders."

All watched as Jake and Schmidt once again demonstrated. Jake did a near-perfect downward dog, his knees and hips moving backward, while Schmidt slowly settled into a weightlifter's squat.

"Hold," Boxwood said.

A few light chuckles came as Jake's rump hovered inches from Schmidt's stoic face.

"And back," Boxwood instructed. Jake rolled forward, straightening back to plank, while Schmidt slowly rose, keeping Jake's ankles in his hands.

"Got it?" he asked, expecting no answer as the wrestlers all assumed their positions.

"Oooonnnnneeee," he began again. Heather could feel the redness rising in her face, trying to ignore the awkwardness of the situation.

"Twwwwoooooo."

Just as she was starting to refocus, she heard Juwann Davies' voice next to her.

"Hey, little Ginger," he said to Willy. "Wanna change places?"

The pairs around them who heard began laughing. Heather almost stopped to tell him to go fu—

"Knock it off over there, or we'll be doing this all afternoon," Wolf yelled from across the room.

Everyone clammed up, but Juwann muttered just loud enough for Heather to hear, "Bet Ginger wouldn't mind." He and Marco chuckled lightly.

Heather bit her tongue and continued.

"And stop. Switch."

The drill was completed without incident.

Wolf stepped in for the next drills. "All right, all right. Let's get in our pairs, but really spread out—all over. I want like ten feet between all pairs."

They moved quickly and were ready when he joked, "Now, I know all of you were big into gymnastics when you were little."

It was a joke he probably should have scuttled, but it got a chuckle.

"Hey, Prince, weren't you a cheerleader?" Juwann joked, eliciting a laugh around the room.

Wolf stopped and took a few steps toward him.

"Davies," he said. "Just how many push-ups can you do?" He asked casually.

"Sorry, Coach."

"One more interruption, and we'll find out. And everyone laughing can do them with you."

He looked around the room. No one made eye contact.

"Now, as I was about to say, we are going to work on your front and back walkovers."

The drill focused on moving over the opponent while he was on his hands and knees, quickly switching sides to control an escape.

"Do not, I repeat, do not just plop onto your opponent's back. Roll onto it while keeping your weight on your hands and your back in contact with each other. Start slow and carefully. Returning varsity, go around the room and spot new wrestlers."

They scrambled around and each found a group. Heather dreaded getting Juwann or Marco but was relieved when the huge guy who had almost crushed her stepped up to her and Willy.

"Mind if I join you guys?" he asked politely.

They nodded.

Heather looked at him this time. She knew his name was Jon Martin, the conference champion heavyweight. She remembered her dad sighing and saying that Jon would never be a state champ because he was too much of a gentle giant.

"Don't worry, it's easier than it looks. I can even do it," Jon said.

Heather thought that must be a sight to see, considering he was probably 40 pounds heavier than she and Willy combined.

"It's Heather, right?" he asked. "Why don't you go first?"

He was ready to reach under and hold her lower back for the first few passes, but Juwann had been right. She had been a cheerleader.

She bounced back and forth twice as fast and twice as smoothly as Jake and Schmidt had during their demonstration.

"Okay," Jon said as he watched.

Around the room, several pairs were on the ground, being chastised by the veterans when both whistles blew.

"Stop. This is sad. If we can't even accomplish basic drills, how the hell are we going to win wrestling matches?"

He let it sink in as pairs returned to their positions.

He thought about something briefly, then decided, *What the hell, may as well say something positive.*

"Prince," he barked, shocking her, as she was sure she hadn't screwed this one up. "Can you please do this at half speed so I can explain it again?"

She complied.

"Now, she may be a little more flexible than most of you, but watch how this is done. Look how she bends her arms a bit so she rolls across his back instead of falling. See the way she keeps her arch close to his back but lets one-foot land before the other."

She kept bouncing back and forth.

"And she uses her opponent's body to push herself back up as she lands."

They watched.

"See how she gets a rhythm going? That's what we're looking for. Good job, Prince."

Maybe he's not a total A-hole, she thought as she stopped.

"Let's go, ladies. Try it again."

The whistle blasted for the hundredth time today.

After five minutes, the majority of wrestlers seemed to have the drill down. Some were flying through it, while others cautiously worked away at it.

The ubiquitous whistle blared.

"Stop," Wolf barked. "Time to take it up a notch. Alder, Schmidt—demonstrate."

It started at the same place as the previous drill but quickly deviated. Instead of bouncing back over, Jake's left arm hooked tightly under Schmidt's stomach while his right shot under Schmidt's armpit and locked around his shoulder. He then did a walkover with a one-foot landing and bounced off the mat quickly, arching back into a kneeling position with his arms still around his opponent. He then quickly drove forward into the other wrestler, bringing him to the ground.

"Keep tight placement of your arms and try to alternate legs when kneeling. Switch after ten walkovers. Let's go on the whistle. Returners, spot newcomers."

The groups scrambled, and the whistle screeched.

Heather completed hers easily.

On the switch, though, Jon Martin barely caught Willy as he tumbled on top of Heather. He reddened and tried to apologize profusely. Not so much for the tumble but for what caused it.

As he shot his right hand under her armpit, he realized his hand had come into full contact with her breast. He pulled his hand away like it had been shocked, which caused him to flop over instead of roll.

"I'm sorry, I'm sorry…" he kept saying until he was overwhelmed by Boxwood towering over them, screaming.

"Get back in position! Let's go. MOVE IT!" he bellowed.

They scrambled back. Willy was more careful but still very tentative as Jon Martin helped him get the arch and rhythm right.

As they switched, Heather quietly told Willy, "Hey, don't worry about it. Just do your job."

Then she flew back and forth as if she'd been doing this her whole life.

The whistle screamed again.

And so it went for another hour.

"All right. That's enough."

Wolf looked around as the majority of wrestlers stood bent over with their hands on their knees, panting and dripping sweat.

"Not awful for day one. But guess what, gentlemen? Tomorrow will be harder, and the next day even more. So let's get our heads on straight and come back tomorrow ready for some real work."

He let it sink in.

"All right, hit the showers."

He and Boxwood strolled to the middle of the room to confer while the wrestlers headed for the door.

Heather was nearly at the door, pulling off her headgear, when she felt a meaty hand impact her backside and linger for a second in a quick grab.

"Good job, Prince," Juwann Davies said with a smile as he jogged past.

She turned toward him, about to rip into him, when a smack hit her on the other cheek. She whirled around as Marco echoed, "Way to go," smirking as he jogged through the door.

No one else seemed to notice.

She just kept walking through the door and to the right as everyone else went left.

Chapter 10

She practically kicked in the door to the girls' locker room. The loud bang as the door impacted the wall reverberated in the empty room. Seething, she went into the small team room. Plopping onto the bench, she ripped open her locker and slammed her headgear into the bottom. The bottom flipped up in the corner, and the headgear stuck in it.

Shit, she thought. *Did I break it?*

But as she reached down, she saw that it was loose and wobbled back and forth, two corners flopping like a seesaw. She pulled the headgear out of the corner and straightened the locker bottom. Taking a deep breath, she began to regain her composure.

Looking at her phone, she saw that there were only ten minutes left before the bus left. She peeled off her dripping-wet clothes, grabbed a towel, and headed for the shower.

From the corner of her office, Ms. Dykstra watched unobtrusively—the initial boom of the door had gotten her attention. She waited as Heather seemed to calm down upon entering the showers.

"Must have been one hell of a first day," she thought.

Her first impulse had been to comfort her, but she knew better. So, she left it alone.

Chapter 11

Friday, and it was unseasonably warm as Heather rounded the corner and headed up the hill, sweating but running freely and easily. Once again, she was way ahead of her nearest competitors but pushed herself to better her time.

"Good job, Prince. Walk it off," Wolf barked as she strode by.

"Ten seconds better," Boxwood added. "She's not exactly wearing down."

"Nope," replied Wolf, refusing to rise to the bait. They waited patiently as Willy rounded the corner and pushed up the hill, followed closely by Davies, Alder, Schmidt, Castaglia, and a lightweight named Warton. They were pushing hard, but Willy stayed ahead and finished strong.

"Excellent, Willy," Boxwood barked as he pushed past.

"What's this? A sewing circle?" Wolf mocked as the group slowed a little on approach. "How about one of you try to win?"

They panted and puffed. In truth, they were spent. Each had put ten dollars in a pot. The winner would have gotten all of it if he'd only been able to catch Prince. But once she skipped past the attempted pushes and bumps, it was impossible. Every time someone pushed to go by her, she just turned it up and opened an even bigger gap.

"The girl is simply a running machine," Alder had said.

They stayed in a group, hands on their knees, catching their breath, while Prince stood off to the side by herself.

"If we all put in again Monday, it'll be a hundy," Marco said. "Whaddya say?"

"I'm in," Warton spat out. "I hate that little bitch. Next time, I'm gonna knock her skinny ass into the ditch as soon as we get around the first bend."

He spat and walked away from the group.

"Yeah, I'd like to knock that skinny ass, too," Juwann joked, putting his hands around imaginary hips and thrusting his pelvis forward, much to the amusement of the remaining group. They broke it up quickly as they saw Wolf look their way.

It was hot. It was brutal. And it was long.

They all breathed a sigh of relief when the whistle finally blared in a short burst.

"Gentlemen," Wolf said, shaking his head. "That was one of the worst practices I've ever seen." He let it sink in. "I think our only choice is to start over. Outside in five. Let's go!"

The whistle shrilled again, covering the multiple groans as they all started to jog to change into their running shoes.

As the group trudged through the beginning of the 2.2 miles, Wolf turned to Boxwood.

"How many didn't come out?"

"Three," he sighed. "But she did. First one out."

"Well, she can definitely hang with the conditioning. But we haven't started wrestling yet…." He let that hang. "How many left totals?"

"Twenty-eight."

"Not terrible. We should be fine for varsity. The rest should be just enough for depth and a few JV matches."

"Just barely. Some will have to swing back and forth. But it will do the young ones good. Remember when we'd have over fifty, every one of them chomping at the bit to get a single match?"

"Times change. Not many want to do the work anymore. Hell, I never thought I'd see the day when the hardest worker was a girl."

"She really is one tough little bitch. Sorry, 'girl,'" he self-corrected. "Still, I think it's bad overall. I hope she has her fill of it come next week."

"She will. She will."

And, as if on cue, she came around the corner—once again, significantly ahead of everyone else.

Chapter 12

Andy Warton's hand-stretched with all his might for the circle. Just inches away, he gave a final, all-out push, knowing the seconds were ticking away. The ref, an actual referee Wolf had brought in to simulate real matches, hesitated for an extra second as time expired.

Heather, however, braced herself and pulled Warton back just as the ref finally blew the whistle. She relaxed and let him go, but he pushed her roughly off and barked at the ref.

"Really?! I was on the line! You can't call it when I'm about to get a fucking reversal!" he snarled, twisting away and standing angrily.

"Hey, knock it off," Boxwood yelled. "That'll get you DQ'd every time. Now, get back in the circle and wrestle. You still have an entire period to get your 'fucking reversal,' so be a man and go get it instead of begging the ref to save your sorry ass."

Wolf thought that was a bit extreme, but he wasn't about to contradict Boxwood in front of the wrestlers.

Warton angrily got back into position on the small circle with the knight emblem in it. Heather dropped over him, locking his near arm in hers and tucking her far arm tightly under his torso. She was ready when the whistle blew for Andy's angry attempt at a fast kick-out, knowing he was losing his cool. She calmly drove her shoulder into his as his body tried to spin out and away from her. Instead of escaping and regaining the point he needed, he found himself on his back, controlled by Heather as she maneuvered him into a pin position.

He heard the ref call points for Prince, and panic began to set in. He scrambled and twisted, but she seemed to anticipate his every move, cutting him off at every turn. He could feel the seconds slipping away. Desperate, he made one last change of direction, and her face was right behind his head. With a quick snap, he popped his head back into her nose.

Heather momentarily relaxed her grip, and he finally spun away, reaching for the reversal he needed until several whistles shrieked.

"That's it!" both coaches screamed.

Wolf grabbed Warton by the arm and pulled him away roughly while Boxwood sprang into action with a towel, making Heather sit and lean her head back.

"Ice," he yelled to the team manager, who scrambled toward the training room.

"What the hell was that?!" Wolf screamed in Warton's face. "You're DQ'd."

Warton spun away and tore off his headgear.

"Y'know what? Fuck you all," he fairly screamed as he started to walk away. "You want a bitch wrestler? You got her."

He tossed his headgear onto the mat angrily. "You think we can't all see it? She's *gotta* be here, and you can't do a thing about it. It's a fucking joke."

"Enough," Wolf said firmly through gritted teeth.

"Well, you want her? You got her," Warton snarled. He threw his hands up. "You know what? Fuck you. Fuck you all." Throwing his hands down in disgust, he turned and stormed away.

Wolf started walking after him.

"Next group, in the circle," he barked.

Boxwood held a towel-wrapped bag of ice to Heather's nose as he led her to the bench. Despite the blood dripping down her face, Heather was smiling.

She was a varsity wrestler. She was a Scarlet Knight.

Chapter 13

She could hardly keep the smile off her face the entire day.

She knew it was just a formality, the posting of the varsity list, but she still felt a tinge of apprehension. *Something could go wrong,* she reminded herself. But the smile still broke through.

She had won.

Even before Andy's overly dramatic, face-saving DQ, she'd had him easily beaten. She won. Nothing could change that, she thought, still smiling as she walked toward her locker.

She didn't really notice the group moving away from the lockers, quietly smiling and laughing.

Heather's smile disappeared when she saw the reason for their mirth.

In a big, bold black permanent marker, *DYKE* was scrawled across her locker.

"That's not even how you spell it," she said aloud to no one in particular.

With a sigh, she opened her locker.

Nope, she thought. *Nobody's gonna take this day away from me.*

She ignored the snickering behind her.

Screw you all, she thought. *I'm a varsity wrestler.*

Chapter 14

It was a relatively light practice. Speed drills, conditioning, and a little work on takedowns. Mercifully, for the first time all season, they ended early.

"All right," Wolf called after the whistle. "Good job today. Get some rest. Tomorrow, we get serious."

He let that sink in as he strolled around, looking at his fit, eager wrestlers.

"Official weigh-ins tomorrow, hydration tests, and we will be wrestling—all out, all the time. You young men," he hesitated, "and women have survived the tryouts. Now, the real fun begins. Now, we wrestle for real. So be ready to fight hard.

"You boys who won the starting spots—you have to win to keep them. You can and will, be challenged constantly by those who want your spot. It only gets harder from here. Bring it in."

The wrestlers all came to the circle in the middle of the mat, the knight emblem full center. With their right foot on the line, they placed their right hands in, all on top of each other's.

Jake barked, "One, two, three—"

"KNIGHTS!" they intoned loudly, hands thrusting down in unison.

"Shower up," Wolf commanded as he and Boxwood walked toward the coach's office.

As the wrestlers milled about, the captains walked up to the new starters and quietly told them, "Team room in 15 minutes. Miss the bus and one of us will give you a ride."

Heather smiled to herself. Only starters got that invitation. She knew she was getting *the* shirt—the one only starters could wear. She was entering that elite club of wrestling Knights, the same one her father had belonged to.

Until now, he had continued to be stubborn, refusing to even talk to her about it. He was tense and short with both her and her mom. She was sure he'd come around by the time of her first match, though.

With a spring in her step, Heather headed for the locker room.

Heather peeled off her singlet and began to pull on a pair of Soffe shorts. Her dri-fit T-shirt was sweaty and sticking to her, and she was still wearing that ridiculous jock. After a second's thought, she pulled off the T-shirt and jock and toweled off quickly. She had a sports bra, which she pulled on fast, but decided that putting on her only clean underwear without a shower was too gross. So she just slipped her shorts back on and grabbed a T-shirt.

She stuffed her sweaty gear into her bag but left her towel and clean clothes on the bench for a quick change later. Letting out a quick breath, she said aloud to the empty room, "I can't believe this is happening."

Shaking her head in bemusement, pleased and thrilled, she slipped on her locker room slides and headed for the team room.

Chapter 15

It had been years since she'd been in this room.

Up until she was ten, she'd come with her dad on Wednesday nights and Saturday afternoons every winter. Her father would regale her with stories of his wrestling days, and she could stay and help him get things ready—until the boys began to arrive. After that, she waited outside in the wrestling room.

Now, it took on a new dimension.

She belonged here.

She was a wrestler.

The room itself was part locker room, part lounge, with a couch and several chairs on one side and lockers with benches forming a horseshoe along the other three sides. The floor was actually wrestling mat material, and in the center was a regulation circle—including the ubiquitous Scarlet Knight.

Everyone looked at her, likely thinking that she was the first girl ever to step into this room as a varsity wrestler.

She was glad to see that everyone else had changed into shorts and a T-shirt as well.

Jake Adler stepped into the middle of the circle, and everyone gathered around the line without any spoken command.

Heather slipped into an open spot.

Jake looked at everyone around him, one by one, and let the silence sink in.

"In this room," Jake began, "have been some of the greatest wrestlers the state has ever known—state champs, NCAA champs, even Olympic gold medalists." He let it sink in. "And we are part of that fraternity. We are part of that select few who can call themselves Scarlet Knight wrestlers. You are special. And responsibility comes with that. We look out for our own. We are there for each other."

Heather smiled to herself. She'd grown up hearing variations of this speech.

Jake continued, "You are expected to behave better, do better in class, do better in all things than anyone in this school." He paused again for emphasis. "And you will be above the drama—no fights, no detentions, no disrespect. And that goes for out in the street as well. You are a Scarlet Knight 24/7. You will always have your brothers' backs. No one comes between us, ever. When one of us needs the others, we will be there. Not just now but always. We are a brotherhood forever. And everything that happens in this room stays in this room. We stick together in all things, share all things, and are completely loyal to each other, first and foremost. Once a Knight, always a Knight."

He intoned, and Heather knew to respond, as they did in unison, "Once a Knight, always a Knight." Like a chorus in a church recitation.

Jake nodded as he started out of the circle. "Juwan."

Juwan strode into the center, holding three shirts rolled up tightly. He tossed one in the air, catching and re-tossing it as he spoke. "Once you put this on, you are special—there is no one else in this school like you. Everything Jake says becomes a commitment. Nothing stops a Knight. We never stop trying. We never stop striving. We never, ever give up. We go to our last breath. We go all out, all effort, until that whistle sounds. And a Knight never loses because a Knight never quits. We may not get every victory, but we never stop wrestling. We never give anything but our best—our 100 percent effort—for ourselves."

He tossed a shirt to each of the three new wrestlers as he walked about, and as he got to Heather last, he flipped her a shirt and added, "And for the team."

As they stared at their shirts, a flurry of activity swirled around them. Behind each of them, a returning wrestler "pantsed" them—simultaneously yanking their shorts down to their ankles. As they stood there in shock, another wrestler jumped on them and pulled them to the mat in a spread-out "figure four," their arms and legs locked down, with their white butts in the air.

The three newbies were momentarily in shock as the remaining wrestlers laughed raucously. They started to squirm and try to get away, but each was in total lockdown. Heather was clamped by Jake, and she could barely budge in his ironlike grip. The wrestlers strolled around the circle, hooting and catcalling. The two boys, Willie and Warren, looked comical with the straps of their jocks tight across their naked cheeks, the front part stretched tight on their frightened "package."

But more attention was drawn to something else, something that captured nearly every eye, causing a slight hesitation in the mocking glances—Heather's perfect, round ass caught them all off guard. For many, it was the first live female derriere they'd ever seen. But more shocking, drawing even more attention, was the fact that she had no jock, thong, or panties—only her perfect female form, in all its glory, on full display. The more she squirmed, the more it moved and spread, making it the most fascinating view many there had ever witnessed.

The moment was broken by Warren Coates' loud threats as he tried to break free.

"You fuckin' faggots!" he howled as he struggled to get loose. "I'm gonna fuckin' kill every one of you when I get loose! Any of you homos touch me, and I'll kick your balls so far in you'll puke them up! ARRRggh!" he screamed and grunted in a final effort to get free.

The laughter grew as they watched his futile efforts.

"Let me go," Heather said calmly and low to Jake.

"Can't. This happens to all of us on the first day," he half-apologized. "Just chill. It will be over in a minute."

"I said, let me go, you bastard!" she said through clenched teeth, trying to jerk free fruitlessly. Jake just tightened his grip and ignored her.

Juwan continued his circular strut, looking around as he moved. "Well looks like we just got one thing left to do."

He paused for emphasis. "It's time to CHECK THAT OIL!" A loud crescendo chant, almost like a drumroll, started, "Check that oil, check that oil, check that oil, check that oil, CHECK THAT OIL! CHECK THAT OIL! CHECK THAT OIL!"

Juwan put his right index finger in the air. As his circle tightened, the chant turned to a chorus of "WHHHHOOOOAAA!" as he dramatically put his finger in his mouth to get it wet, then put it in the air as he stopped behind Warren.

"Time to check your oil, son," he said in a deeper tone. The crowd clapped and chanted lower, "Check that oil, check that oil, check that oil…."

"I'm gonna kill you, you fuckin' faggots" Warren threatened to no avail.

Juwan dropped to his knees and stuck his finger into Warrens tight, resisting rectum. Warren's grunt was covered by the crowd's laughter. Then, one by one, the remaining wrestlers followed Juwan's example until finally, the wrestler holding him let go with his right hand and gave

Warren one last poke as he tore free, rolling away and pulling his shorts quickly over his violated behind. He shoved the wrestler back to the ground and wanted to punch someone, but instead, his reddened face started to break into a chagrined smile.

"You're all a bunch of fucking faggots!" He yelled again. But he didn't push away from Juwan's big hug or those that followed.

The redness began to settle back from his face as he returned high fives and playfully pushed a few away as some huggers playfully tried to grab his buttocks.

Juwan returned to his task as MC and ringmaster and restarted his strut. He stopped as Willie let out a slight whimper as he vainly tried to escape his viselike hold. Juwan stopped as if shocked.

"What in the hell do we have here?" he added in a high-pitched voice, exaggeratedly staring at Willies concave cheeks and scrawny legs. "That's not even an ASS!" he looked around the room. "What should we call it? A heinie? A coolie?" The laughter roared around him.

He raised his index finger in the air again, the chant of "check that oil" softly starting up again. He seemed to be considering his outstretched finger thoughtfully. "I don't know, fellas, this might kill him." And he tucked his index finger back into his fist and stuck up his pinky, looking around seriously as a disappointed 'ahhh' started in the room.

After a dramatic pause, he shouted. "Fuck that!" and shot his index finger back in the air.

"Let's check that oil!" The cheer rose as he started moving his finger toward his mouth but pulled it back quickly in disgust, to more laughter. Instead, he spit in his left palm and rubbed it on his finger.

As he knelt, he intoned with mock seriousness. "I'm sorry, son. This will hurt me more than it's gonna hurt you." ....

"NOT!" he shouted to the chanting, laughing throng. Willie let out a gasp as Juwan violently penetrated his exposed behind.

"Help, help. I can't get it out." He mimed being stuck and fell back as if he had to yank with all his might.

"Watch out, fellas, this one's dangerous!" Warren Coates, freshly indoctrinated, jumped the line to join the fun. He kneeled and thrust his finger in. "Hey, that makes you a faggot now too, Coates." And they all laughed and loosely lined up.

One by one, they passed through, Willie no longer making any sounds. He couldn't stop the tears from streaming down his face as he endured more than a dozen anal penetrations. Like Warren, he tried to push the others away as they hugged him and pounded his scrawny back.

With a sniff, Willie tried to regain his composure and surreptitiously wiped the wetness from his face as he also cursed them for a bunch of homos.

But it was done; he'd survived and was one of them. A dream he'd had since he was seven years old had come true—he was a Scarlet Knight.

His thoughts were broken as he turned to a long-breathed exclamation.

"Wwwhhhheeeewwww!" Juwan dragged out like a whistle.

"Oh my God. Now that IS an ass." Juwan smiled and looked around.

"For those of you who have never seen one before."

A few uncomfortable laughs arose, but mostly, there were incredulous stares—for what Juwann said was true. Most had only seen such a thing on the internet or in magazines.

"I usually like 'em a little bigger, but I gotta admit—it's damn near perfect."

During the awkward pause, Heather told Jake one last time, in a low, firm voice, "I said, let me go," as he shifted slightly to respond, she saw her opening and snapped her head back sharply, fully catching his nose and lips.

"Fuck!" he screamed, with blood spraying with the sound. She tried to twist out of his slightly loosened grip, but Juwann jumped to his aid, throwing himself against her back and shoulder and forcing her back into Jake's grip.

"You bitch." He slurred through the blood as he regripped and locked her down.

Juwann remained kneeling next to her and started screaming.

"What's the matter, bitch. You are too good for it. You better than us! Yeah, that's right," He sneered.

"You wanna wrestle with the boys—you get what the boys get! Right, fellas?"

"Yeah!" several voices responded halfheartedly.

Most eyes were still fascinated by the female form before them. Juwann paused, still kneeling. He then reached out and patted her naked behind.

"AHH, whatsa matter, honey? You don't want your oil checked." He spoke with mocking gentleness. "That's ok, we won't do that." After one last pat, he stood up, stuck two fingers in the air, and shouted.

"We'll just dip that honey instead." After a confused second.

Several responded gleefully as they realized what he meant. A short chant began,

"Dip that honey, dip that honey." Juwann strutted in a short circle. Index and middle finger together thrust in the air. Jake's eyebrows tightened, trying to think what to do as Juwann dramatically began to swing his arm in a slow arc toward her vulnerability, when a large body stepped in the way, putting his huge paw a few inches from Heather's exposure. Jon Martin firmly told Juwann.

"We can't do this."

"No? You don't want me to touch her?" Jon shook his head, his hand hovering protectively over her, and Juwann seemed to slouch a little as if in surrender, and then his hand shot forward pushing Jon's.

"Then you do it," he barked as he forced Jon's surprised open palm fully onto her spread-eagled privates.

Jon yanked away as if shocked by a thousand volts. He turned to step toward Juwann, but three other wrestlers stepped in, pushing Jon back. He acquiesced, all the wind taken from his sails, as he stared at his unintentionally guilty hand.

Jake had watched the quick altercation while still holding his grip, too surprised to think. He was about to come to his senses and let go when Juwann seemed to read his mind, once again throwing his weight on top of the two of them.

"Don't even think about it." He almost whispered. "She wanted this—now she got it." The two captains locked eyes, and Jake moved his arm just in time as Heather's teeth almost snapped to his forearm. He repositioned quickly under her jaw, and his anger kicked in—he put her on lockdown. The chant started again, "Dip that honey…" and Juwann pulled his weight off them. He slid a bit to his right, but instead of standing up, he stayed kneeling behind her. They saw his hand move down between her legs. Many craned their necks to see but couldn't as he was kneeling too close.

Then, Juwann pulled away a bit, and those near could see that his shorts were pulled down, and his fully erect manhood was exposed. Some were momentarily confused but quickly realized what he was about to do, and some eyes widened as they realized what the gasp that burst out of Heather meant. As they watched Juwann start arching and thrust back and forth, the room took on a strange silence.

As he penetrated her, everything changed for Heather. In that instant future, things would now never be—no awkward fumbling with her first boyfriend. No romantic first time after prom. No virginal honeymoon night. Her innocence was gone, forever. With one violent thrust, it had all been stolen from her.

Jake looked into Heather's eyes, and they took on the deadly stare of a shark. Looking up at Juwann's enraptured face, he realized he had done much more than touch her with a finger. And once again he moved to release her.

But Juwann, in his fully aroused state, had finished only seconds after he'd started. Quickly realizing what was about to happen, he pulled out and again leaped onto them—locking them down. This time, his sidekick Marco joined him, pinning Jake and Heather in position.

Juwann's shorts were still pulled down as he wrestled against the two beneath him. The howl that escaped from Heather's lips momentarily froze the room. The three burly wrestlers could barely hold her as she struggled with all her might.

Most were transfixed by the scream and were startled by how quickly Warren Coates jumped down, tugging his shorts down on the way, a third body onto the pile, yelling "Dip that honey" as he forced himself on her just as Juwann had.

Heather stopped moving in resistance, almost drawing inward on herself. As Warren pulled away laughing, another took his place. The chanting had stopped, but the focus had not. Some squirmed uncomfortably yet couldn't look away. Others grew very excited, even rubbing themselves as they adjusted the extreme tightness in their jock straps. Jon Martin had turned and walked to the other side of the locker room, his back turned to the proceedings. Willie croaked a "Stop!" and tried to push through but was quickly grabbed by several strong arms and held back.

Bobby Holario could not take his eyes off what was happening before him. He was a quiet young man, likely because of the scarred and red acne that covered his face. Bullet-headed and powerfully built, he was a great wrestler.

However, he was socially awkward and had never had a girlfriend. Regardless, he spent several hours a day viewing and staring at a computer screen, dually guilty and fascinated at the acts he saw played out before him. Try as he might, he always found himself aroused and always did what he swore to himself he'd stop doing. And now, the real thing stood before him—so much more amazing than he could have imagined.

Bobby couldn't even consciously be aware of it as he knelt, his shorts dropping to reveal a massive erection. As he paused, a small voice inside him told him to stop. Juwann noticed and joked, "Damn, Hammer, don't hurt her," and the laughter seemed mocking to Bobby, so he quickly pushed in.

Heather grunted and cursed in anger as she tried one last time to pull away from the assault. Again, her eyes locked with Jake's, hers with hatred, his with resignation; he looked away first.

As Bobby finished and guiltily pulled away, no one else stepped forward. A strange rustle rippled through the room until Juwann spoke one more time. He'd been watching Willie and worried that he was freaking out. He decided Willie was a problem if he was not a part of this, so he stepped in.

"Oh, no, we ain't done yet. We still have another wrestler to go. C'mon now, Willie, step up to the plate."

Willie was horrified. He backed up as if to bolt the room, only to find his way blocked by a wall of wrestlers. He turned left, then right, only to be grabbed firmly by Marco and Warren. They led him forward as Juwann beckoned with a curling finger.

"Willie, you got to, son. She ain't really one of us until everyone goes."

He shook his head and tried to pull away but to no avail. His shorts were yanked down, and even though his flaccidity clearly showed he wanted no part of this, he was pushed against her.

Juwann took matters into his own hands as Willie refused to push in, grabbing his hips and forcing him back and forth. "C'mon boy," he hooted, "git some!" to a chorus of raucous laughs that drowned out Willie's croaking, crying.

"Please stop." When they finally let go, he whirled away, yanking up his shorts. For the second time, tears streamed down his face.

Jake looked into Heather's glazed stare and quietly said, "I'm gonna let you go now." She kept staring at him dully as he loosened his grip.

Out of nowhere, she furiously sprang forward, snapping her forehead, this time fully getting his nose and upper teeth. He let out a roar and sprang back at her. They began to wrestle with a ferocity no one there had ever seen. The crowd watched, enthralled as they moved and rolled, Jake's face streaming blood and Heather nearly naked.

Despite Jake's superior strength, Heather's rage drove her like a mad woman.

Finally, Jake overpowered her, forcing her onto her back. As she tried one last move to escape, he sprung upon her, finding himself between her legs as she tried to arch away.

Despite himself, perhaps at first unaware, Jake found that he had a violent erection, half of it pushing out of the waistband of his shorts. As she arched to get away, he pushed against her, and he heard himself say it. "Is this what you want, bitch." And with a thrust, he joined all the others. He pushed several times and their eyes once again locked.

Jake froze—what have I done—and he pushed her shoulders away as he jumped off of her. Pulling his shorts back, as he rolled, he immediately loathed himself. But it was done.

Heather rolled onto her hands and knees, instinctively trying to escape. As she was crawling away, she felt every eye on her. Something inside her screamed, "STOP CRAWLING" STAND UP!" She became aware of herself, her shorts twisted around one ankle, her sports bra pushed high above her breasts. She rolled away and pulled her shorts as she moved. With her back to the crowd, she pulled her bra back down and adjusted it over her reddened breasts. Her legs were shaking. She was totally disoriented. The only thing she saw was the door.

Unsteadily, she started to move toward it, only wishing to leave. After several steps, she felt she was going to make it. And then she heard it, a soft snort and snicker. She was sure it was Marco. She stopped; steel began to rise in her, her legs stopped shaking, and her steps ceased. The snicker stopped. Heather turned and strode past the shocked and guilty throng. Without any eye contact, she stepped toward the circle.

On the floor, her still rolled shirt lay untended; she grabbed and shook it loose with a determined scoop. Toeing the line, she pulled it over her head and shoulders and waited. After a pause in which one could hear a pin drop, they all cautiously moved toward the circle.

Even if Heather had wanted to look in any of their eyes, she would not have been able to; every stare was directly at the mat as the enormity of what they had just done began to sink in.

Juwan finally broke the silence and stepped into the circle. He tried to look at Heather, but her gaze was fixed straight ahead.

"You have now finally joined this brotherhood. Every wrestler who's passed through these doors has endured this moment. Everyone," he paused for effect, "myself included. It's a hard thing, but it bonds us. No one, NO ONE! Knows us like we know each other." He waited as if to find the right words.

"And no one ever knows of this but us, but this brotherhood. What happens in this room stays in this room. We are loyal to each other in all things." He tried to catch Heather's eye, but her gaze was like a sphinx.

"Everybody in," he commanded. Warren and Willie hesitatingly put their hand on top of Juwan's, but Heather strode forward and firmly covered all three. The remaining wrestlers gradually pushed forward and joined.

"On three, Juwann commanded "Knights forever!" and the chorus responded in kind. Heather spun on her heel as the hands pulled away, pushing those around her, and strode forcefully toward the door. Every eye was on her as she left without a word or backward glance. No one moved for quite some time.

Chapter 16

Ms. D. nearly jumped out of her chair as the sound of the locker room door slamming open resounded like a gunshot. She leaned out and peeked out of the office door just as Heather turned into the small team room. The next sound was of a slamming, or punched, locker. She almost went to investigate, but decided it would be better to give her some space.

The sound indeed had been a punched locker. She teetered on the edge of breakdown and rage. Rage won. She tore off her t-shirt and was about to throw it, but caught herself and roughly folded it and placed it on the bench. Red blotches and hand prints covered her torso as she tore off the sports bra. Finally, the shorts came off, and she retched as she saw the amalgam of blood and fluids coating them and running down her thighs. Furiously, she threw them into the bottom of the open locker, where they wedged into the corner of the loose seesawing base. A long ragged intake of air controlled the explosion writhing inside her.

Grabbing her towel and kit she strode into the showers and snapped a nozzle on full hot, not waiting, she stepped into the cold water , closed her eyes, and leaned one hand against the cool tile. Bowing her head, a single strangled sob fought it's way up her throat and was quickly followed by a rattling sigh of intake as he tried to breathe. The water grew intensely hot and mixed with the tears starting to flow down her face. The water also mixed with the blood and fluid on her legs, and it began to run to the tile floor. In a panic she began to scrub furiously, everywhere, trying to get all of it; blood semen, sweat and their touch off of her. Her breath became frantic quick sobs, finally coming back as all of her skin reddened with the heat and scrubbing.

Ms. D had wandered to the team room, hoping to talk to Heather. She felt a bit of embarrassment as she glanced in the shower room, and pulled back as she saw Heather scrubbing. She noticed a trickle of blood tinged water running down her legs to the shower floor, and all she could think of was the movie "Carrie" and how embarrassed the poor girl was when the gym teacher confronted her. Imagine the stress she's under already, all the harassment, the challenges physically, and now her period on top of it. Heather seemed to stop washing and took in a deep breath, stepping further under the water. No, thought Ms. D – better to give her some space.

Chapter 17

Most of the wrestlers had headed home.

Jake was pacing, somewhat nervous and frantic. He headed straight for Heather as she exited the building. She veered quickly away.

"Wait… can we talk?"

"Go away."

"C'mon, let me drive you home," he said as she kept striding away.

"Stay the fuck away from me."

"Heather, c'mon, please wait."

She stopped, turned, and looked him in the eye.

"Leave me alone," she intoned menacingly.

She turned on her heel and kept walking while he stood there, frozen and staring.

Her gaze was down, and when she looked up, she saw a wall named Jon Martin. Unlike Jake, he didn't try to stop her.

"Are you OK? Can I take you to the hospital?"

She stopped and tried to read his expression, which seemed a mix of sympathy and guilt. She felt a slight calming.

"No. Jon, I'm fine. I just wanna go home."

"Do you want me to drive you home?"

She touched his arm lightly. "I'm good, Jon. I've got a ride."

He looked as if he were going to cry.

"Heather, my dad's a captain in the state police. We could go report it all. I'll confess. I'll tell them everything."

She sighed. "No, Jon, please don't."

She looked into his eyes, filling with tears.

"Let me handle this my own way. Please."

He sniffed. "OK. But it's not right. They shouldn't get away with it!" Anger was starting to rise in him.

"They won't."

She touched his arm again.

"Jon, it's OK. You didn't do anything."

"I know," he choked out a sob, "but I should have. I should have done something."

She looked at him for a moment, and strangely, she wanted to comfort him.

"It will be all right, Jon."

She saw her Uber pulling in and started toward it.

"See you at practice tomorrow, Jon."

"Bye," he croaked.

Chapter 18

It almost knocked over his coffee. Pulling back his paper quickly, he looked up to see his daughter's defiant stare as she stood, arms akimbo, waiting for a response.

On the table in front of him was her shirt. Staring up at him from the tabletop was a Scarlet Knight emblazoned and surrounded by the school's name and the year.

"I am a varsity wrestler," she taunted. "They couldn't stop me." She paused. "You couldn't stop me. So all your little world is now different because a girl can do it. This girl."

She was almost screaming.

"I'm sorry you didn't get a son. I'm all you've got. And I can do anything you did!"

She couldn't help but tweak him for coming up short as state champ all those years ago.

"And maybe even more."

She grabbed her backpack and headed out the door, letting it slam behind her as she bounced down the front steps.

"Can't you see what you're doing to her?" her mother finally spoke.

"Me?" His voice rose incredulously. "What you've done to her! Look at the anger, the frustration. That's all on you. I wanted to protect her from it." He paused. "But you insisted."

She shook her head. "All she wants from you is your support. Why is it so hard for you to admit you were wrong? Now you're just in a tug-of-war with her. Can't you at least try to meet her halfway?"

He shook his head firmly. "If I go along with it, she's only going to get deeper into it, and that will really break her heart when it all comes crashing down. Better she quits and blames me than gets crushed and humiliated. You just don't get it. Everywhere they go, she's going to be a target. She'll be mocked, booed, and harassed. And she's going to get beat badly and hurt again—badly. Why do you refuse to see that? You think this is about me?"

Now, he was nearly screaming.

"No, you've made it about you. You pushed her to do this to prove something to yourself about being a woman. Well, when she's in the hospital crying and broken, maybe then you'll believe me."

He punctuated his rant with a fist pounding the table.

Though it almost made her flinch, she wouldn't show it. Instead, she shook her head, picked up her coffee, and got up gracefully before leaving.

He stared at the shirt for a long moment. He picked it up and refolded it so that the logo sat in the middle of a neat square.

He sighed. It was quite an accomplishment.

Still, he was sure it was going to end badly.

Chapter 19

The halls bristled with the normal morning rustle and flow. Heather, however, found it particularly annoying and irritatingly crowded. She grew tenser by the moment as she dodged contact with the careless brushing and bumping of bodies pinballing their way toward homeroom. She almost breathed a sigh of relief as she entered the wing where her locker was located. Thankfully, the crowd seemed to open a bit to let her pass.

The feeling was short-lived as she realized they were actually moving out of her way. A hint of a hush seemed to settle in, and she noticed the movement had stopped as groups coalesced against and near lockers. The sense of others trying not to watch her as she passed was becoming obvious. A few chuckles and snickers grew as she neared her locker. Two small cliques parted like the Red Sea as she approached.

Stopping dead in her tracks, she stared at her locker, and a white-hot wave seemed to rise in her like steam from an ignored kettle. At the last moment, she grabbed hold of it and pushed it back down. With a barely perceptible deep breath, she stepped closer and took a good look at the Sharpie-drawn caricature on her locker. It was actually fairly well done.

Depicted for all to see was a female figure in a wrestling singlet, her legs spread and in the air with a muscular wrestler between them. The word bubble above screamed in all caps, **"PIN ME, BABY! PIN ME HARDER!!"**

She let out a kind of harrumph and chuckle, then said aloud for everyone and no one, "It doesn't even look like me."

After a moment, she took out her phone and snapped some shots of the cartoon from several angles. She tucked the phone in her pocket and gathered her books and necessities for the morning. She made a point of closing her locker calmly. Instead of turning right, as she normally would for class, she turned left and headed for the front of the school. The Red Sea parted again, surreptitiously watching her stride by with her head held high and her jaw firmly set.

Ms. D, standing outside her door, said a pleasant good morning as Heather whizzed by but received no reply.

Wonder where she's going, Ms. D thought. *She usually goes the other way.*

"Ms. D," a boy with braces and wild hair interrupted her thoughts, "can I go to the bathroom?"

"Sure, there's still five minutes until the bell rings."

She greeted several other students as they entered and began her day.

Heather stood in front of Mrs. Calhoun's desk for several seconds before she was finally acknowledged with an annoyed sigh.

"How can I help you, young lady?"

"I need to speak with Mr. Dale."

Reaching for a pink half-slip of paper, she offhandedly held it out for Heather. "Fill this request form out, and he will call you down when he has time available," she intoned monotonously.

"I need to see him now," Heather said as politely as she could.

"That's not possible," Mrs. Calhoun responded icily. "He is in the middle of a meeting." She shook the form toward Heather. "Fill out the form, and he'll call you down."

Heather took the form and turned away. Mrs. Calhoun went back to her paperwork. Instead of turning to leave, however, Heather turned in the opposite direction, threw open the door to Principal Dale's office, and stormed in.

"Wait—" Mrs. Calhoun started to rise from her chair, but it was too late.

Surprised, Jim Dale paused just as he was about to take a bite from his ham and egg sandwich. It took a second for him to react, but he did, properly offended by her impertinence.

"Excuse me!" he barked just as Mrs. Calhoun pushed her ample bulk through the door.

"Young lady," she said, trying to grab Heather's arm, "get out of this office right this minute." She demanded it with all the sternness she could muster.

Heather yanked her arm roughly away, and Mr. Dale was about to reprimand her when a small alarm went off in his head as he realized who she was.

Not again, he thought.

Putting down his sandwich, he raised a hand. "Thank you, Mrs. Calhoun, but I'll handle it from here. I will deal with her, don't you worry."

Mrs. Calhoun glared at Heather, her wide face crimson with indignation at Heather's brazen effrontery. She stepped out slowly, closing the door quietly.

"Now—" Dale began.

"Deal with me?" Heather practically screamed at him. "Deal with me? How about you deal with this!"

She was nearly spitting with rage as she shoved her phone in his face. He took it gingerly and studied the picture.

"Where was this?"

"Where the fuck do you think it is? That's my locker, you idiot."

"Control your language, or you'll be in ISS PDQ, young lady. Now slow down and tell me what this is all about," he stalled.

Taking a calming breath, she began again. "Last week, I showed you the graffiti on my locker, and you promised you'd take care of it. Obviously, you didn't because this morning I walked up to this on my locker."

He studied the phone, gathering his thoughts. "Now, I can't discuss other students in particular, but the boys responsible for last week's incident were caught and appropriately disciplined. This is obviously an entirely different situation."

"It's not a situation. It's harassment and bullying."

Snatching her phone back, she snapped, "And you obviously aren't doing anything about it. Well, maybe a lawyer and the newspapers will motivate you to do something!"

The alarm was now screaming like a five-alarm fire. He quickly shifted to his "best buddy" mode and tried to calm her down. "Heather, let's take a breath. Have a seat, and we'll get this figured out."

After a brief pause, she plopped into the large leather chair facing him.

"Believe me, I'm as shocked and horrified as you are. And I'm sorry. I was sure the two boys who admitted to defacing your locker last week were the only ones who'd do such a thing." He paused for effect. "I promise we will get to the bottom of this immediately and make sure that it doesn't happen again." He added with all the earnestness he could muster. "Would you like to take the day off? It won't be an absence, just kind of a break. Should I call your mom?"

She closed her eyes and shook her head. "No, I am not running and hiding from these assholes. I just want something done about it."

"Right, right." He quickly agreed. "How about this, though? We have a bank of lockers right across the hall from this office, in full view of Mrs. Calhoun at all times. What if we moved your locker to that area?" He smiled as he threw her a brilliant olive branch.

"Let's see. I have had my locker vandalized twice in one week. I am sexually harassed in front of the whole school, and your solution is that I should take the day off and be inconvenienced by moving to the opposite side of the building from all my classes." She looked at him, shaking her head. "I would say that's kind of blaming the victim, don't you think?"

"No, I'm absolutely not saying that. I'm just suggesting things to try and take some of the pressure off you. I can see that this is really affecting you."

"I'll be fine. I just want it stopped. Isn't that your job?"

She is really pushing it, he thought, but he still put on his best-concerned look. "As I said, I promise we'll get to the bottom of this. But, Heather, let's be real, you had to expect…"

His logical mind almost dove to try and stop the thought his emotions just let slip out, but it hung there, heavy, in the silence between them.

"I see," Heather said calmly as she rose. "So you think it's kinda my own fault? I deserve this? Well, whether I deserve it or not, why don't you use the hundred cameras in the halls and some of this fine security and do something about it? How about you do your fucking job?" she added frigidly.

"Now that is enough." He started to lean forward in his chair, but he was talking to her back as she strode out and slammed the door behind her.

He took a second and gathered himself. Looking down at his uneaten breakfast, he mused, "Ice cold." Quickly balling it up in the wrapper, he tossed it in the trash.

"What a little bitch," he actually said the thought aloud. Then he punched the intercom for Mrs. Calhoun, having regained his composure.

"Esther, could you track down Big Ed and Officer Smiley and have them meet me in the security office?"

"Yes, sir, right away." She hesitated. "Is everything all right?"

"Fine, fine," he said casually. "You know, same crap, different day. Oh, and could you have one of the custodians go to Heather Prince's locker and clean off the graffiti immediately?"

"Right away," she replied but thought, *What the hell is going on around here?*

Chapter 20

All around, wrestlers were just going through the motions. As he stood musing over it, Box came up next to him.

"Worst practice I've seen in years," he stated quietly. "Not one of them is showing a bit of energy. Should we run them?"

"No. The last practice before the opening match usually sucks. I was kinda expecting it."

His whistle shrilled, and all movement stopped.

"All right," he bellowed. "That's enough of this bullshit!

"I don't think I've seen so many heads planted firmly up their own asses in 30 years of coaching. I hope you get them out by tomorrow, or it's gonna be a long season." He shook his head with visible disgust for emphasis. "You know what, screw it. You're either ready, or you're not. Shower up."

The smiles that appeared at the idea of a half practice were short-lived as he followed with, "And I want every one of you across the hall in the team room in exactly ten minutes. Anyone who's not showered and dressed—everybody runs."

They all ran for the locker room, highly motivated. Box looked at Wolfe curiously.

"Figure it's as good a time as any for my pre-season pep talk," Wolfe replied.

"Should we give them popcorn?" he joked.

"Fuck that. We should make them run," Box grumped. "Half their fat asses might not make weight."

Wolfe smiled at Boxwood's sunny disposition, and they headed toward the coaches' room.

84

Chapter 21

Heather was standing outside the team room, finding it a little difficult to breathe, when her growing anxiety was interrupted by Coach Wolf's low growl.

"They better all be dressed, but I'll check and give you the thumbs up."

He pushed open the door and barked, "Who's ready to run?"

But they were, to a man, fully dressed and waiting on benches and seats.

He pushed the door back open. "All right, Prince, it's clear."

She forced herself to walk in, heart pounding, not making eye contact. Most of the boys also looked around at other things as she slid into a chair near the benches.

Wolf thought to himself, *Is everything going to be weird this year? I hope not*, he mused as he shook his head. Then, trying to keep a jovial tone, he added, "Well, you guys let me down. I bet Coach Boxwood 20 bucks that one of you would still be wrapped in a towel, and we'd all have a nice run."

"Sorry to disappoint, Coach," Juwann joked, and a light chuckle went around the room.

Coach Boxwood came in with an armful of ties. He was starting to sort them when he asked, "What joke did I miss?"

Before Wolf could explain, he saw Juwann with a hand up as if to shush everyone and a cell phone to his ear.

"Davies!" Boxwood snapped. "Put that damn thing away this instant."

"Sorry, Coach," he said, making as if to pass the phone to him. "It's the eighties. They say they want those pants back."

He delivered the line with all seriousness, and after a brief pause, the room erupted in laughter. Even Heather joined in as Wolf shook his head.

"I'll have you know, Davies, these are classics. They are the best pants money can buy. I've been rocking these since… well, the eighties." The laughter rose again.

"Speaking of fashion, though, here's a little something that's been around since before the eighties." He started going around the room, tossing scarlet-colored neckties to each wrestler. "Do not lose them, drip ketchup on them, or use them to wipe your… nose."

The seniors groaned, having heard the joke several years running, but the newbies smiled at Boxwood, lowering his usually dour demeanor slightly.

As they all looked at the silky red ties with the knight emblazoned on the bottom, he tossed two to Willie and Heather, the only ones he had ordered in a boy's size.

"Simple look. Neatly pressed khakis, white dress shirt, black shoes." He hesitated for a moment, then looked at Heather. "Of course, we can make some adjustments if…"

"No, it's fine," she responded. "I have all those things and was planning on it."

"Okay. Fine."

"Dang, I was hoping she wanted to wear a skirt," Juwann chimed in. "Cuz if she was gonna, so was I. And it's nice too. Not too short, pleats in the front. And," he stood and stuck out his backside a little, "it doesn't make my butt look big."

He sashayed a little to a chorus of guffaws.

"That's enough. Let's get serious. We dress as a team on match days. No exceptions. And after we win, everyone wears their team shirt." He paused. "And we need to make a few adjustments to our schedule this year. In case you haven't noticed, we have a young lady with us…"

"No way! Who?" Juwann looked around with mock seriousness but stopped swiftly and gazed down beneath Wolf's withering glare.

"So," he continued, "after home matches, we will meet right here. Ten minutes, and everyone is showered and fully dressed. You just showed you can do it. For away matches, I want everyone on the bus in fifteen minutes. We'll meet and then head home."

His glare returned to Juwann to preempt any wisecracks.

"All right. Let's get a good night's rest. Eat lightly stay hydrated, and I want all of you ready to wrestle like champions tomorrow afternoon. Bring it in."

He stretched out his hand, palm down, and every hand rested atop his. He glanced at Jake.

"On three! One, two, three…"

"KNIGHTS."

Chapter 22

She was on her way up when she saw a faint light coming from the front room. She walked over quietly and peered in. Her dad was sitting silently, looking at a book with just the small table lamp glowing softly.

Watching for a moment, she felt a surge of tears almost well up. She had the urge to rush in like she did when she was little, leaping into his lap and knocking whatever he was working on flying. He never cared what it was. He'd pick it up later. She half wanted his arm to wrap around her as she snuggled in, and they both ignored the rest of the world. But she didn't. She wasn't five anymore.

Something made him look up. "Hey, Peanut," he said softly, just like when she was five. "How you doing? School okay?" He turned the book over in his lap.

"Fine. Everything's good." She cut to the chase. "My first match is tomorrow." An edge started to sharpen between them.

"I know." He took a moment. "Look, it's amazing that you've come this far. It's awesome. But," he hesitated, "I wish you'd reconsider. You've proved your point. Why not just stop right now?"

"Quit? On my team? Really?" She started to get hostile. "That goes against everything you ever taught me," she added incredulously.

"No, I taught you to be smart and reasonable." He paused, searching for the right words. "Look, up to this point, it's been under control. A few okay competitors. But now…"

She cut him off. "So I only made it this far because there were just some mediocre *boys* in our school? You still believe I'm not good enough? Well, I've proven myself so far, and I will again tomorrow."

About to turn and storm away, she hesitated when she saw his hand go up, as if to apologize.

"It's not that at all. You have proven yourself beyond anyone's wildest expectations. It's just that it's going to get ugly. Really ugly. Ugly, mean, and violent in ways you can't imagine." He paused again, looking for the right way to proceed. "It's kind of like puberty. Having a boyfriend at ten and having a boyfriend now are completely different. It's dangerous. The innocence is gone. It can get really… crazy."

"So is that it? You're worried about me being around these guys?"

"No. And yes."

A smirk had started on her face. "Shall I assume then that everything you told me growing up was a lie?"

"No, not at all. It was true." Another pause. "Then. It's just that things change. You're not ten, and believe me, it's not innocent. And I never thought you'd come face to face with it."

Too late, she thought, growing angrier by the second.

"We wouldn't be having this conversation if I was a boy, though, would we?"

"No. It would be an entirely different conversation. He would have to learn to live with these things. There'd be no avoiding it. But I'd hoped you'd never have to see it, let alone deal with it."

Too late! She wanted to snap back, but she swallowed it down.

"So, I'm guessing you won't be coming tomorrow."

"Heather, please. I need you to…" He was talking to her back.

Tossing behind her like a casually dropped grenade, she added, "Don't come. I don't want you there if you're not one hundred percent behind me. I'm fine on my own." She headed up the stairs.

He watched the empty space where she had been for several minutes. Taking a deep breath, he flipped the photo album he'd been looking back over. It was turned into a picture of him in this very chair, with a very happy and beautiful five-year-old smiling brightly as Mom had snapped the picture.

A choking sound escaped his throat, and he had to close the album.

Chapter 23

Even though she had him wrapped up, he was inching toward the line.

"Thirty seconds!" she heard someone yell.

It was 5-4. If he got to the line, it was an escape and a draw. The clock was ticking, and he was redoubling his efforts. A thought struck her, and she acted on it.

Letting go with her legs, she brought her body perpendicular to his shoulders. He sensed what he thought was her mistake, let his chest hit the mat, and stretched with all he had for the line. He was shocked when she put her forearm right across his shoulder blades. Then, harking back to her cheerleader days, she executed a perfect round-off, using his back as a brace. With her feet landing just inside the circle, she repositioned her arms under his outstretched one and drove back against him, actually turning him and gaining a control position. With twenty seconds left, she was going for the pin. Focusing completely, she was oblivious to the uproar from the benches and the bleachers behind her.

The whistle shrilled. The air horn blasted.

"Time," shouted the official.

Heather relaxed her grip and leaned back. The Hispanic boy was not smiling now. He pushed her away as he scrambled to his feet, then turned and stormed off, not waiting for the official to acknowledge the victor.

The opposing coach stepped to the circle, practically foaming at the mouth.

"What the hell was that? That was an illegal move! She should be disqualified!" he screamed.

Before the ref could respond, Wolfe, who had stepped up to congratulate Heather, did.

"How?"

"You saw it. She totally left her feet. She can't do that!"

"Every time a wrestler hops back away from a takedown attempt, he leaves his feet. His entire body is in the air. Every time he crosses over the top of another wrestler, he leaves his feet. Happens at least ten times every match." Wolfe calmly shook his head. "No rule against it."

"Not like that! It was a fucking cartwheel, for God's sake! You can't do that in wrestling!" He continued to rant.

The official jumped in. "Hey, watch the language, Bobby. One more, and you're outta here." He paused. "But Wolfe's right. At the same time, I've never seen that before, there's nothing in the rule book against it. The decision stands."

Turning his attention back to the official scorer, he held up two fingers. "And two for riding. Green."

"What?!" The coach screamed again, the bench joining in behind him. "That's fucking bullshit! He was escaping!" The boys were off the bench, pumping fists and jumping forward.

"He was seconds from being pinned when the horn saved him. And you're done. You've got thirty seconds to leave the gym, or it's a total forfeit." The official stood with his arms firmly on his hips.

The visiting coach's face was crimson and ready to explode. Then logic grabbed him, and he turned and yelled at his boys. "Everybody sit down. NOW!" he bellowed.

Turning to his assistant, he gave some instructions. Before leaving, he got inches from the official's face and said through gritted teeth, "I'm officially protesting this decision. Hell, I'm officially protesting this entire match."

"Duly noted," the official responded calmly. "I'll send in my report first thing tomorrow."

"Oh, and since I'm getting kicked out anyway," he paused for effect, "fuck you."

He turned and stormed off, the few visiting fans standing and cheering while the home crowd booed and laughed.

The official returned to the circle and held up Heather's hand. The crowd politely cheered. She looked up at the scoreboard. It read:

113 Prince 8-5

Not only was she a varsity wrestler. She had won.

As she ran off, Wolfe had a big smile despite himself and almost smacked her behind. At the last minute, he put a big hand right on her back.

"Great job!"

She practically ran down the bench, getting a high-five from the next wrestler and just about everyone. She didn't even notice as Juwann had to tie his shoe as she passed, and Marco suddenly had something urgent to get out of his bag behind the bench.

She almost lost her breath when she reached the end as Jon Martin scooped her up in a bear hug.

"That was awesome! You rock!" he shouted.

She returned a quick hug around his massive shoulders.

"Thanks," she puffed out in the middle of one last squeeze as he put her down.

Willie was ready with a high five and a huge smile full of crooked teeth.

"Wow, I've never seen anything like that before. Where'd that come from?" he squeaked.

Heather shook her head. "No idea." She was still breathing hard and starting to cool down. "I had to stop him from getting to the line, and I thought of that walkover drill." She paused. "I can't believe it actually worked."

"Did you see their coach's face? I thought he was gonna have a heart attack."

They quickly sat in their spots as the official signaled in the next wrestlers. Willie reached over for one last high-five.

Heather settled in and scanned the stands. Hoping but not surprised, she saw only her mom sitting, clapping, and waving frantically to get her attention. She smiled and waved back to her mom's double thumbs-up.

Oh well, she thought, steeling herself. His loss.

As she looked away from her mom, she saw another smiling thumbs-up—Ms. D. Heather smiled back and gave a quick wave. It was nice to have a few faces there for her. She turned her attention back to the match.

The Scarlet Knights were on fire. They won every match, five by pin. The stands were rocking as Jon Martin closed it out with a last-minute pin of a huge 300-pounder. Even if he was a bit flabby, 300 is 300.

Wolfe and Boxwood couldn't stop smiling.

Chapter 24

"All right, all right." Wolfe walked around the circle in the middle of the team room. "Awesome job tonight. Obviously, everybody won, but I was most impressed by the effort. Tremendous job—everyone brought it tonight."

"Yeahhhh!!" Juwann screamed as he jumped and gave a full flex for effect. "Bring it on, boyzzzz!!" He started around the circle, slamming high fives as he hopped around. "All out! All out! Every time!" He slapped high as hard as he could. "Do it! Balls to the walls, boys!!"

The hooting and hollering slackened, and a few laughs and snickers kicked in.

"All right, that's enough, Davies," Wolfe said, shaking his head, knowing Box was probably holding back laughter behind him. "Wrong phrase, right sentiment. If we bring that every match, we will be going places."

He paused and rubbed his hands together. "So, whaddaya think, Box? Did these guys earn a day off or what?"

Boxwood snorted. "Horseshit," was his one-word answer.

"Sorry, boys, but he's absolutely right. As good as it went tonight, we have a long way to go." He gazed around, letting it set in. "That was a decent team we crushed tonight, but not a great one—not even a really good one. We have some great ones coming up, and even with tonight's effort, we'll be seriously challenged at every weight class by them."

He paused and made sure he had total eye contact. "So be ready. Tomorrow's practice will be the toughest yet. We are just getting started." He spoke evenly for emphasis. "We have places to go and a long way before we get there. So tomorrow, we dig in and do the work. Everybody in!!" he bellowed.

As one, they hopped into the circle. Hands piled on top of his. He looked around at all the intense faces.

"Prince," he barked out. "I've been in wrestling for forty years, and I have one question."

They all waited.

"What in the hell was that!!??"

They burst out laughing as a team. Heather reddened a little but responded.

"Secret weapon, Coach." She raised her eyebrow a little and added, "And there's more where that came from."

The laughter rose again as Wolfe shook his head, smiling.

"I can't wait. All right, Prince, take us out."

"One, two, three. KNIGHTS!"

The hands pushed down in unison, and they broke—chatting, laughing, slapping backs.

Heather smiled as she turned to head back to her locker room.

She was a Scarlet Knight.

Chapter 25

Heather checked her makeup again. She didn't often wear it, but she'd hardly slept last night. Excitement, adrenaline, and replaying the day in her head had kept her from falling asleep. And when she did, she kept jumping awake in a panic, dripping sweat.

Oh well, she thought. *It'll calm down after a few matches,* she assured herself. Adding a few more touches to smooth out the dark circles, she sighed.

Stepping back, she checked her look in the mirror. *Not bad.* The victory shirt fit her just right. Her jeans were a little tight—Mom must have tossed them in the dryer again. The hair was good. Makeup didn't look over the top. She smiled, a little forced, but okay. Taking a deep breath, she headed downstairs.

Mom was at the table drinking coffee. "Well, look at you. Winner. Ready to go strut your stuff today," Mom beamed.

"It's just one win, Mom."

"Maybe. But it was an awesome one. You rocked. That last move—oh my God, it was amazing. And it was historic."

"No, Mom. We've shut out teams before. They did it a bunch of times in Dad's day."

"Not that," she retorted, shoving the newspaper across the table toward her. "This."

There, in bold headlines, read: **"Prince Makes History in Scarlet Knights' Rout of Central."**

Her jaw dropped as she read the article, which led to several paragraphs about the fact that she was the first female wrestler to ever win a varsity match in the state. It also pointed out how she won on a spectacular and controversial move with seconds left. The article finished by mentioning Jake's, Juwann's, and Jon Martin's pins and how big things were predicted for the Knights.

"Oh my God," Heather said breathlessly. "But I wasn't even one of the big wins. I mean, Jake pinned his guy in 12 seconds. That's amazing. That should be the story."

"Nonsense," Mom insisted. "You did something amazing, something every young girl in America can look up to. That is definitely the story. Jake will probably pin ten more guys. No one can ever be the first girl to win again. It's you and you alone."

Part of her wanted to argue that she wanted to be a wrestler, not a *girl* wrestler, but another part did feel amazed and proud. She had done it—something no one else had ever done.

"Wow," she said softly.

"Wow, indeed. Give me that back. It is going right in the scrapbook. No," she reconsidered, "I'm getting that framed!"

"Mom…"

"Don't even start. I'm doing it."

Heather smiled, shook her head, and headed for the kitchen to grab her lunch. She paused when she saw her dad pouring his coffee. She felt heat rising in her, ready for another battle.

"Hey," he said evenly as he stirred in cream and sugar.

"Good morning." She matched his tone, keeping a grip on her rising anger.

Nodding toward her shirt, he added, "Looks good on you. You really shook things up yesterday, I hear."

"Why?" she snapped back. "Because I shocked their little world? Dared to beat them on their own turf?"

He held his hands up in surrender. "Just saying it was a big win for you. The first one is always the hardest. Congratulations." He raised his coffee cup with a half-smile and turned toward his office.

Shit, she thought. *Why'd I do that?*

"Thanks," she said as he walked away.

She waited a second, took a deep breath, and headed toward the door.

Chapter 26

She felt a little uncomfortable with the congratulations and high-fives as she headed down the hall. Lots of smiles and woo-hoos, but also a number of people watching her and then turning to make some hidden comment to those around them.

Oh well, she thought. *I guess I'm a one-day wonder. After tomorrow's match, it'll die down.*

She smiled back as some girls from the basketball team shouted, "Way to go, Heather! Give 'em hell!"

Once again, her reverie was broken as she neared her locker. Everyone seemed to drift away as she saw today's entry. It showed a small wrestler on all fours with his eyes bugging out and his mouth open in a shocked gasp. Behind him, positioned firmly against his rump, was a well-muscled, larger girl in a wrestling singlet that sort of resembled her, albeit with exaggerated musculature. The caption read:

"Fuck with me, and you get..."

Once again, she was impressed with the creativity.

While she looked it over, Ms. T, the custodian, arrived with a bucket and cleaning solvents.

"Sorry," she sighed, shaking her head. "Guys can be such assholes. Don't let them get you down. You're doing great."

"Thanks," Heather responded, surprised. "Sorry, you've gotta deal with it."

She laughed. "If not this, some other mess. Just wish I got it before you had to see it. For what it's worth, Big Ed and Officer Smiley were here almost instantly. They dragged half a dozen punks down to the office. One of them will talk. They always do."

"Oh. Well, sorry again. I have to get to class."

"No big deal. Like I said, don't let a few a-holes ruin it for you. They're just jealous."

"Thanks."

Chapter 27

It had been a good day so far, she thought, as she headed into the lunchroom. Weaving in and out of the milling crowd, she made her way to her usual table. Several of the girls saw her and waved.

In the fall, the table had been full, with no seats available and every girl squeezed in. Almost entirely soccer players, they were a tight-knit pack. But with the season change often came a shift in friendships. Not that they weren't still friendly, just that those who played a winter sport began to spend most of their time with their teammates. Basketball players now sat mostly with other girl b-ballers, and the swimmers moved like a school of fish, always together.

In addition, the mid-sophomore year was when many girls started getting their licenses and cars, opening up new social circles. Not to mention that for many, it was the advent of the serious boyfriend. In short, things changed.

Still, the table was three-quarters full, with many year-round soccer girls and several friends—a nice group, she thought as she plopped her books onto the table.

"Uh-oh," Sara Mears joked, "we've got a superstar sitting with us now. Are the paparazzi gonna harass us?"

"Shut up!"

"Seriously, though. Holy shit, that's awesome. Cover of the sports page. Damn!"

"I know," Madison Manford chimed in. "My mom freaks out and buys a hundred papers if my name's in the box score on page twelve."

"Like you're ever in the box score!" Sara teased.

"Hey, I scored five goals this year!" Maddie countered. "And like ten assists."

"My mom's got all those tiny little box scores on one page of her scrapbook."

"What about that picture where you were jumping all over us at the North game?" Heather added.

"Oh, that one..." Maddie started turning red. "My mom framed that one."

"And sent a copy to every relative," Sara kept teasing.

"Yeah." Madison sighed, still blushing.

"Your dad's probably having a poster made of it. Isn't he like *Mr. Wrestling*?" Sara added.

"Yeah, probably." Heather bit into her sandwich, not wanting to tell everyone about what a dick her dad was being.

The conversation moved on, bouncing from boys to bitchy teachers, what other girls were doing, and general nonsense. Heather joined in here and there, laughing along with everyone else, totally enjoying the casual meaninglessness of it all.

Finally, she took her tray and headed out, dropping it in the bin near the garbage and grabbing a pass for the lavatory.

The hall was empty and quiet at first. Then she heard them.

At first, it was just footsteps. As they grew louder, she looked over her shoulder and saw them striding toward her from behind, one from each side—Juwann and Marco. Her heart started to race, and she quickened her pace.

"Well, if it ain't our biggest star," Juwann stated with mock seriousness.

"Yeah, I'm sure we'd have lost everything if she didn't inspire us," Marco chimed in.

"I'm inspired right now. Ain't you?"

"Yeah, just that walk gets me real inspired."

They were getting closer.

"I know, it's exciting, isn't it?" They both chuckled.

She took several quick steps and turned into the ladies' room.

Her heart was pounding, and she could hardly breathe. Rushing to the last stall, she stepped in and pulled the latch. Something between a sob and a cough exploded from her chest. She could barely breathe.

Then she swallowed a gasp as the door banged open.

A little whistle sounded, followed by a lightly spoken, "Hello, hello."

Two sets of footsteps echoed in the nearly empty room.

"Come out, come out, wherever you are," the mocking voice continued.

Heather's hands tightened into fists as she waited silently in the last stall.

The silence and footsteps were interrupted by a strident voice.

"What the hell are you two assholes doing in here?" an incredulous voice boomed. Heather recognized it as Ellen Kyle.

"What the hell are *you* doing in here?" Juwann feigned shock. "Are you doing that gender thing, using the men's room?"

"Do you see any urinals, moron?" she barked back.

Juwann hammed up a look around. "Damn, I knew there was something different about this one, Marco. Whoops, our bad, excuse us," he said with mock seriousness, hands up as if apologizing.

"You've got five seconds to get out." She stared them down.

"Or what? You're gonna have your brothers beat us up?" Marco snidely replied. "We're so scared."

Ellen, whose twin brothers were the starting tackles on the football team, eyed him coolly. "I don't need my brothers to deal with a punk like you." She stepped forward.

"Whoa, whoa," Juwann interjected, stepping between them. "We cool. It's all good. Just walked into the wrong door. C'mon, Marco, gotta get to class."

Marco let himself be led out but kept staring her down as he backed out.

"Sorry, didn't mean to bug you during your period," he said with false sincerity.

"Fuck off, asshole," Ellen snapped as the two boys chuckled on their way out. Shaking her head, she turned to wash her hands. A bang to her left made her look up, eyeing Heather exiting the last stall.

"What was all that?" she asked as she bent over the sink, partly to wash her hands, partly to hide her face as her hair hung down.

"Two of your wrestling buddies," she said, shaking her hands and heading for the air dryer. "Apparently wanted to see what a girls' room looks like. I can't stand either of them." She punched the dryer button. "Juwann is such a phony, and his little butt boy is just a total scumbag."

Heather tried to laugh. "Okay, Ellen, but don't hold back. How do you really feel about them?"

"I know they're your teammates, but I've known them since, like, third grade. They've always played football with my brothers. They were jerks then, and they're even bigger jerks now."

"Teammates, yes. 'Buddies,' definitely not," Heather responded, splashing some cool water on her face. "They are two of the biggest jerks I've ever met."

Ellen watched her for a second. "It's pretty cool what you're doing. I mean, being the first girl ever and everything."

"I just want to wrestle," Heather sighed. "I wish none of the other stuff mattered. But it's such a big deal for all the wrong reasons." She hesitated. "I mean, it feels like 90 percent of the people hate me, and they don't even know me."

"Yep, no doubt about it. People suck." Ellen shook her head as she tore paper towels from a dispenser. "Still, it's pretty cool. I mean, there are probably a lot of girls who want to try things but are afraid to get in there. You're, like, showing them they can."

"Thanks, but like I said," Heather dabbed at her eyes with a paper towel, "I just want to wrestle."

"I get it." She hesitated. "You know, until, like, seventh grade, I used to play football with my brothers all the time. And I was just as good as they were." She shook her head as she tossed away her paper towel. "I stopped, not just because they and the other boys got so much bigger, but because it started getting weird. It was like… I don't know. They'd touch me too long or try to grab the ball and accidentally 'miss,' and their hands would go other places.

"The last time I played with all the guys, I stopped and whipped the ball in this kid's face after he 'touched' me even after I was out of bounds, and all his buddies were laughing. He called me a bitch, and I was gonna fight him, but one of my brothers came flying in and tackled him, and the other punched him in the face and broke his nose." She shook her head. "They got in a bunch of trouble, but my dad was mad at me. I got a whole lecture on how I should 'be a young lady' and 'why was I playing with the boys,' and I was 'forbidden to play football'—just go play 'my sports with other girls.'"

Heather half laughed in response. "I was so pissed. It just wasn't fair. They were the assholes, but I had to stop playing. I mean, I get it now. He was just trying to look out for me. Still, it sucks."

Heather nodded. "It absolutely sucks."

"Anyway, you're doing awesome." Ellen held up a hand for a high-five as they headed out the door.

Heather looked both ways, a little hesitant to head back down the empty hallway as Ellen turned and went the opposite way. But she took a deep breath and willed herself ahead. One foot in front of the other, she headed back toward the lunchroom.

Chapter 28

The entire bench rose as one, clapping as Willie sprinted off after the ref let go of his upraised arm. His first pin. Heather, being the next wrestler up, was the first to greet him. She had her hand raised for a high-five but quickly caught him as he practically knocked her over with a full-body hug. She could hear the laughter from the bench and the stands. It sounded great.

"Way to go," she laughed as he jumped off and headed toward the gauntlet.

Coach Wolf was first, and the laughter rose again as he held both hands in front to ward off a possible hug leap. But he surprised everyone by grabbing Willie's attempted high-five and pulling him in for a bro hug, practically dwarfing Willie in the embrace. An "Awww!" rose from the crowd, followed by more laughter.

Heather jogged toward the center of the circle with a big grin on her face. She did her best to shake it off and regain her game face. The ref stood mid-circle, arm already raised, whistle ready in hand, standing in Semper Fi erectness with a gray buzz cut. He gave a quick burst from the whistle as he watched the home team wrestler saunter toward the circle. The boy didn't even have his headgear strapped tight yet.

The ref's jaw tightened slightly, and he barked, "Let's go!"

The boy stopped at the edge of the circle and raised his hand toward his chin strap. Instead of tightening it, though, he dramatically pulled it over his head. With a flourish, he held it out and dropped it on the mat. Like a marcher in a parade, he executed a crisp 180, turning his back on Heather, the ref, and the circle. He crossed his arms and stood there defiantly.

The ref's jaw was as tight as a drum. Crimson ran up his neck in contrast to his whitish hair. Striding to the edge of the mat, he stared at the coach. "You've got till the count of ten to get your wrestler on this mat," he hissed through clenched teeth.

The coach responded by putting his clipboard in one hand, crossing his arms, and turning his back on the fuming ref. The team rose as one from the bench and followed suit. As if on cue, the stands rose and joined in the silent protest.

The ref forewent the ten count and strode to the center of the mat, raised Heather's hand, and shouted in his loudest voice, "Winner by forfeit!" Shaking his head, he turned and walked to the scorer's table, leaving Heather alone and shocked.

She walked slowly off. Her bench looked shocked but angry, and instead of the normal cheers, they were all talking to the wrestler next to them. Almost zombie-like, she moved past Wolf, whose hand shot out and grabbed her arm.

"Hey, head up. You were ready to go. He didn't have the balls to wrestle you. Remember that—you scared the shit out of him. That was just a big show to save face."

She bobbed her head up and down and kept walking. There were a few high-fives and arm slaps that she hardly noticed. Three-quarters of the way down, a solid grip halted her shoulder. It was Jake.

He got right in her face. "That was absolute bullshit!" He looked enraged. "We are gonna fuck these guys up!"

Again, she shook her head, croaking out a "Thanks" as she went by.

When she arrived at the end, Big Jon gently placed a hand on her shoulder and tried to comfort her. "Hey, that's all on them. You're awesome. They're a bunch of chickenshit assholes."

She smiled and nodded. At the very end, she received a second, but less joyous, hug from Willie.

Jake wasn't kidding. Every wrestler went out to the circle angry, and every wrestler came back victorious. It was a complete rout, including six pins and an overall 64-0 victory. The energy and testosterone were explosive as they headed for the bus afterward. The opponents' gym cleared out quickly, and the team boarded with lots of joking, pushing, and posturing.

As they milled about, climbing into seats, Wolf stood up front, waiting with a huge smile on his face. They began to settle.

"Gentlemen," he started, "that was one of the finest efforts I've ever seen." He looked over the quieting group. "Talk about an ass-whoopin'. Damn!" he dragged out.

They burst into energetic laughter at the unexpected praise—and phrasing.

"Seriously. All of you wrestled with the kind of focus and ferocity it takes to become a state champion. We definitely have something to build on here." He paused. "But it was a weird night. One of your teammates was disrespected."

He turned and looked at Heather, who had hoped her match would be forgotten in the uproar of victory—but no.

"In all my years of wrestling, I have never seen anything like that. What a total pus—punk—move."

He nodded his head and said to Heather, "They were afraid of you. He knew you were going to beat him and embarrass him. So, instead of being man enough to compete, he went for some BS show. What a shame. You were more than ready to test your skills. But he was afraid. Despite the show he made, he was, is, and always will be a loser. You, though," he paused for emphasis, "are a winner."

"Yeahhh!!!" Juwan hooted as he ran around the room, powerfully slamming high-fives with everyone. The room started a slow chant— "Knights, Knights, Knights"—which grew in volume and rhythm until the room was practically shaking. Even Heather smiled and joined in.

The coaches pulled back and watched the room celebrate themselves. Boxwood leaned over and shouted in Wolf's ear to overcome the din. "I think we just found that 'team' attitude we've been looking for."

"You may be right, Box. You may be right."

Chapter 29

He was wrong.

When Heather came down for breakfast, her mom was beaming. "You made the front page of the sports section again." With a flip, she tossed the section over.

Heather scooped it up, and there it was—a picture of her and the ref standing in shock as the other wrestler defiantly turned his back. Despite the caption saying he quit, the photo was centered and timed perfectly to make him look like the hero.

"Great," Heather said wryly.

"It is. The whole story is about you and how brave you are to face their ignorant behavior."

"But we crushed them, shut them out, and it says nothing about the team besides the score. We had seven pins. Jake's was in five seconds. The story should be about that, not about me," she said, shaking her head. "And certainly not about that asshole."

"Language, young lady," her dad said evenly as he sat down and poured some coffee from a carafe. "Just because you're around a bunch of meatheads doesn't mean you should start talking like them."

She responded with a smirk.

He continued, "Tough one last night, huh?"

"Total bull...oney," she adjusted at the last moment.

"Indeed." He paused, measuring his words. "This is the kind of bullshit I have been trying to warn you about. Are you sure you want to continue exposing yourself to this?" He tilted his head rhetorically. "It's only going to get worse."

She bit back the angry retort she wanted to throw at him and curtly stated, "Aren't you the person who's always told me, 'Never quit. Once you start something, you have a moral obligation to see it through'?"

"Yes, that was me. And I still mean that. But this is not a normal situation..."

"Why? Because I'm a girl?" she snapped back.

"Partially!" His voice also rose.

"Okay, okay. Can we at least agree to a truce during breakfast?" Mom pleaded. "It's not healthy for any of us to start the day like this." She paused. "So, let's take a deep breath."

Heather scooped her eggs onto her toast. "I've gotta get going. I'm going to be late." She threw her backpack over one shoulder and gave Mom a quick half-hug. "Bye," she said generally, then headed out.

Mom waited a second until she heard the door slam. "Really? You couldn't even start with something positive? She's on the front of the sports page. Couldn't you at least toss in an 'Attagirl' and let her enjoy the moment?"

He sighed. "Oh, I read it. You think that's a good thing?" He raised his eyebrows. "It's not. It's the beginning of a shitstorm for her. Her teammates are going to be irritated and will ride her for it. The school wise-guys are gonna give her all kinds of crap." He paused. "You think her anger is all about me and how hard wrestling is?" He shook his head. "Wrestling's probably the easiest thing. The hard part is the shit she's getting from every angle."

"That's just your stubbornness talking. You can't admit you were, and are, wrong."

"She's not telling me about any of it because she doesn't want to hear 'I told you so.' But she's not telling you because she wants you to be happy about your decision, and she doesn't want you to feel bad about all of the things that are happening to her."

She threw up her hands, her head almost shaking in a shiver. "Your paranoia is incredible. You're making all this up in your head to try and justify your position." She pushed away from the table. "I gotta go. I can't even talk to you anymore. The things you're saying are just... just... crazy."

She stormed away.

He looked at the paper and said to no one in particular, "I wish they were."

Chapter 30

She walked quietly down the hall. There was very little commotion around her; almost everyone was busy at their lockers or in private conversation. She arrived at her locker, expecting nothing, but much to her chagrin, she found another wonderful marker drawing.

This one was particularly well done. It depicted a wrestler with his back turned, looking almost like Michelangelo's *David*, only with a headgear dangling from his hand instead of Goliath's head. She sighed. Looking around for the usual snickering, she found no one watching. Was that a statement, or had they all tired of it? She gave her own locker the finger, grabbed her things, slammed it shut, and headed down the hall.

Her teeth were clenched, though she didn't notice—this was becoming her normal state. Looking straight ahead, she strode toward homeroom. At an intersection, she paused for a millisecond, then took a quick turn down the hallway toward the office. Principal Dale had promised this was taken care of, yet here it was again.

Her fuming was broken as she heard a familiar mock-serious voice.

"Hey, superstar," Juwann said loudly. "Nice article today. Damn, you are the shit, aren't you?"

A few half-hearted claps emanated from his crowd of lackeys.

She stopped and glared back, but before she could reply, Marco joined in.

"Wow, you and the reporter must be close to getting such an exclusive," he said almost sincerely. He then moved his closed fist back and forth toward his mouth while simultaneously pushing out the side of his cheek with his tongue. This elicited great laughter from the throng of sycophants.

Her gaze hardened and narrowed as he continued his vulgar simulation for the crowd.

"You're really good at that. Get a lot of practice?" she shot back.

"Ooohhh," the crowd responded.

"Your mom showed me how," he retorted, displaying the limits of his imagination and intelligence. The crowd swayed his way.

"Juwann should thank her then since you seem to love doing him."

"Whoooa!" The crowd cranked up.

"Fuck you, bitch," he replied with the tried and true.

"Castaglia!" a booming voice bellowed as Mr. Cranston lumbered out of his classroom doorway. "Get in here this instant," he demanded, pointing into the room. "And the rest of you, get moving. Anyone standing in this hall when I count to five will have detention. Move!" he shouted for emphasis.

A quick flurry of movement cleared the area, with Juwann and Heather glaring at each other as they grudgingly moved in different directions.

Cranston turned into the room and shut the door behind him. "Sit down," he sternly commanded Marco. "Now, what in the world was that all about?"

"She was being a total b... brat. Talking stuff about me and Juwann."

"Really? Seemed like you were the one doing the talking."

Marco remained silent.

"Correct me if I'm wrong, but what happens if you get suspended?"

"Off the team." Marco hung his head.

"Exactly. And you're a senior. You should know better." He shook his head and went over to the phone on the wall. Punching in three numbers, he waited for the pickup.

"Coach. Cranston. Got one of your boys here." He paused and listened. "Yeah, he was screaming obscenities at some girl in the hallway." Another pause. "Exactly. Well, I figured I'd see if you wanted to handle it. You know, a little physical torture. If I send him downstairs..." He let it hang, listening. "Uh-hmm. Oh yeah, definitely. Right." A conspiratorial chuckle. "All right, he's on the way."

He paused, then lowered his voice. "Oh, and I think the girl might have been your girl wrestler. So..." Another pause. "All right, you too." He hung up.

Turning his attention back to Marco, he said, "Okay. You are damn lucky it was me. Your coach and I go way back, so as a favor to him, I'm gonna let you see him about this. Hope you like running."

Marco took the proffered pass and muttered with his head down, "Thanks."

"You're welcome," Cranston responded and added, "and I recommend that you get your head out of your ass."

He shook his head as Marco headed out the door.

Chapter 31

Practice was fairly easy, almost just going through the motions, so when Wolf's whistle shrilled, most inwardly groaned. "Here we go," they thought. It hadn't been hard enough, so he was about to ramp it up. Surprisingly, though, he said, "All right, that's enough for today. Don't shower yet, though. Team room in five—we'll change after."

They looked at each other curiously as they jogged off the mat. "What's up?" they wondered but were glad they weren't running. Heather had a few minutes, so she went to grab a water bottle from her "team room" and slowly headed back. She waited outside until she saw the coaches coming. They both smiled at her and headed in. Wolf had a few packages in his hands, so Box held the door for both of them and followed them in.

"All right," Wolf bellowed, "let's cut the grab-ass and have a seat." Like a game of musical chairs, they all scurried about. Heather went to her go-to spot, a desk off to the side where she half sat, half leaned. They settled quickly as Wolf looked around.

"Good." He started to pace a little. "Yesterday was a tough one." He paused. "On the one hand, it was the most dominating victory we've had in years. On the other hand, some truly disturbing things happened." All eyes were on him as he gazed from wrestler to wrestler. "I was appalled that a wrestler could quit like that. I didn't think I'd ever see that in my sport. I was also shocked that a team and a coach would allow such a thing—to try and embarrass an opponent like that." He shook his head in disgust. "Fortunately, our wrestler is way too strong a person to let that affect her." He turned to Heather and gave her a positive nod. She smiled in response. A smattering of applause and a few "Yeah" and "Way to go" comments arose.

"I was also pleased to see that, as a team, we rallied together and made them pay for that insult." Another round of congratulations rang out.

"Unfortunately, though, some negative things popped up today that I need to talk to you about." He weighed his words. "Sometimes people outside the sport can miss the point. They get all excited about the sensational thing and miss what's really going on." He hoped he was putting this right. "For instance, newspapers. Usually, we get a little blurb on the second or third page, just a few paragraphs on some highlights." He picked up a folded sports page from the table and waved it for effect. "Front page today. But I'm pretty sure Heather didn't want any of this. Am I right?" He looked her way.

"Definitely not!" she replied, shaking her head.

"No. The writer sort of mentions her and then makes it all about this loser asshole, as if he were some sort of hero for taking a stand." He tossed the paper in the trash can for emphasis. "What a crock. Half a page on quitting and being gutless. And," his voice rose, "not a mention of the score—an incredible shutout, with seven pins. Seven pins!" He was almost screaming. "And I'm damn sure it would have been eight if that weasel had dared to step in the circle." The noise rose as the audience bought in. "And there were a couple of milestones that were totally ignored. Sickening."

Doing an about-face, he strode back to the desk and grabbed one of the packages.

"Jake got a little something for you." Jake took the small wrapped package with a quizzical look. "Go ahead, open it."

Looking around, Jake tore off the wrapping and pulled out a small timer. It was set at the lowest setting—five seconds.

"Come on, push it," Wolf encouraged.

Jake was still looking around, wondering what was up, when the timer went off shrilly almost immediately. Several people, Jake included, jumped back, and laughter followed. Wolf let it die down before he explained.

"Five seconds," he nodded. "That's how fast you pinned that guy yesterday. According to the record books, it's the fastest ever—only been done three other times in the state. I found an article that said it's the fastest possible. Physically impossible to do it in less. I sure as hell never saw it before."

Another round of applause. Jake looked chagrined as he stared bemusedly at his memento but scowled when the inevitable "That's what she said" turned it into laughter.

But he recovered quickly. "Let's leave your mom out of this, Marco." That shifted the direction and volume of the laughter.

"All right," Wolf raised his hand. "Enough of that." He paused and strolled around. "All kidding aside, that is one hell of a feat. If the scientist is right, no one will ever top you, Jake." He let that sink in. "But that's not the only amazing feat that our local a-hole writer missed."

He stopped strolling and looked right at Juwann. "In this program's illustrious history, we've had seven—count 'em, seven— wrestlers who have won one hundred matches. Two of those seven went on to compete at the Olympics." He nodded. "And every one of them went on to wrestle at Division 1 schools. Yesterday, Juwann Davies joined that elite club." Again, he shook his head in amazement. "One hundred victories." He whistled softly and started clapping. One by one, everyone joined in. Soon, it was a standing ovation, boys reddening their hands with the noise and not a single joke.

As nearby wrestlers pounded his back and embraced him with bro hugs, Wolf walked back to the desk and grabbed another wrapped package, this one larger and flatter. He handed it to Juwann.

"Thanks, Coach." For a moment, Juwann seemed overwhelmed, but his nature took over. He held it up and looked it over. "Is it a close-up of my beautiful face?" He gazed around to chuckle.

Wolf shot back, "That was our first thought, but every time we tried to snap a picture of you, the camera broke."

"Woooohs" and "Oooohs" circulated in response.

"So we went with this instead."

Juwann tore off the wrapping and stared at the frame. At the top was his name and yesterday's date. At the bottom, all in caps was the phrase "100 WINS!" In the center, framed neatly, was a crisp one-hundred-dollar bill.

More "Woooohs" followed as he showed it around.

"Did you get one of those little hammers like they have on fire extinguishers?" someone joked. "Y'know, break in case of emergency."

"All right! Applebee's on Juwann tonight," another joked.

He shook his head. "No, no," he said, for once seriously. "I'm gonna be saving this. Thanks, Coach. This is awesome."

The coaches nodded. "Seriously, gentlemen and ladies, we have to stick together. Let's not let the outside stuff tear us apart. Bring it in."

They pushed their hands together.

"On three," Wolf barked. "One, two, three—KNIGHTS!"

They started to wander off when Wolf added, "Oh, by the way, Castaglia."

Marco winced. "Time to grab your running shoes."

They were surprised when Heather jumped off the desk she was sitting on and added, "Meet you out there."

Juwann looked at her for a minute and chimed in, "Yeah, I could use a little jog, too."

Jake looked sternly at both. "I'm in."

A rustle of whispers went around. It seemed like they were all in. Some looked a bit confused, while others, like Jake and Jon, looked serious. Regardless, five minutes later, they were all outside.

Chapter 32

The coaches stood off to the side, their ubiquitous clipboard and stopwatch in hand, as the wrestlers milled about the start point.

"Interesting," Wolf mused. "Sticking together for Castaglia seems a bit weird, but what the hell. Maybe we're starting to gel."

"Hope so," Box added dubiously.

Marco strolled over toward a stretching Heather. "Way to make it about you, Prince," he smirked and acted as if he was also stretching. "What's wrong? Didn't like Jake and Juwann getting the attention?"

She controlled her urge to punch him in the face. "Number one, I figure I did as much as you. But you got caught, so I kinda deserve this, too. But"—she looked firmly into his eyes—"mostly, I was hoping it was just gonna be me and you."

"I knew it. You want me."

She closed her eyes for a second. "I actually think I just threw up in my mouth. You are so disgusting, I can't even think of the proper word for it." Shaking her head and stretching over her right knee, she offered quietly, "No, I have a proposal for you. If you can beat me, I will quit this team right now."

"You're on." He didn't even let her finish.

"Wait," she called his attention back, "but if I win—again—you never speak to me or about me ever again." She locked eyes with him and even came closer as she softly added, "And my name never even crosses your lips again. Agreed?"

"Agreed." He stuck out a hand to shake on it.

She looked at it with disdain and turned back to stretching her left leg. He laughed and started to jog away. "Oh, it's on," he offered in parting.

Again, she ignored him.

As she stood and shook her legs out, ready to run, she saw Marco talking to Juwann and a group of others. They all stared right at her.

So that's how it's going to be.

She steeled herself. Focus filled her face, and she didn't notice as Jake walked over to speak with a very concerned Jon and Willie.

The shit was about to hit the fan.

Wolf looked at Box. "What's going on here?"

"Damned if I know."

Wolf shook his head and blew the whistle.

Heather was off like a shot. The throng of Juwann, Marco, and Warren Coates were caught off guard and took a moment to jump into a sprint, only to run directly into a "tripping" Jon Martin. They all went down in a pile.

The coaches started to move toward them to check, but the threesome hopped up quickly, loudly cursing Jon's fat ass, and scrambled to restart.

They all broke into a sprint, but Heather was already a hundred yards ahead. Jake and Willie were running smoothly side by side, halfway up the course. Bobby Holario had started out jogging with the oblivious throng but seemed to come to some revelation and tore into an all-out sprint to join Jake and Willie.

"What the fuck," both coaches croaked together.

Wolf tried to whistle them back, but they were long gone.

“Shit.” He turned to Boxwood, who still ran daily. “Can you catch them?”

“Not a chance,” he replied.

“Fuck!” was all Wolf could think of to say.

Chapter 33

The chase was on, and the fox was winning. Heather cruised at her strongest pace and was surprised when Jon Martin came sprinting up next to her.

"What are you doing?" she asked, her breath slightly accelerated.

"Don't slow down," he panted. "C'mon, let's race."

She glanced over her shoulder, surprised at the crowd coming on strong. She expected Marco, maybe Willie, but the six or seven vying like the starting gate of the Kentucky Derby caught her off guard. Realizing what was up, she turned back toward Jon.

"Don't worry, they can't catch me."

"Maybe not," his breathing was choppy, "but they're gonna try something."

Her brow knit as she took Jon's advice and picked up the pace.

Juwann decided to make a move and broke out in a sprint, the linebacker in him seeing a running back head downfield. He began closing the gap rapidly but was bumped off his rhythm by a jarring hit to the shoulder. Looking up, he saw the firmly set jaw of Jake glaring right at him.

"Leave her alone," Jake hissed.

Juwann laughed mirthlessly, resetting his intense stride as Jake kept up a step for step. "What, she your little bitch now?"

"Just let her be."

"Uh-uh. She loses to Marco, she quits," he spits out with rapid breaths. "And she needs to get the fuck off this team."

He tried to pull away, but Jake matched him and added firmly, "She stays."

Juwann turned it up to full volume. "Don't fuck with me."

Jake still kept up. Juwann began to smile as he inched ahead.

"What the—" he shouted as Jake slammed into his shoulder with all his body weight behind it. They both rolled into the brush on the side of the trail.

Heather and Jon both turned their heads toward the commotion twenty yards behind them, just in time to see Jake and Juwann go down. Jon seemed to let out a long exhale and, despite his all-out effort, began to fall off the pace.

Heather turned and picked it up another notch, consciously loosening her jaw and trying to relax her shoulders for full breathing.

So that's how it's going to be, she thought. Well, bring it on.

Behind her, Willie and Bobby Holario watched Jake and Juwann go down and start to grapple as Juwann tried to jump back up. They passed the cursing and whirling pair at a breakneck pace—Willie smooth but all out, Bobby with square shoulders pumping for all he was worth.

Their attention was broken by a voice-over their shoulders.

"Move, faggots!" Warren Coates barked, with Marco right beside him.

They did not. Instead, with a silent glance between them, they put on the brakes.

Marco ran straight into Willie's back, both suddenly in a tangle.

"Mother—" he bit off in surprise.

Warren, Juwann's backup at running back this year, was ready, though. He instinctively went into a spin move, like sliding right off a tackler, and completely missed Bobby. He laughed as Bobby stumbled over his own feet, having expected contact.

He was looking back as his feet regained the trail at full stride. The laughter stopped abruptly as he swung his head forward. His neck snapped in a whiplash as he hit a 260-pound wall.

Unfortunately for Warren, when Jon Martin realized he could no longer keep up with Heather, he slowed to a stop and waited in the middle of the trail.

No tangle this time. Warren just dropped like he'd been hit with a sledgehammer.

Jon dropped his hands to his knees and tried to catch his breath. He wasn't quite quick enough to stop Marco, who had untangled himself from Willie. Jon's lunge just missed as Marco skipped around on the edge of the trail.

"Watch it, fat ass!" Marco snapped as he broke into an all-out sprint to regain the trail.

Looking up, Marco saw nothing but daylight between him and his quarry. With a quarter mile or so left before they exited the woods and turned back up the school drive, he had about fifty yards to make up. Piece of cake, he thought, and he turned on the jets.

Seeing the turn up ahead, Heather increased her stride and closed on the last half mile with determination. She had just glanced back and knew Marco was coming all out. The race was on.

Marco was faster in an all-out sprint, and he knew it. A smile crept onto his face as he opened up and could visibly see how quickly he was closing. It was obvious. He would catch her before the turn, knock her on her skinny ass, and sprint to the finish before she could recover. Finally, they would be rid of this irritating, pushy bitch.

She didn't look back, but she could feel him gaining. Not quite at an all-out sprint, but close. She pushed toward the turn but felt he was going to catch her. No way he could keep up this sprint, she thought. But I still have a little left.

He was almost there, closing just beyond her left shoulder, when she instinctively veered off like a receiver with the safety on him just before the end zone. It was timed perfectly, just missing his forearm. The effort threw him off balance, and he stumbled, having to stagger and put his hand to the ground to keep from wiping out.

Heather quickly turned the corner and headed up the drive. With the coaches now in plain sight, Marco's last chance was to simply run her down and pass her. He broke into an all-out sprint.

At first, he began to close, but Heather had a finish left and turned it all the way up. With 200 yards to go, he was holding on. At 100 yards, she was pulling away. At 50 yards, he knew it was over and began to back off. It wasn't even close at the end. Heather strode through strongly and slowed into a cooldown as she passed the coaches.

"Nice job," they encouraged as she passed.

"Hey, best time all year. Way to go, Marco. You almost caught her!" They clapped as he passed, and he gave them a tight smile. He jogged out, head down, as he slowed and finally stopped, bending over his knees by Heather, who stood with her hands on her hips.

"Nice try, dickhead," she said, just loud enough for him to hear. "Now be a Knight and keep your word," she paused, "and never speak to me or about me again."

He nodded, and she walked away toward the locker room.

Wolf had been watching and was trying to figure out what the hell was going on when Box whistled and spoke lowly. "Look at this." As the next six came around the turn, he added, "They're all way ahead of their normal times. Whaddya think, some sort of bet?"

"Yeah," Wolf replied. "But what were the stakes?"

"Damned if I know," Box said, shaking his head. "But they sure were motivated."

Chapter 34

Friday's meeting, for the most part, was uneventful. No in-school drama, no locker drawings, no confrontations, and a long but boring bus ride to Rolling Hills.

Willie's match was an easy win, but he couldn't quite get the pin. Heather stepped in against a much shorter and stockier wrestler. Being nearly six inches shorter, he was pound for pound much more powerful, so she knew she had to be careful.

Not careful enough, though, as she quickly found out. He got her off her feet, and she paid for it. Once he had her moving, he took her down violently, essentially body-slamming her and throwing all of his weight onto her as he drove his shoulder into her sternum when she hit the mat.

The referee's whistle almost matched the grunt of the wind leaving her chest. She couldn't breathe for a second as the ref grabbed the other wrestler and pulled him off her.

"One!" he shouted and gestured toward Heather as he placed a hand on the shorter boy's chest and held him back.

Wolf was already on his feet, screaming. "DQ! That was out of control!"

The opposing coach was two steps behind, shouting, "Come on, you gotta be kidding me. That was clean!"

The ref looked down at Heather. She had forced a gasp of air into her lungs and was turning over to get up.

"Can the wrestler continue?" the ref asked with some concern.

Heather was nodding as she got to one knee, but Wolf was still yelling. "No way! He probably broke her ribs. DQ him now."

The ref looked at Wolf and then at Heather. "Yes or no?"

"I'm fine," she said, looking at the ref and then back at Wolf. "Really, I'm good." She started bouncing on the balls of her feet as if to emphasize it.

Wolf started to move as if he was going into the circle, but the ref reminded him, "Wrestler's call."

Wolf backed off, watching her carefully. The whistle shrilled again, and the ref repeated to the scorer as he held up a finger, "One for red."

Heather's opponent shook his head in disgust as he assumed the position. She adjusted her grip on his arm and wrapped her opposite arm tightly around his torso.

When the ref's hand came down and his whistle blasted, the boy went for a quick kick-out, but Heather anticipated it. He found himself on his back, with Heather trying to close her grip and drive her weight into a pin. He panicked and managed to turn over, but his face was quickly pushed into the mat as Heather locked him down with an arm bar. He turned and tried to inch toward the edge of the circle for an escape.

Heather was fine with that. In fact, she drove his arm and shoulder forward in the direction he was trying to go. As a result, his face was being rubbed raw on the mat. He tried harder to move forward, but Heather just drove down with everything she had. She vaguely heard Juwan's loud "That's gotta hurt!" in the background. She was focused on her opponent's anguished grimace, which she found herself enjoying, and the ref's half-raised hand, getting ready to break it up.

With a quick turn, she changed direction and started to roll him over again, the redness of his face evident to everyone. The ref jumped back as they moved.

"Two for riding, Red," he bellowed as he danced lightly around the combatants.

The next two periods were more of the same. Heather had learned her lesson and consistently danced away from his grip. He lost his cool and overextended himself several times, only to find his face ground into the mat again. Heather had settled into a cold determination and made him pay each time.

Mercifully for the shorter boy, it ended. The ref held up Heather's arm. "Red. 8-0."

The team jumped up cheering, even Marco. As she jogged off, Wolf grabbed her.

"How are your ribs?"

She stopped and put her hands on her knees as he placed his large hand on her back.

"Fine," she replied. "Just knocked the wind out of me."

"Let's try to keep our feet on the mat, okay?" he said with a half-laugh.

She smiled. "Yeah, I gotta work on that."

He patted her back as she jogged down the gauntlet of high-fives.

"Good match."

"Good match."

"Damn, you fucked him up!"

"Did you see his face?"

And so on, until she reached the end, where Jon and Willie were just nodding in approval as she high-fived them.

Taking her place next to Willie, she whispered, "Damn, that hurt."

He nodded knowingly.

Chapter 35

The buzz and hum were that of an easy victory. Light laughing and teasing filled the air as everyone spread out for the hour-long bus ride home. It was already fully dark, and before long, half of the bus would be sleeping off the exhaustion that came after extreme physical and emotional exertion.

Heather settled into one of the three seats near the front, her bag on the seat next to her, a semi-conscious buffer when Gina Angelo slid in beside her.

"Are you okay?" she half-whispered.

Gina was the team manager—the job Heather had not wanted—and she was good at it. In her lap was the ubiquitous book, a giant red scorepad that was the team's statistical bible. Scores, pins, takedowns, and records lined its pages. Gina was perfect for the role. Like Heather, she was a wrestling brat. Her two older brothers wrestled—one had been the state champ who graduated last year—and her younger brothers were already making a name for themselves. The twins were dominating at the middle school level and were expected to be the next great wrestlers after Jake and Juwan graduated.

Gina was perfect in other ways, too, but it was hard to tell at first glance. She dressed in baggy sweats, frequently wore an oversized wrestling shirt or loose jacket, and never wore makeup. Her long dark hair was always pulled back in a ponytail. If you looked closer, though, you'd notice perfect, if slightly rounded, features, a ready and radiant smile, and a fit, decidedly feminine form beneath the baggy clothes. She might have been the girl One Direction sang about, and she truly seemed unaware of herself. Genuinely nice, she was mostly left alone by the wrestlers, partly because of her unobtrusive look and demeanor and partly due to a healthy fear of her brothers.

Heather casually moved her bag to the floor to let Gina slide in comfortably. Gina put her own bag and the book on the floor beneath her.

"I thought you broke your back!" she continued.

"Just bruised," Heather responded softly as the hum of the bus settled in while they merged onto the highway.

"I don't know how you do it. That would have killed me." Gina shook her head and smiled, bringing Heather back to when they were both ten, sitting in the front row together while their fathers coached the youth wrestling program. They had both watched in awe as if beholding gods. Gina had been really kind and sweet back then. Heather's brows knit together for a second as she remembered why they had stopped seeing much of each other.

Gina's mother had battled breast cancer for several years—a losing battle. Everyone had felt bad for them and helped as they could, but the family had mostly drawn inward, circling the wagons. Now it was Gina and all the boys, and it was mostly wrestling all the time. But Gina seemed pretty happy on the surface and was still a great person.

"Oh, come on," Heather joked. "You'd probably be kicking ass if you were doing this. I seem to remember somebody pinning her little brothers and making them eat handfuls of grass."

Gina laughed. "Yeah, when they were little. They'd kill me now."

"Well, they have 30 or 40 pounds on you."

"Not quite that much," Gina pouted as she patted her belly.

"Yeah, right," Heather mocked.

"Seriously, I'm almost 140 pounds. If I tried to wrestle, I'd have to take on Warren and guys his size. I would get my back broken."

"If you were wrestling and doing the workouts, you'd probably be near 120 and wrestling guys like Marco. I think you could take him."

"Yeah, but then I'd actually have to touch him." She mimed throwing up in front of her. "He's the only one on the team I truly can't stand," she whispered.

"Join the club." Heather mimicked Gina's faux vomiting. They both stifled their laughter as heads turned their way.

"So," Heather casually started, "big Friday night plans?"

"The biggest," Gina said with feigned excitement. "Pick up the twins after their match, grab some pizza, and veg out over a few episodes of *Sunny with a Chance.* And you?"

"Almost as exciting. Ice bath for the back and continuing my *CSI* binge-watch—I'm up to season three."

"Damn, I'm jealous. We are just two social butterflies, aren't we?"

"Indeed." Heather shook her head. "Although I do have an opening in my schedule tomorrow. You?"

"Let me check my calendar." She turned up her palms and gazed at an imaginary book. "Hmm, look at that. It seems I have a cancellation—I think I can squeeze something in."

"Remember how we used to do sleepovers?"

"They were awesome!" Gina said excitedly. "And remember the tournaments? We used to get our own room—girls only!"

"No boys allowed!" they said in unison.

"Yeah, that was pretty cool," Heather said wistfully, hoping it didn't make Gina think about her mom. "Up for a sleepover?"

"Only if I can bring the movie."

"All right, if you insist. How about five-ish, in time for dinner?"

"Is your mom cooking?"

"Yeah. I'll check, but I'm pretty sure."

"Awesome. I'd love a home-cooked meal."

Heather drew a breath, sorry she had steered the conversation toward Mom. But Gina seemed unfazed. With a big smile on her face, she plopped open *The Book* and sighed. Every match was an hour's work for her.

"By the way, congrats."

"Thanks. Again."

"Not for today. For the other thing."

Heather was puzzled. "What other thing?"

"Well, the basic rule is that a wrestler either participates in six matches or wins four matches. You're 4-0."

"And…?"

"And that means you've already won your varsity letter."

"Wow, I didn't realize. I thought it would be up in the air till the end of the season."

"Nope. You are golden, girl!" Gina held out a palm for a high five. After a second, her big smile faded. "And now, the highlight of my night—*The Book*."

"Can I help?"

"Nah, it's about an hour of tabulating and adding everything, then I enter it in the computer. I usually do it before going to bed. But we got an hour, right? You get some sleep. It's a long night."

"Okay, Mom," Heather taunted, hating herself the second it left her lips for slipping again. But again, Gina didn't seem to notice.

"Okay, young lady, if you don't get to sleep now, I won't let you stay up tomorrow."

"All right, I guess," she said mock petulantly, balling up her jacket as a pillow and leaning against the bus window.

"Good night."

Chapter 36

Things finally seemed to be settling into a rhythm. No drama, no more locker drawings, no more newspaper silliness.

The bell rang for homeroom, strangely placed after the first period. It never made sense to Heather, but whatever. She waved to Mr. Carson and headed for the nurse's office. The boys always went down to the team room for their match day pre-weighs. Heather went to the nurse.

She waved to the nurse as she walked into the reception area. There were half a dozen seats along the wall, where one pallid-looking freshman hunched over, holding his stomach. The nurse sat behind a sliding glass window, on the phone, likely talking to the boy's mother. She nodded as Heather came through the door to the back exam room.

Heather slipped off her shoes, socks, and top, then stepped onto the scale in her shorts and sports bra, adjusting the weights. 112.5. *Good*, she thought.

The nurse stepped up behind her and gave the weights a slight tap to get them to balance perfectly.

"Looking good," she intoned brightly. "How's your hydration?"

"Fine. Already had two bottles of water today."

"Okay, make sure to have at least one more before your match." She reached for a set of skin calipers. "I know body fat hasn't been a problem, but let's check real quick."

She went through the procedure and did a few quick calculations.

"Just over eleven. Not even close to an issue. Ready to roll, kiddo." She lightly tapped Heather's shoulder to let her know everything was done.

As Heather pulled her game day outfit out of her backpack and started to dress, she tossed in a few questions.

"Any injuries or skin issues?"

"Nope, all good."

"Soreness? Bruises you can't account for?"

Heather smiled. "No, I know where I got them all from."

"Okay, I'll call Coach Wolf and let him know you're good to go."

"Thank you."

"No problem. Us girls gotta stick together." She smiled and offered Heather a fist bump, which Heather tapped. "Give 'em hell today."

But the moment was broken by the sound of retching from the outer room.

"Really?!" she sighed as she rushed out.

Heather smiled and finished dressing, hoping for the nurse's sake that the freshman grabbed the wastebasket. She finished getting ready and headed to the second period.

Chapter 37

Willie slipped out of his slides and handed his T-shirt to Heather. He stood still on the scale as the official tapped the metal slide.

"105 and a quarter," he intoned disinterestedly as Gina and the visiting team's manager jotted the weight down next to the wrestler's weight class and name.

Wolfe, Box, and the visiting coaches stood off to the side, exchanging bits and pieces of information about wrestlers their respective teams had already faced.

Heather slipped out of her slides, keeping on her Dri-FIT T-shirt. The official slid the bar to 112, then began tapping toward 113. His brow furrowed as the weight didn't cause the expected flop of the bar. He tapped back and tried again.

Heather stared, wondering what was wrong. He tapped past 113, then 114, then 115, and finally stopped at 115 and a half.

"Step off for a moment, please," he said. "Coach." He gestured toward Wolfe.

Wolfe strolled over. "What's up?" he asked calmly.

"When was this scale last checked?"

"Two days ago. It's right there on the sticker."

"Just checking. Miss, would you step on again?"

He repeated the drill, starting at 112, once again finally getting a balance at 115 and a half. He tilted his head and said to Wolfe, "Even if I give her the half for the shirt, it's still two over." He paused and looked at his watch. "We're under 30 minutes. I'm sorry, I can't re-weigh her. Do you have an alternate?"

Both Heather and Wolfe were in shock.

"What the..." He paused and stared at her.

"I... I don't know. It doesn't make sense."

"Well, you can't go." He turned away from her, whispering under his breath, "Fuck," as he marched toward Box, who had been watching quietly. "Get Wainwright out here. I can't fucking believe this."

"Problem," Box countered. "He came in with a cast this morning. Skateboard."

"Johnson?"

"He's way over. Barely makes 121."

"We can't forfeit."

"We could bump Willie up. Little Carmine makes 106 easy."

"Shit. He's not ready."

"Only option."

"All right, go get him."

Heather, who had been standing mutely, tried to get his attention. "Coach..." she started.

He held up his hand to silence her. "Nothing to be done about it now. We'll talk later." He turned to the official. "All right. We're bumping up our 106 to 113. We just need a minute to get our JV 106 out here."

The official looked to the visiting coaches. They nodded their assent.

Wolfe strode toward the locker room, muttering, "Jesus f—Christ," to no one in particular.

Chapter 38

Carmine bounced nervously from foot to foot. At 98 pounds, he easily made weight, but he was one of the few wrestlers whose singlet was actually a bit loose on him. Barely hearing the official's instructions, he toed the mark as the whistle shrilled.

Hesitantly, he moved forward as if to go for a takedown but froze as his opponent sidestepped quickly to his right. Before Carmine even processed it, the wrestler drove through him, swept out his legs, and slammed him to the mat.

An audible "OOOFFF!" escaped from Carmine's throat as the breath was knocked out of him. With a quick spin, a hook of the leg, a wrap of the neck, and a firm interlocking of the hands, Carmine's opponent had his shoulders on the mat and his legs in the air.

By the time Carmine was able to suck in a breath, the official was slapping the mat.

"Red, by pin."

The visiting 106 jumped to his feet and looked at the clock. Thirteen seconds—his new personal best. Yanking off his headgear, he nearly flew into the throng of congratulating and whooping teammates at the end of the mat.

Carmine got up and headed back toward a silent bench. Wolfe stood with his mouth agape and had to shake himself before patting the dejected Carmine on the shoulder.

"That's all right, Antonuzzi, first one's always the toughest." He forced an encouraging look onto his face. "Shake it off. We'll learn from it."

Carmine's head was hanging as he went through the gauntlet of wrestlers.

"Hang in there, kid."

"Pick your head up."

"Good try, good try."

Juwann grabbed him and pulled him into a bro hug.

"All right, popped your cherry, little man. The first time always hurts." He pounded Carmine's back loudly, bringing snickers from the surrounding wrestlers.

Carmine finally reached his seat at the end of the bench and plopped down dejectedly, finally removing his headgear.

The recovery was short-lived as Willie faced the returning runner-up from states at 113. Willie tried gamely for a takedown but was quickly overwhelmed and reversed. Just like Carmine, Willie was wrapped up and pinned within 30 seconds.

The visiting crowd jumped to its feet, while the home crowd, even the Knights' Knation, sat in stunned silence. Willie jogged off, his face red from exertion and from being rubbed across the mat. The only face redder was Wolfe's. His jaw was clenched firmly as he patted Willie's shoulder when he passed by.

Wolfe signaled to Marco, who was on his way out. Marco jogged over.

"Castaglia, we need to stop the bleeding. Pin this guy," Wolfe hissed through clenched teeth.

Marco attacked. He was relentless and firmly in control. With ten seconds left in the first period, he saw an opening and went for the kill. Unfortunately, he missed and lost his balance enough that his adversary not only reversed him but had him down and started driving all his weight to collapse Marco's high shoulder toward the mat.

With only two seconds remaining, the official slapped the mat for the third consecutive time. The lead was now nearly insurmountable.

The visitors smelled blood in the water. Every match was hotly contested, even Jake and Juwann had their hands full. It all came down to Jon Martin. He had to pin to win.

Unfortunately, his opponent was no slouch, and the first two periods went back and forth. As the ref sorted them to begin the third, Wolfe clapped enthusiastically.

"Come on, big man, you know what we need. You got this!" he emphasized.

Jon nodded assent and was about to turn and assume his position when a voice cut through the murmuring crowd.

"Come on, send out the girl!" someone shouted. "I'd like to see her get pinned!"

The fan stood, smiling at the chuckles and guffaws that rippled through the crowd.

Jon's brows knit together, and he looked at Heather, stoically sitting behind the bench, once again the target of ridicule. He knelt over his opponent, but it was pointless. His mind was elsewhere, and he was easily reversed. He tried to respond to Wolfe's shouts of encouragement, which grew more desperate as the seconds ticked away. He tried counters but to no avail. The visiting wrestler felt victory within his grasp and reached down deep to foil Jon's final move.

The horn sounded, and no one even heard the official's call. The gym erupted with cheers and celebrations from the visiting team and their fans. The newspaper writer, who had expected an uneventful match, was tweeting out the incredible upset.

The Knights milled about in shocked silence as Jon shambled off the mat. Wolfe shook himself out of it and walked across the mat to congratulate the opposing coach.

Boxwood turned to the stunned bench. "Team room in five. No showers yet. Just go take a seat." He walked off to join Coach Wolfe.

Chapter 39

They sat in relative silence, with only a few whispers of encouragement and comfort. The boys spread out in chairs and on the couch while Heather, as usual, leaned on a small desk near the door. A few wrestlers grabbed cups and poured water from the Gatorade cooler on the table in front. Everything stopped as the door swung open and slammed against the wall in its arc.

All eyes were on Wolfe as he paced back and forth in front of the table, fury obvious on his face. In a controlled voice, he started, wagging his right index finger in front of him. "That may have been," he paused for effect, "the single worst performance I have witnessed from a Scarlet Knight team." He paused again.

"The…"

"Single…"

"Worst!" His voice began to rise.

"Not one…NOT ONE!" He clenched his fist beneath the raised finger. "SINGLE WRESTLER WRESTLED TO HIS ABILITY!"

"NOT EVEN ONE!" he shouted.

He looked around the room, his tone starting to come down. Everyone was looking at the ground or their feet. Heather felt tears rising and stifled a sob with a cough.

Wolfe swung toward her, the fury rising again. "And you. Two and a half pounds. TWO AND A HALF POUNDS!" he fairly screamed, taking a step toward her. His hands went to his hips; his jacket pushed back as he leaned forward. "This all starts because you can't control yourself. What did you have? A cheeseburger and a shake for lunch?"

She stared at the ground.

"Well, I hope it was worth it. 'Cause you know what you did—do you—DO YOU?! YOU SCREWED THE ENTIRE TEAM—THE ENTIRE TEAM!"

Heather looked up as if she'd been slapped, her jaw dropping in absolute shock.

Wolfe turned and emphasized his tirade by sweeping the Gatorade jug off the table and into the far wall. Water and ice flew everywhere. He was about to storm out of the room when Jon Martin's voice made him turn on his heel.

"Coach," Jon called out, "that's too…"

"Too what?" Wolfe raged. "Too what?! Now you have some nerve, now you want to take a stand? Where the hell was that when you were rolling on the mat like a beached whale? Huh, Jon?" He was nearly face-to-face with him now. "Where was it then?"

Jon stared back hard but said no more.

After a tense second, when you could have heard a pin drop, Wolfe turned and strode out, flipping the table on his way. Granola bars and fruit flew to join the ice and water. The door once again bounced off the back wall and slammed shut.

A murmur started to rise when Boxwood held up his hands to get their attention.

"Okay, let's all take a deep breath. Tough loss all around."

He paused as they looked toward him.

"Fast showers. I want everyone back here fully dressed in ten minutes. Let's use that time to cool off and wash off today. Got it?"

Everyone nodded and started to mill toward their lockers. Heather was almost to the door when he called to her.

"Prince, could I have a sec?"

She thought about just storming out but took a breath and waited for him.

He couldn't help but put an arm around her shoulders as they stepped out of the door. They started down the hallway toward the girls' locker room as he spoke in a calm voice.

"I am so sorry. That's just not true. Every wrestler in there is responsible for their own performance," he paused. "Coach was way out of line."

He surprised himself, having never once before contradicted Wolfe to a wrestler.

"Both in what he said and even more so in how he said it." He paused again. "I've known him for over thirty years, and I know he didn't really mean it the way it sounded. He let the anger get the better of him."

He reached for the right words.

"What he said, he's said things like that to guys, meaning it one way." He hesitated. "But he's got to learn it comes across so differently to someone like you."

"Doesn't excuse it," Heather said tonelessly.

"You're absolutely right. He—we—went way too far." He nodded. "And however you want to handle this, I've got your back. One hundred percent. I promise I won't sugarcoat or try to excuse anything."

Heather gazed at him, thinking hard.

"I'll be back in there in ten. I'm still a Scarlet Knight," she said firmly.

"Whatever you decide." He patted her on the shoulder and turned down the hall toward where Wolfe had stormed off.

At the far end of the hall, Wolfe stared out of the plate glass window into the darkened parking lot, letting the emotion drain out of him.

"Excuse me, Coach."

He turned, surprised to see Gina.

"Hey, Gina. Sorry, I just need a minute here, okay?" He tried to gently ask her.

"I know. I'm sorry, but I just wanted to show you something real quick." She held out her phone to him.

He steeled himself, ready to read the already growing tweets about tonight's terrible loss. Instead, he was confused by some article from Web DRx. His brow knit as he read it:

"It is not uncommon for a fluctuation between three and five pounds at the onset of one's menstrual cycle. Fluid retention and bloating can cause sudden weight gain in as little as six hours..."

He sighed internally, beginning to realize what an ass he'd been.

"It's just, y'know, I was with her at lunch, and she had celery and carrots. And I know you encourage them to stay hydrated, so she did have a large amount of water. And with that," she gestured with her head toward the phone he still stared at, "it just kinda, well..."

"Thank you, Gina. I appreciate it. I have to admit, I didn't know..."

"It's just, you know, not something we talk to guys about. You know."

He returned the phone. "Thanks."

"Yeah, no problem. I just thought you should know. Well, uuuhhh, see you tomorrow?"

"Absolutely. Good night."

He forced a smile as she hugged "the Book" to her chest and headed down the hall toward the parking lot. Wolfe looked up to see Boxwood heading his way. He started walking toward him, shaking his head at himself, knowing he'd just screwed up royally.

They met in the middle, Wolfe still shaking his head. "Not exactly my finest moment, huh?" he started with chagrin.

"You've had better," Box agreed. "I'll be totally honest. That could well have been your last moment." He tilted his head and crossed his arms over his chest.

"I know. I'm definitely going to face the firing squad for this," he sighed. "No excuse, but I lost it. I was sure this was an undefeated state champ group. I never imagined we could come apart like this. Still, I really blew it."

"You did indeed." He gathered his thoughts. "I'm not saying 'I told you so,' but the dynamic with a girl changes everything."

"Yep, and you'd be right. Still doesn't excuse what I did. Do you know what Gina just showed me? Did you know that a girl can gain three to five pounds on the day her period starts? How in the fuck am I supposed to know that?" He shook his head again.

"Hhmmpphh," Box retorted. "Maybe I should've. My wife and daughters always complain about it. I usually just block them out. Guess I should've paid attention."

They both stood there shaking their heads until footsteps in the hallway made them look up. Heather was heading back to the team room. They strode forward to meet her.

Wolfe stopped in front of her. "Heather, I apologize for everything I said. I was completely out of line, and I was completely wrong. I know I can't take it back, but I am truly sorry." He stopped and started again. "First thing tomorrow, I will be in Principal Dale's office with a true and complete story of my actions." He nodded. "And I will tender my resignation as coach and submit my statement to the board of education for whatever discipline they deem necessary."

There was a pregnant pause as Heather looked evenly at both coaches. "Please don't do that," she said calmly but sternly.

"I'm sorry, I really have no choice…"

"Yes, you do. You can make this about you and fall on your sword and be all noble," she paused, "but when it's all said and done, it won't be your fault. It will be all on me—the little bitch who ruined Scarlet Knights wrestling. The girl who stole our chance at a state championship. I'd get to be the no-good, rotten little whore who destroyed the great Coach Wolfe's career. No," she stated firmly, "I won't be that person."

They both stared, shocked at her resolve.

"If you want to go in there and apologize, great. I wasn't the only one you attacked." She paused for emphasis. "But it ends there. If your conscience needs salving, go to church or something. Or wait until the end of the year. But if you're really sorry, you won't make me the bad guy."

"Okay." Wolfe nodded.

They went in.

Everyone quieted and headed for their seats, preparing for another tirade. Wolfe paced again, surveying the mess he'd made with his fit. He started calmly. "You know, I've stood up here before and talked about character. I know I've said that adversity doesn't build character—it displays the character you already have." He gazed around the room. "Tonight, we faced the first real adversity we've come across this year, and one person—just one person—showed a real lack of character. That person would be me." He looked around again, seeing some surprise but also full attention.

"I had high expectations, and still do, for this group." He stopped and crossed his arms over his chest, his feet planted wide. "I got cocky and thought, 'Hey, we got this.' I just wasn't ready and didn't get you ready to deal with adversity. So, I failed. I failed all of you." He hung his head. "And to make it worse, I tried to blame you—a bunch of wrestlers who had just wrestled their hearts out in a tough situation. I was wrong, and I am truly sorry."

He turned toward Heather and gazed right at her. "And I truly apologize for my language. It was completely inappropriate and couldn't have been more wrong." He took a deep breath. "I was the one who didn't prepare you properly, who didn't help and support you with what you needed to be ready. I screwed up, both before the match and absolutely in my comments and personal attack on you. I know it's unforgivable, but I still apologize with all my heart."

Heather nodded in assent and looked away.

Wolfe turned back toward the boys and focused on Jon Martin. "And Jon, you were right. It was too much. Both in what I said to everyone and to Heather, but also in what I said to you. You wrestled like a champion, regardless of the outcome. I was wrong to question your courage. In fact, you showed the most courage of anyone in this room. You stood up to me when I was acting like an ass. You stood up and didn't back down." He hung his head again. "I was wrong, and you were right. I apologize to you and thank you for trying to straighten me out."

Wolfe looked out over the crowd of shocked faces. "I apologize to each and every one of you. I'm ashamed of myself, and I'm not even sure if I deserve to coach this team anymore. I leave it up to you." He turned and looked at Boxwood. "Coach, I'm going back to my office. If you could let me know what the team decides…" He strode out, this time the door closing with a gentle click.

After a silent moment, Juwann's hushed voice uttered, "Fuck me."

"Hey," Box said firmly. "I do not want to hear that word ever again this entire season. Got me?" He stared Juwann down.

The silence resumed until it was broken by Heather. She stood up from her usual perch and took a few steps forward. "I'd like to say something." Surprise spread across their faces.

"I think you guys get just how rough that was for me." She let it sink in. "It was like getting punched in the face by Conor McGregor. But…" She paused and tried to make eye contact with as many of them as she could. "I'm still standing, and we have a lot of season left. I didn't like how Coach handled that one bit, but I missed weight. That's on me. It won't happen again."

She paced a little. "Coach lost his shit. Yeah, he went too far, but he was sort of right. We all fell apart. If we are going to win anything, we need to come together. We need Coach Wolfe. We need Coach Box. We need each other. Remember how you guys all promised that what happens in this room stays in this room?"

There was some uncomfortable fidgeting as they passed quick glances at each other.

"Well, tonight needs to stay in this room. No matter how hurt or offended anybody feels, we gotta tough it out. Tomorrow, we pick it up and start to put it back together. All of us and both our coaches."

She stuck out her right hand, palm down. "Everybody in?" she asked, almost as a challenge.

One by one, they all stepped forward, looking at her.

"On three."

"One."

"Two."

"Three."

"KNIGHTS!!"

They broke off, and Heather headed for the door. Boxwood watched her go, her face a mix of determination and anger. He was impressed, but he was even more convinced—having a girl wrestler changed everything.

Chapter 40

She had skipped dinner last night, and her stomach grumbled as she got out of her car for the first time as a driver. It had been a nice respite for the family Saturday as she turned sixteen. They weren't big on parties—just Mom, Dad, and Gamma—and a nice dinner. When they came home for her cake and candles, everyone was happy. No talk of school or wrestling. Her parents seemed to agree to a truce with Gamma there.

Heather thought nothing of it when her dad asked her to help him with something in the garage. It even took her a second to register what the strange white car with a bow on it meant. Her hand went to her mouth just as Mom and Gamma, who had snuck up behind her, yelled, "Surprise!" She jumped right into her dad's arms, and they hugged like they hadn't in months. He couldn't get the grin off his face as she kept saying, "Oh my God! Really? It's mine?" She ran to the car and tried to hug it like a toy at Christmas. Mom and Gamma both snapped a picture, immediately adding it to their Facebook pages. It was a great night.

"I still have to go to the DMV Monday, but Tuesday morning, she's all yours," Dad had said. He gave her the keys and a lecture about safety and drinking, which she hardly heard.

But Monday's events sucked some of the joy out of this morning. Mercifully, neither Mom nor Dad said anything about the match, although the story screamed at them from the front of the sports page. They told her to have a great day and be safe. She smiled and thanked them again. Then, Dad took his coffee and headed for his office. Heather grabbed her backpack and headed out—not for the bus, but for the first time, her own car. Mom picked up the plates, noticing but not mentioning that Heather's eggs had merely been pushed around the plate, not eaten. She shook her head, keeping her thoughts to herself.

School seemed quiet enough as she strolled in. Normal milling about and chit-chat. It wasn't until she neared her locker that she once again noticed the furtive glances and smiles.

"Oh great," she thought. "Another locker, Picasso."

The crowd parted like the Red Sea as she approached. Most were surprised when she let out a snorting laugh at the sight—a perfect rendition of Porky Pig's girlfriend in a wrestling singlet, albeit with her curls added and a turkey leg held up in one hand. The caption above the marker art read, "FEED ME!!!"

People joined in the laugh, first uncomfortably, then fully as she said aloud to no one in particular, "All right, that one's pretty good." She calmly opened the locker and placed her things inside. She didn't even bother going to the office to complain. She was sure it would get back to Dale soon enough.

Books in hand, head held high, she headed for class. Period one was uneventful, which was a relief. Since she hadn't been called down and Wolfe had been in his classroom as usual, she was glad her plea for letting things go had apparently been heeded. She took notes mindlessly, enjoying the relative quiet.

Things were fine all day, except for one minute before the gym. She had changed, trying to ignore her grumbling stomach, when a sudden urge made her turn quickly into the ladies' room. Being part of the locker room, there was no door, just sinks and stalls open to the room. She had just made it into a stall when the water and juice she'd sipped during breakfast made a reappearance.

She wondered how loud it had been as she wiped her mouth.

"That's it," she said to herself. "Gotta eat something."

As she washed her hands and rinsed off her face, she saw Big Marty—that is, Coach Martin—in the mirror.

"Everything okay, Prince?" she asked with a concerned look on her face.

"Fine." Heather pulled down some paper towels. "Skipped breakfast and just chugged an ice water," she paused for effect. "Bad idea." She smiled as she wiped her hands and face.

"All right, but take it easy out there today."

"Volleyball?" She joked. "I just have to avoid the boys diving in front of me to get the ball."

"True," she nodded, moving her impressive bulk toward the locker room door. "Back when I was in school, I'd trip them as they went by." She gave Heather a conspiratorial wink and headed out.

Heather tossed the towels and jogged out, still with a slightly sour taste in her mouth and throat.

The day meandered on with no surprises. She headed into her private team room, pulling on her practice equipment. She had one foot up on the bench, tying her wrestling shoes tightly when she heard a tap on the doorjamb behind her. She looked up and saw Ms. D's smiling face leaning in.

"Hey, Heather. Got a minute?"

"Sure. What's up?"

"Heard yesterday was a tough one."

Heather almost panicked, then realized D was only talking about the loss.

"Yeah, things kind of went crazy after I missed weight," she said, switching feet on the bench and raising her brows for emphasis.

"Yeah, but you can only be responsible for yourself. What everyone else does is their responsibility."

Heather shrugged her shoulders, not wanting to argue the point but not believing her.

"Last year, I had a freshman playing second base, and she'd played great all year," D went on. "First inning of the county final, she makes a bad throw on a routine ground ball that would have gotten us out of the inning." She paused to let it sink in. "We walked the next batter, and their big hitter came up, hit it about five hundred feet. Three to nothing." She shook her head. "We battled but came up short, left the bases loaded in the seventh, lost three to two. Total bummer."

She waited as Heather finished tying and sat to face her.

"After everyone was gone, I heard someone in a stall—it was the freshman second baseman. I pulled her out, and she was still in full uniform. 'It's all right,' I told her. 'We tried our best, just came up a little short.'"

"But it was all my fault. I ruined our whole season," she said, unable to stop crying.

"I'll tell you what I told her," Ms. D continued. "That play, yes, it was bad. But we never would have made it to the finals without all the good plays she made throughout the season. She didn't walk the next batter. She didn't throw the pitch that got crushed. She wasn't one of the ten strikeouts we had, and she wasn't the one who grounded out with the bases loaded to end the game. When you are on a team, you can only do your part. Win or lose, succeed or fail, you can't control what your teammates do. It's a series of challenges for each individual. Don't ever try to take on more than your part."

She watched Heather's steady gaze. "All right, I know you don't believe me now, but you'll agree later. I promise." She shifted gears. "So, what do you think was up with the weight thing?"

"Damned if I know." Heather shook her head. "I hardly ate a thing, and I was half a pound under when I weighed in at the nurse's office that morning."

"How much did you drink?"

"Like three liters of water. Coach is always on us about hydration."

"Hmmm. Let's see. Each liter is about a pound and a quarter, so maybe three and three-quarters total."

"But that shouldn't have added that much weight."

"For a guy, no. And most of the time, for us, no," Ms. D said, pausing. "But at certain times, like just before our period, we can retain every ounce. Sometimes between three and five pounds."

"I've never heard that," Heather argued.

"Then you weren't paying attention in health class," Ms. D teased. "Look, I don't know the perfect way to manage it. Maybe next month, just sip water near those days and weigh yourself a few times."

Heather's face showed deep thought.

"But one thing that isn't going to help is making yourself vomit," Ms. D added.

Heather looked up in surprise. "So you talked to Big—uhh, Coach Martin."

"Yeah. She mentioned it to me. She didn't want to go to Coach Wolfe or make it a big thing, so she thought I might have a little talk with you." She raised her palms. "And here we are."

Heather considered her response. "It's just like I told her. I skipped breakfast and chugged down an ice-cold water. It came right back up." She looked at Ms. D sincerely. "No fingers down the throat. I swear." She placed her hand over her heart.

"Okay, but a lot of wrestlers do that to make weight. However, you, being female, are at a much higher risk of it turning into something more serious."

"I know, I know," Heather agreed. "I was paying attention that day in health class. I promise I didn't, and I won't." She made an up-and-down, then side-to-side motion. "Cross my heart."

"Okay. But if it seems like a problem again next month, come see me a few days before. We'll figure something out. Something safe. Okay?"

"Okay. I promise."

"All right then. You better get out there before Wolfe comes pounding on the door." Ms. D nodded and turned toward her office.

Heather jumped up, bouncing on the balls of her feet to check the snugness of her shoes, then jogged off toward practice.

Chapter 41

A short blast from a whistle got everyone's attention.

"All right, let's get started," Wolfe bellowed. "Thank you for your vote of confidence. It means a lot."

He looked around and gave a slight nod when he made eye contact with Heather. "But like any loss, today we hit the reset button. And that means everyone has to wrestle to keep their spot. So, everyone, take a seat against the wall."

They all settled in, and a few giggles and catcalls arose as Box entered in a complete official outfit. He ignored them, striding to the center circle as Wolfe called out.

"First up, 106. Carmine, Willie—into the circle."

Both jogged out, snapping up their headgear and assumed the position facing one another. Box dropped his hand, blew his whistle, and danced back on his toes as the wrestlers began. It was over quickly as Willie dropped and pinned Carmine in a flurry.

"Good job, good job. Nice try, Carmine, keep up the good work," Wolfe encouraged. "Way to go, Willie," he yelled as he clapped. "Next up, 113. Prince, Johnson—get to the center."

So that's how it's gonna go, Heather thought. They don't trust me to keep weight, so they're gonna try to get him down from 121. Good luck with that, she mused, both for him making weight or beating her.

They circled after the whistle for a few seconds. Then Johnson dove in for a leg grab, but Heather pushed his weight to the side as she skipped away. He tried a feint and scooted to the side, but she countered quickly and fended him off again. Johnson fainted several times, and each time, Heather danced back. On his third feint, she hesitated a second too long, and he drove hard for her front leg. His arm found only air as she deftly drew back, swept into his off-balance torso, and followed his weight down onto the mat.

Box's hand flew up, showing her takedown points. She locked an armbar and pushed hard to turn him. His effort to resist only gained him a serious face drag around the mat. No matter how he tried, he could not escape. The period ended with Heather gaining more points for riding.

As Heather settled into the superior position to start the second, she held Johnson's arm lightly. He fell for that gambit, too, trying to pull it in and sit out quickly. He never noticed her lightning-quick drive into his turning shoulder until his back slammed firmly into the mat. He valiantly arched and twisted but to no avail. About ten seconds in, Box slapped the mat.

"Excellent job, both of you!" Wolfe hooted. "Really good match. Way to move, Prince! That was awesome," he praised. "Grab some water, Johnson. You're doing double today. Castaglia, you're up!"

Johnson was pinned again, and the matches continued. By the end of practice, the starting lineup remained the same. However, some JV wrestlers pushed hard. If nothing else, it gave them hope and a good contest to hone their skills.

Everyone headed for the showers. Heather jogged off, determined to gain weight and regain the team's confidence tomorrow.

Chapter 42

The bus ride to Auburn Central was quiet. There was a subdued and slightly nervous hum to the conversation, with little of the usual rowdiness and, as the coach called it, "grab-ass." Heather sat silently next to Gina, deep in thought. She had checked her weight just before they left and hadn't had so much as a sip of water since then. In fact, she had even spit out most of the moisture in her mouth to avoid swallowing it. She was determined to gain weight. The team couldn't afford another debacle.

Upon arriving, they filed off the bus. Like most away matches, Heather was curious if she'd have access to a locker room or if she'd have to change into a bathroom stall. At first, she believed the excuse—"Oops, sorry. There are no female coaches around to open it up." But after several times, she remembered that every custodian and most coaches had master keys to everything. She knew they were messing with her on purpose. Whether it was for a competitive edge or just plain obnoxiousness, she didn't know or care. She wasn't going to give them the pleasure of responding to it.

This school had a locker room. There was even a friendly woman coach inside to check if she needed anything. Before heading out for weigh-ins, Heather stopped in the bathroom to try to get rid of any unnecessary ounces, to little avail.

Once again, she stood nervously, holding Willie's T-shirt and passing her own as she stepped up. She watched apprehensively as the official stopped at 112. A smile crept onto her face as the scale balanced right there. A little tap and it held firm at 112 ¼.

"Take the ¼ off for the T-shirt. Make it 112 even," he intoned as Gina and the other manager scribbled it down. Heather smiled as she stepped off, and Wolfe breathed a sigh of relief. Crisis averted.

She stepped to the side as Marco stepped onto the scale, bare-chested. He turned and flexed for his buddies until the official scolded, "121, exactly."

Willie and Heather strolled off together.

"You can take a drink now," Willie teased as he handed her his bottle.

"And get cooties from you? Eww!" she laughed but then grabbed it and took a swig.

"Better cooties than mono," he responded, animatedly wiping the top of the bottle. A second of guilt hit him, and he glanced at her to see if she took it the wrong way. She seemed unaffected, so he kept it up, holding the bottle away at the last minute as if afraid to drink.

Heather helped him by smacking the bottle and splashing water all over his face.

"There, now you have it everywhere," she laughed.

"Gross!" he whined.

"Are you crying? Are you crying?" she said in her best Tom Hanks impression. "There's no crying in wrestling!" She mocked him as she put him in a headlock.

"When you get sick," she continued as he tried to pull away, "everyone will want to know who you've been kissing." She then proceeded to plant a few loud smacks on his cheeks. He didn't try too hard to pull away.

"And there's no kissing either," he laughed as he tried to reverse the headlock.

Their fun was interrupted by Box. "Okay, lovebirds, enough of that," he said with mock seriousness. "How about we get changed and start thinking about wrestling?"

They both let go and turned a little red, but as they started toward the opposite locker rooms, Willie shot a stream of water just as Heather turned to say something.

"Oops."

"Jerk!" she yelled, but she laughed.

A half-hour later, the thinly filled stands cheered lightly as the home team jogged out to warm up. Auburn was a smaller school with little interest in wrestling. Lately, they had barely been able to field a team, so when Willie, Heather, and Marco started out with pins, there was little reaction from the crowd.

It was almost embarrassingly easy. The only challenges came for Warren Coates and Bobby Holario. Warren faced Auburn's only truly competitive wrestler, just squeaking by on a late reversal. Bobby, however, surprisingly had his opponent nearly pinned three times, yet somehow let him escape all three times. He won, but everyone was looking at each other, asking "WTF" under their breath.

Regardless, they won every match, making it a solid victory.

The mood on the bus ride home was upbeat and a bit more raucous than the ride in. Boxwood sat down next to Wolfe after stowing the first aid kit and spare equipment.

"Now that's more like it."

"Definitely. Seems like we're back on track."

"Nice effort," he nodded. "Although having Auburn scheduled didn't hurt at all."

"No doubt," Wolfe agreed. "But everybody—well, almost everybody—was on point today."

"Yeah, although what's up with Holario?"

"No clue." Wolfe shook his head. "Though he has been pretty quiet lately. Anything going on at home?"

"Not as far as I know." Box looked over his shoulder toward the clowning around in the back of the bus. There was Bobby, sitting by himself, head down. He was never the loudest, but he usually sat with the others and joined in. Guess he's bummed about the match, Box thought.

"I'm gonna go settle those jokers down," he said as he rose and headed back, holding onto the edge of the seats as he went. Stopping briefly, he spoke across Gina.

"Prince, nice job. Way to set the tone."

She smiled in response as he kept going.

"All right, let's settle down. Everybody is in a seat. The last thing we need is some stupid injury from grab-assin'. Let's go."

They milled about, settling.

Juwann, of course, couldn't let it go. "Coach, you need to grab a seat too. The last thing we need is a broken bone. I hear bones get brittle as you get older," he paused for his punchline, "and I'm thinking yours must be awful brittle!"

Laughter erupted.

"Yeah, yeah," Box answered, "and I wouldn't be at risk if I didn't have to deal with a bunch of comedians back here!" He turned and headed back toward the front as the bus pulled onto the main highway. He glanced at Bobby, sitting alone in a three-seater, and plopped down next to him.

"Hey, champ. How you doin'?"

Box was surprised to see that Bobby had been intently reading a Bible and had a set of rosary beads in his hands.

"Oh, hey, Coach. I'm good," he responded quietly.

"Tough breaks today. You almost had him, like, three times," Box said, trying to joke. "What was he, covered in butter?"

Bobby smiled. "He was pretty slippery." He paused, sensing that Boxwood wanted some sort of answer. "I don't know. I guess I couldn't quite make that last move quick enough."

The box stayed positive. "Hey, no harm, no foul. You won, right?"

Bobby nodded in agreement.

Box changed tack. "So, how's everything at home?"

Bobby looked a bit confused. "Uh, fine. We're all doing good."

"Glad to hear it. Well, don't worry about tonight. Next time, you'll get him." He reached over and patted him on the shoulder. "Hey, you know where my office is, right? If you ever need to talk about anything, just stop in. No need for an appointment. Just pop in."

"Sure, Coach," Bobby said, still looking confused. "Thanks."

Box stood back up and headed to his seat next to Wolfe.

Wolfe looked up. "I think we got another problem," he sighed.

Wolfe shut his eyes for a second, his head sinking down. When he reopened them, he looked at Boxwood. "What now?"

With his head, he gestured toward Bobby, whose head was back down, attention again on his Bible and rosary beads.

Wolfe looked for a moment and muttered, "Just... great." They both shook their heads.

Chapter 43

Thursday and Friday were light practices, mostly just conditioning. Everyone was gearing up for the big tri-match with Winslow and Tuscarora, both of whom were also ranked in the top ten. The stands would be full, college recruiters would be there, and the local public network would be televising it live. To some degree, this could be a precursor to states, as both the teams and many of the individual wrestlers would be standing between the Scarlet Knights and their goals of team and individual state championships.

To add a little extra drama to the match, Wolfe announced on Thursday that they would all have to arrive an hour early on Saturday.

"The wonderful chemists from the state will be here," he mocked. "So everybody needs to pee in a cup." He arched an eyebrow and looked around. "There better not be any surprises, gentlemen," he said, letting it sink in.

Juwann couldn't resist. "Not the ladies?"

"Of course. Everyone gets tested." Wolfe looked squarely at Juwann. "But I'm a little more worried about some of the guys."

"Moi?" Juwann responded with mock seriousness. "Not to worry, Coach. I'm clean as a whistle." He gestured toward himself with both hands. "My body is my temple."

Marco and Jake both snorted, and Jake called out, "Yeah, you sure worship it enough. The rest of us can't get near the mirror in the team room."

"Well, boys," Juwann stood up and posed, "it's not easy being this beautiful."

Boos and catcalls rained, and he sat down, flipping a quick finger to the crowd.

Wolfe restated, "Seriously, no surprises. Make sure you are rested, hydrated, and ready to go. All right, everybody in."

All the hands came together as they ended the practice.

Chapter 44

Even though it was several hours before the tri-match, the gym was already buzzing. Three teams' worth of wrestlers, trainers, coaches, and managers were scattered about. Plus, just about every JV wrestler (and freshmen for one team) was there to support, as well as learn. At least fifty or so parents, siblings, and girlfriends had already arrived, chatting and greeting each other, most knowing one another from the circuit.

Juwann and Marco were out walking around, strutting and joking, when they found who they were really looking for.

"Boys," Juwann greeted Johnson and little Carmine, putting his arms around them.

"How'd you like to get a little education on some of the intricacies of high school wrestling?"

They both nodded, interested but a little confused.

"Tell you what, meet us in the team room in five, OK?"

Their eyes lit up. In general, the team room was off-limits to JV during matches. This was big, they both thought, looking at each other with a tinge of excitement.

"Cool. See you in five then," Marco chimed in as Juwann squeezed their shoulders, then turned his attention to an attractive redhead from Tuscarora.

"Yo, Marguerite. What's up? Been a minute." He strutted over, his lackey nodding to the intrigued boys and following his fearless leader.

The boys wanted to be cool, so they didn't want to take off right away. After a short pause, though, they made a beeline for the team room.

They opened the door a little cautiously, not one hundred percent sure that Juwann and Marco weren't setting them up. They tried to look cool as they stepped onto the mat with the Scarlet Knight logo in the center. They were in the Holy of Holies, and a sense of awe filled them.

Their reverie was interrupted when one of the seniors elbowed Big Jon Martin, and they both turned toward them with a quizzical look. A look of some revelation seemed to hit Jon, and he whispered something to the other wrestler, who nodded his head in response and turned back toward his locker. Jon gave a little nod and a smile.

"Boys," he said in semi-greeting, then he too turned back to his locker.

They were unsure of where to go or what to do when the door opened, and Juwann and Marco strolled in.

"All right. My men!" Juwann sauntered over and held out a palm, which each boy nervously slapped.

"Y'all ready to help the Scarlet Knights win a state championship?"

They nodded vigorously as Juwann steered them to the bathroom stalls near the showers. Meanwhile, Marco went to his locker and retrieved what looked like a small shave kit. He then followed to join them.

When they arrived, Juwann checked that they were alone and started.

"Now, gentlemen, I'm going to share something with you that was passed down to me by a senior when I was just a freshman like you."

They waited expectantly as he spoke softly now.

"Occasionally, the state comes in and asks us to pee in a cup. To make sure everything's on the up and up." He paused as they came closer, drawn in by his conspiratorial tone.

"But we got to be careful. You know how it is, you go to a little party... Who knows what people put in a drink? Maybe somebody is smokin' a little something and you get some of that secondhand smoke, know what I'm sayin'?"

They both nodded vigorously, though neither had actually been to a high school party yet.

"And Carmine," Juwann said as if they were longtime buddies, "I know you may wanna use some of those powders to put a little muscle on."

He held a hand up as Carmine started to object.

"I ain't judgin'. But who knows what's in that stuff? Shoot, ballers fail tests all the time, and they were using legal stuff — but it messes up the test sometimes." He repeated for emphasis, "Like I said, got to be careful."

Meanwhile, Marco had pulled some supplies out. Juwann stepped back into the stall so as to be out of sight from the team room. Marco handed each of the boys a foil-wrapped condom.

Both looked like they wanted to run for their lives when Juwann chimed in.

"Calm down," he smiled. "We both like girls; it ain't nothing like that."

He tore open his package.

"What y'all are gonna do is pee into those condoms, carefully, so that they're both half full." He looked at them seriously. "Can you do that? Can you help a brother out?" he asked in his most earnest tone.

The freshmen looked at each other and shrugged, stepping into the stalls. After a nervous moment, both boys came out dangling a fluid-filled condom.

"All right, lookin' good," Marco added.

Juwann called the boys closer.

"Now watch and learn, boys, this is how it's done. First, you wanna get some pee that you're sure is clean." He looked at the two in rapt attention. "It is, isn't it?"

They both bobbed their heads up and down.

"You also have to make sure it's body temperature. If not, you fail right away. That's why we do it this way. Plus, you are going in a stall in nothing but shorts, with a dude behind you watching — so you can't just pull out a cup or something. So here's the solution."

Juwann dropped his shorts, revealing a penis significantly larger than the youngsters', who self-consciously tried not to stare.

Juwann took the condom and rolled it tightly over himself, all the way to the base, and took a rubber band that Marco handed to him.

"You want it to be tight enough to stay on but not too tight. You don't want it to cut off circulation, know what I'm saying?" Both boys nodded, fascinated.

"Then," he said, taking the pee-filled condom that Marco handed him, "you carefully pull this one over the first." He snugged it gently upward, letting trapped air escape, until the urine was tightly up against his phallus, with several inches of condom reaching up toward the base. He then added a second rubber band to snug it all together.

Overall, it gave the image of a larger, but seemingly real, penis. They all watched, fascinated.

"Oh, and don't forget," Juwann added, holding up his right index finger, "you do this the night before." Marco held up his next to Juwann's, both revealing a fingernail that had been cut in a small V close to the edge, the small part having been filed to a sharp point.

"You gotta have something to puncture a little hole. Then it comes out in a little stream, just like the real thing — even sounds like it."

Marco headed into a stall to repeat the process on himself. Juwann tucked himself back into his shorts.

"So that's it. When we win states, you know you helped. And, you may need it yourself when you're wrestling as varsity Knights." He stroked their egos. "Don't forget, though," he added almost in a whisper, "you gotta pass this on before you graduate."

"Cool," they excitedly nodded, thrilled at being part of a special thing, one of the boys.

Juwann put a hand on Johnson's shoulder and guided him out, Carmine following.

"C'mon, let's give Marco a minute. He's a little shy about his size."

"That's not what your sister said!" a voice rose from the stall.

"Yeah, right," Juwann told the boys. "My sister'd break him in half."

They all laughed.

Chapter 45

The mobile lab was efficient. Wrestler after wrestler stepped into the trailer in shorts and slides and peed on demand. Several took quite some time, performance anxiety and all that. Eventually, though, they all strolled out smiling like Juwann and Marco, laughing and slapping high-fives.

In line, Jon Martin and the senior from the locker room exchanged a whisper, both of them shaking their heads.

They all had some time on their hands, with two more teams to go through testing, then weigh-ins, and finally, the thumbs-up from the pee techs that everyone was clear. There was one wrestler who would have even more time, as they had set up a separate station for her in the nurse's office. Wolfe had made sure the state sent an additional tech — female — to avoid any potential questions or delays. She was a pleasant woman who sometimes picked up extra money in addition to her regular job in a women's health clinic.

Heather's test went uneventfully as the tech waited patiently outside the nurse's bathroom, with the door open, of course. It took Heather a little time, as she was again drinking sparingly for weight reasons, but she produced a sufficient amount. The tech capped and labeled the specimen and headed back to the mobile station to run the sample with the others.

Heather put in her earpods and went toward her private "team room." She had time to kill.

Chapter 46

Near all three bench areas, the coaches paced nervously. They hated these days, as someone invariably lost a wrestler. It got worse every year — partially because the testing got better and better, partially because the wrestlers seemed to be increasingly more likely to be getting into things.

"What is taking them so long?" Wolfe fumed, gazing at his watch. "We're barely going to have enough time for weigh-ins."

His pacing was halted by a buzzing in his pocket. Looking at the number brought a muffled "Fuck," to his lips.

"God damn it," Boxwood echoed.

Both men strode to the mobile lab, the other coaches watching closely, hoping their own phones wouldn't be buzzing next.

Wolfe gave a light tap on the open door of the trailer as they watched the techs intently going over results on a clipboard. They looked up simultaneously.

"Oh, hi Coach — coaches," one tech said, pausing. "C'mon in, have a seat."

They remained standing.

"Unfortunately, we have a little problem," he began tentatively. He looked over at the female tech and cleared his throat.

"Ahh, as you probably know, one of our sub-tests is for estrogen — it's often used to support and mask certain PEDs: HGH, testosterone, a number of anabolics," he explained, as Wolfe and Box nodded impatiently. "Sooo…" he continued, "we contacted the state and got some numbers from their guidelines for women's track and field — you know, some of the throwers like to bulk up too." He paused.

"And?" Wolfe grew impatient.

"Well," he finally got to the point, "your female wrestler is exceeding those proscribed levels."

Wolfe gathered himself. "Well, she just had her, uh, period a few days ago. Can that have an effect? And can that be an exemption here?"

The male tech looked over to the female tech as if for help.

"Certainly, menstruation can cause a significant rise in estrogen. However, that range is factored into the state guidelines," she added calmly. "So we can't make an exemption based on that," she said firmly.

Boxwood chimed in. "But they can vary greatly, can't they? I mean, I have three daughters, and one of them had to go on the pill just to regulate... things," he said uncomfortably.

"Yes, that's definitely true. But again, these are items that are factored in to establish a top range."

"Okay, we understand," Wolfe cut to the chase. "But can we get a waiver for today and then have her checked on Monday for a permanent ruling?"

She shook her head. "I'm sorry, but in all good conscience, we can't allow her to wrestle today."

"Occasionally, though, waivers are granted if the levels are close," he argued. "Or a retest can be run." He tried to keep a calm, professional tone. "What are we looking at here?"

"We are talking about four times the allowed level, and we ran the test twice, using a fresh sample the second time," she continued, shaking her head. "No exemption possible."

Wolfe was shocked. "That sounds crazy. I'm telling you — no way this kid is using anything. What the hell is going on?" His voice started to rise.

She glanced briefly at her partner. "It could be any number of things. I couldn't say on the basis of these tests," she tried to be reassuring. "I see numbers like this all the time during the week..." she hesitated. "So, she definitely should be checked right away. Hey, if it's cleared by a doctor, she can return," she paused for emphasis, "but not until."

The coaches were stunned, stumped.

"All right, thanks. We'll get her to the team doctor first thing Monday." They turned to go.

"Actually," she held up a finger to hold them back, "I think she'd probably need to see a women's doctor. It's probably not what your regular wrestling doc deals with."

"Yeah, you're probably right. We can probably get a recommendation from him."

She already had her card held out to them. "Well, if not, give me a call," she tried to make firm eye contact. "Like I said, we see things like this all the time," she added. "It's one of our specialties."

It felt like both techs were staring them down.

"Good luck, gentlemen," she finally added as they headed out of the trailer.

"Un-fucking-believable," Wolfe quietly complained, slapping the hand with the card into the opposite open palm. "I don't think I can handle any more of this female shit, Box," he shook his head vigorously. "My head is going to fucking explode! And don't say I told you so. I may literally kill you."

Box shook his head with a slight smirk on his face. "Hey, I didn't say a thing. But we gotta get going. Our replacement has to get tested, muy pronto!"

"Can Johnson make weight?"

"I think so. He was half a pound over yesterday," Box replied. "And I told him not to eat a fucking thing until today. I'll go grab him."

"Thanks," Wolfe said absently and handed Boxwood the tech's card. Box glanced at it before putting it in his pocket when he stopped in his tracks.

"Holy fucking shit," he sighed.

Wolfe stopped and turned, "What now?"

Box passed him back the card. Wolfe looked at it and asked, "So. 'Women's Health Clinic.' What am I looking at?"

"The specialty."

"OB-GYN. And…"

"Obstetrics. She sees this all the time."

Wolfe was a bit slow on the uptake, but then it hit him. He stared at it for a second. "It can't be... no fucking way."

"Yeah, well," Box replied. "That's what I thought about my daughter. Yet I'm getting used to being called Pop-Pop."

Wolfe shook his head. "Okay... okay. But let's not jump to conclusions." He paused. "Can you get Johnson ready? I need a minute before I talk to Prince."

"You got it, Coach." Box patted Wolfe on the shoulder as he headed back into the gym.

As he entered, he looked around at the quickly growing throng and saw Johnson. He practically sprinted to intercept Johnson, who was strolling toward the stands with a hot dog and a Coke in his hands. Quickly snatching the untouched items out of Johnson's shocked hands, he quipped, "Thanks for the snack, buddy. But you, son, need to get ready to wrestle."

Johnson's eyes grew wide.

"And you better have lost that half pound," Boxwood added.

Johnson was nodding up and down as Boxwood steered him out of the gym toward the mobile lab. Box took a big bite of the hot dog, followed by a long sip of the Coke.

"What a way to start the day," he thought. "C'mon, son. Let's pick up the pace," he chided. "You've got your first two varsity matches to get ready for."

Johnson didn't know whether to whoop out loud or faint, but he started speed walking.

Chapter 47

Meanwhile, Wolfe stood staring at the door to the girls' locker room. He was trying to decide if he should knock, just go in, or call Coach D to find out if it was all clear.

"Hey, Walt. Everything okay?" D's smiling face was right behind him.

"Oh, hey. I was just..." he replied distractedly. "I need to tell Prince something. And I..." He let it trail off.

"What, you didn't want to stroll right in?" she joked. "I'm sure the girls appreciate that. Not to worry, though. Heather's the only girl in there today." She started to push open the door. "You want me to send her out, or you want to talk to her in my office?"

"Yeah, that'd be..." He paused. "Uhhmm. Actually, do you have a moment? In private?"

"Sure." She raised her eyebrows teasingly. "Ooohh. Sounds ominous."

His only reply was to arch his eyebrows back at her. She stopped joking.

"This way," she said, and they headed for her office.

She sat quietly as he fumbled through his explanation.

"... and I'm not sure what the procedure is here." He put his hands in the air as if surrendering. "Privacy, HIPAA. How much should I say? Should I call the parents — can I even call the parents?" He was overwhelmed. "Have you ever had to deal with this?" he implored.

"Unfortunately, several times," she sighed. "Number one — we shouldn't jump to conclusions." She waited, then asked, "Do you normally call the parents in a failed test? And what do you tell them?"

"Usually, that night or the day after. We just tell them that a test came back positive and that they need to see Doc the next day so he can see what went wrong." He added, "I also usually tell them not to get ahead of themselves. Most of the time, it's a mistake, and Doc clears it up, and they can get right back to it."

"Do you tell them what they failed for?"

"No, we tell them they need to see Doc, or he can fax the test over to their own doctor if they want."

"Ok, so let's proceed the same way here. Call them tomorrow, and since it's Sunday, they can reach Doc on Monday."

Wolfe let out a sigh. "Yeah, you're right. I'm freaking myself out here before I need to."

"Exactly. But," she added seriously, "we do have to be really careful here if it is the worst-case scenario. There are a whole lot of privacy issues and her rights involved in this. So, I wouldn't even hint at the possibility or say anything about the nature of the test issue." She contemplated. "To be honest, the tech really went out on a limb to hint like this. But I get it. She probably doesn't want her in practice or anything until there are clear answers. Still, if it's true, we have to handle it by pretty strict guidelines."

They both gazed at each other for a moment. Then D continued. "I'll go get her in a minute, but I actually shouldn't be here since I'm not her coach or advisor. If it comes down to it, we can say I was here at your request to keep propriety." She kept running it through her head. "Go ahead and tell her what she failed for. You can even toss in how high it was, but no conjecture, and don't mention the tech's card.

Just say she'll have to be cleared by Doc. Then tell her you'll call her parents like you normally would, ok?"

He quickly nodded, glad to be relieved of some of the responsibility.

"After you leave, I'll comfort her and feel her out a bit," she added. "But even if she tells me some details, I won't be sharing anything with you. Whatever we talk about will stay private between us. And don't forget, nothing extra to the parents, and you can't even suggest this to Dale or Doc."

She tried to soften it. "I know you've been around longer than me, but I'm assuming this is not something you've ever even considered before. Her privacy issues are huge here, so we need to tread very lightly. Trust me on this one."

He nodded and put his hand over his heart. "Promise. And I'll fill in the Box. He was there, too. Thank you, I was blown away with this."

"Hey, let's wait and see," she tried to reassure him. "It might be something completely different. But we'll just be careful." She rose from her desk. "Okay, I'll go get her. Ready?"

"Ready as I'm gonna be, I guess."

She nodded and headed out of her office and down the hall. Wolfe rubbed his temples as he waited.

Heather entered, fully uniformed for the match but with slides on and a pair of shorts pulled over her singlet. Around her neck were a pair of noise-canceling headphones.

"Hi, Coach. Thought we weren't meeting for a half hour yet?" she asked.

"No, you were right," he tried to be pleasant. "It's just that something's come up." He gestured toward the open chair next to him in front of D's desk.

She tried to smile. "Don't worry, Coach. Just weighed myself. I'm a half-pound under." She jokingly patted her stomach.

"I don't doubt it." He regrouped. "It's something else. The screening came back with a positive on you."

She was shocked. "But… how? I've never taken anything but vitamins. I don't even use the muscle builders or protein powders." She threw up her hands. "And I've never had a drink or smoked anything," her voice rose, "not even once, ever."

"I'm sure, no doubt at all. It's not that." He tried to lean forward as if to console rather than criticize. "It's for the hormone estrogen."

"But I'm a girl. Of course, I have high estrogen. They can't compare to guys' levels. That's ridiculous!"

"I know, and they're not. They used the guidelines established for girls track and field athletes." He leaned back. "Unfortunately, yours exceeded that by a lot."

She was confused. "Can't they test it again? It's gotta be a mistake. I haven't been drinking much because of that weight thing. Maybe that screwed things up."

"I'm sorry. I tried my best. They re-ran the test a second time. They won't budge."

"But… it can't… there's just no way."

"Look, they're not saying you did anything wrong. Just that something's not right with your blood work. They said it could be all kinds of medical issues, so they can't take a chance."

"Can't I sign a waiver or something? Go see Doc first thing Monday?"

"Well, you will need to see Doc, but no dice for today." He shook his head.

Her shoulders slumped, crestfallen.

He slid forward to the edge of his chair. "Look, Prince. This is not like the weight thing," he assured her. "It's a medical issue, totally out of your control. We totally have your back on this. Whatever it is, we'll get you the treatment you need, and as soon as it's addressed, you're right back in your spot." He looked at her for a response. "OK?"

She sniffed back a tear. "Ok, Coach." She wiped her nose lightly. "Ok, I just hope Johnson cut enough weight."

"You and me both," he added. "Look, are your folks here? I can go explain this…"

She shook her head. "No, Mom's away for the weekend, and Dad…" She paused. "Well, you know."

He nodded, aware that Paul had not come to any matches, remembering the earful he got when Paul called and told him of his disapproval.

"All right. Just tell them I'll give them a call tonight or tomorrow. We'll set something up with Doc Monday or send the info to your doctor if they prefer." He added, hoping to calm her down. "The quicker we get to the bottom of this, the quicker you're back on the mat. And... you know we need you."

He nodded. She faked a smile.

"Well," he stammered, "I gotta get out there. If you're up to it, change and come join us on the bench. Everybody will understand."

Yeah, right, she thought. This time, her smile was a little more like a smirk. "OK." And he rose.

"Good luck, Coach," D chimed in, almost dismissing him. He jumped at the cue and left, closing the office door behind him.

Heather took in a deep breath and exhaled, trying to regain her composure.

"That's a tough one," D started. "I would ask if you're ok, but I know you're not."

Heather shook her head, holding back tears. "I just can't imagine what it could be!" she objected. "I've never done anything."

"Like Coach said, it's most likely medical," she started in slowly. "Could be a lot of things. Maybe an endocrine thing," she tried to sound calm. "Sometimes, before a growth spurt, we can have big surges. Not to sound scary, but it could be a cyst."

She smiled when Heather looked up, her eyes growing big.

"Whoa, calm down. Don't mean cancer. Just a little growth. I've had several and had them removed — no problem. Honestly, I was back at work the next day."

She watched Heather and let her calm a little.

"And that's exactly how I found out. Well, not a test for a match, but from a blood test that showed really high hormone levels. I would never have known without the test. I didn't feel anything, no symptoms at all, thought I was doing great. Then — surprise!" She laughed.

Heather did not join her.

"Have you taken any antibiotics recently?" D changed direction.

"Like two weeks ago."

"There you go. A side effect of some antibiotics is estrogen spikes. Could be from that." She shrugged. "Make sure you bring the bottle when you see the Doc. He can check for that."

"None of that is a reason not to wrestle, though. It doesn't make any sense."

"Well, the cyst thing is somewhat of a danger. One good slam to the mat, and it bursts, and you could have some serious internal bleeding."

"I guess."

Ms. Dykstra weighed her words carefully on the response. "But what they're really covering their butts on is the big one."

"What's that?"

She couldn't help but pause. "Well…" she dragged out. "The most common cause of a rapid rise in estrogen is pregnancy."

Heather tensed. She didn't look up, but D could see every muscle in her body go rigid.

"Hey," she tried to soften it. "No one's accusing you of anything. I just happen to know about it, well, because it's come up before. With students." Her voice dropped softly. "And myself."

She could see Heather was beginning to crumble as the rigidity began to move toward muscle collapse. D waited and gazed at Heather, whose head was down, shoulders slumping. She decided to break the silence.

With a soft, comforting tone, she began a story. "When I was a sophomore, like you, I had my first experience." Heather's head stayed down, but D could tell she was listening despite the slight sniffle she tried to cover up.

"God, it was great and scary and painful," she let the story breathe. "Physically and emotionally."

"He was a hot shot senior, so cool, so handsome, so popular. And yes, he had a cool car." She chuckled, trying to lighten things. "He asked me — a dorky sophomore — to go to prom. I was on cloud nine." The silence of the room surrounded them.

"My friends were so jealous, but it was all we talked about. Buying the dress, the shoes — my hair!" She sighed. "I felt like Cinderella. He, of course, was cool about it. After all, he was a guy. Plus, he was the main pitcher on the baseball team, and they were going to states."

She sat back. "I'd wait for his call. We'd chat about the game, who we'd be sitting with, who we were going to drive with. Then he casually said we were going to his family's lake house after. 'Oh, not just us, the whole gang was going.' I didn't want to be some dumb kid, so I said, 'Sure, sounds awesome.'" She shook her head at the memory.

"You know, I think that's the first time I ever lied to my parents," she continued. "I told them I was sleeping over at one of the girl's houses. And they trusted me. After all, I never gave them a reason not to — until then."

"Long story short, there was drinking. The night was like a fairy tale. I had so much fun, and once we got to the lake, it was a great big party. It was also my first time drinking, and I got sorta drunk. I remember it pretty clearly, so I wasn't too drunk. Everybody started pairing off, and we did too." She reflected thoughtfully again. "I sort of liked it. It was scary but thrilling, kind of. And he was actually kind of gentle."

She looked at Heather, who looked up and made brief eye contact, tears streaming down her face. D continued.

"Of course, I cried after. He held me and stroked my hair. I actually thought it was the beginning of a great romance." She coughed a little chuckle. "Silly me."

"The next day, he dropped me off at the end of the block so my parents wouldn't see. I thought he'd call me that night. He didn't. I looked for him in school, but the seniors were busy with all that graduation stuff, so it was like I always just missed him."

"I finally got up the nerve to call him. His sister said she'd tell him I called. I thought she must have forgotten because he never called back. I went to graduation and even brought him a little present. But by the time I got through the crowd — well, they were all heading out with friends and family."

She was feeling a bit sad as she continued with the story.

"Oh well, I figured, now that that's all over, he'll have some more time. We'll have a great summer."

"Wrong again. After a few days, I called him again. Got the sister again. She told me he was spending the summer at the lake house and then straight to college. I asked for the lake house number. But you know what she said?" she asked rhetorically. "'I'm sorry, it's unlisted, and I can only give it out to close friends.'"

"I started to tell her, 'But I'm…' — 'Sorry, I'll tell him you called.'" She paused. "I was devastated."

Heather watched D's face, wiping the tears from her own.

"I was just starting to get over it. After all, it had been over a month since I'd seen him. Then I realized it had been over a month since I'd seen another 'friend.' In fact, it had been over six weeks." She let it sink in.

"I didn't know who to turn to. He obviously didn't care, and I couldn't even reach him anyway. I was sure my parents would be crushed — and likely kill me," she added. "So I did what any red-blooded American teen would do — nothing."

"I procrastinated, ignored it, tried to act like nothing was wrong," she let out a sigh. "It was just about two months, more than half through the summer, and my parents wanted me to go to some get-together. I begged off, saying I didn't feel well — which was true. I'd actually been secretly throwing up for weeks."

A thought hit her, and she glanced at Heather. *Oh, no,* she thought.

"And I laid down in my bed, well, cuz I was feeling like shit when I started getting these sharp pains in my stomach. I ran for the bathroom."

"I actually screamed when I looked down, and blood was just pouring out of me. I didn't know what the hell was going on. There were a couple of really bad cramps, and the blood started to slow down a little. I just sat there and cried for like an hour."

"I should have called an ambulance. I could have bled to death." She spoke like a warning. "But I was more afraid of anyone finding out. At that moment, I thought I'd rather die than have anyone know." She let it hang in the air.

"Then I cleaned myself and everything and went to sleep. My mom woke me up at like 10 the next morning. 'Hey, sleepyhead, you must really be sick. Oh, and you've got a little fever.' I stayed in bed the next two days."

"I never told her." She looked down, guilty. "Until now, I'd only told one other person." She nodded. "Definitely one of the low points of my life." She wiped a tear from her own eyes.

They sat in silence for a while, D finally breaking it.

"You know, anything you tell me from this moment on is in total confidence." She paused. "Not just because I give you my word, but legally, I can't tell Coach, the principal, or even your parents without your permission. Okay? So if you want to share..."

Heather nodded in understanding.

She waited. "Is it possible?"

With a sigh, Heather nodded a second time.

It was D's turn to nod. "Do you know for sure?" She waited. "I mean, have you gone to a doctor or taken a test?"

Another negative nod.

"All right then. Might still be a false alarm." D pondered a moment. "Well, we could wait until Monday and go see a specialist, or how about this."

She leaned over and rummaged through a file drawer. Tampons, sanitary napkins, band-aids, Tums, Advils, and several other sundry items. Then she found what she was looking for — an EPT test.

"You could take this. It takes about ten minutes." She watched Heather's face carefully. "It might be easier than waiting and wondering all weekend, and it would give us some sense of direction on where we might want to go come Monday."

D waited and watched.

"It's up to you." She took a deep breath. "Again, from this point on, anything you say, or what that might say," she nodded toward the kit on the desk, "is completely confidential. I can't tell a soul unless you instruct me to."

Heather wiped her eyes, took in a deep breath, and reached for it. "I'm pretty sure I already know." She began to regain control of her voice and breathing. "Guess I might as well confirm it."

D watched her closely, looking for any signs of desperation or breakdown, but Heather seemed ready to face it — or was really good at putting on a mask. She couldn't be sure.

Heather rose from her chair and turned to head to the locker room.

D had a short panic. *Alone is bad!* Her brain screamed.

"Wait," she blurted. "You can use the bathroom here." She gestured with her head toward the door behind her. "There's, uh, not much privacy out there."

Heather paused, then nodded and turned.

"Good point," she tried a smile, which came across more like a grimace.

"I'll step out a minute." D rose.

"No need, I'll be right out." She tried to joke. "Apparently, it's the day for peeing on demand. Just wish I drank more water." And she closed the door.

A quick sob escaped from D as she put her head in her hands. She had to keep it together, she knew. So she got a grip quickly. She shook her head to try and shake it off.

After all, she'd been here before with several girls. But this one was tougher, she thought. Such a great kid with so much on her plate — and now this.

She sat up straight as she heard a flush behind her.

Okay, here we go.

Heather held the stick with a paper towel. "I guess we wait now," she said, placing the paper towel with the stick, view window up, on the desk. There was silence.

D decided to distract her. Ten minutes was a long time.

"You know what the worst part of my situation was?" She refocused Heather on her story. "Even though he didn't call me all summer or write me from college, I still thought there was something there. I just thought, you know, he's all caught up in his big moment... college, baseball scholarship." She paused, shaking her head at her 16-year-old self's naivete. "I was looking forward to Homecoming," her tone took on a bit of nostalgia. "I was sure he'd be there, then we could talk, and well, you know, then everything would be good again."

"Well, I wasn't disappointed," she said matter-of-factly. "I was at the game with a few friends, and then I saw him. He was hugging and back-slapping a few of his buddies. I tried to be cool about it, told my friends I'd be right back, and I walked toward him; my heart was racing." Her eyes did a kind of roll as she shook her head lightly. "And I was a few steps from him; he had just glanced at me when a gorgeous college girl, probably in her twenties, came up and threw an arm around his waist."

'There you are!!' she playfully punched him in the arm.

"I think my mouth was hanging open when they both noticed me. By then, his arm was around her shoulders. It seemed to take him a second, and then he crushed me."

'Hey, Darleen, right?' He waited for confirmation. I nodded. I was in a dazed shock. 'How's it goin'?'

There was a pause, and his girlfriend casually jumped in. 'Hi, I'm Cassandra,' and stuck out her hand. 'Do you go to school here?'

Again, I nodded mutely.

He chimed in, 'Yeah, what are you, a soph or a junior this year? What do you... play field hockey, right? How's that going for you?'

'Good,' I said, even though I actually played soccer. I just stood there in shock.

"I guess it was a bit awkward, so his girlfriend politely ended it. 'Well, we've got to get to our seats. It was nice to meet you.' She stuck out her hand, and I shook it, still staring. He pulled her toward him and started to turn away. 'Yeah, good to see you. Good luck with the field hockey thing.' And they turned and walked away.

"I felt weird just standing there, so I started walking too. I was still a few steps behind them and could hear them.

'That was kinda weird,' she said as he pulled her close to him.

'Ahh,' he laughed. 'Just some kid who used to have a crush on me. You know how it is. You're nice to them for a minute, and they follow you around like a puppy dog.'

"I stopped in my tracks, but I just heard him as they moved away.

'You know what,' he joked. 'I think her name is actually Donna — my bad.'

'You're terrible!!' she laughed and leaned into his squeeze.

D nodded her head up and down for emphasis. "My education in guys was complete."

She looked at Heather, who had been following the story raptly.

"Wow. That. Truly. Sucks."

"It does indeed." They both sat quietly.

Then, almost simultaneously, their eyes returned to the stick.

"Here goes nothing," Heather said fatalistically. She picked it up and looked at the view box. She turned it towards D, who let out a slight sigh as she saw the big positive sign staring back at her. They both sat silently for a moment.

"I know my guy was awful, but do you think yours will be, uhmm... supportive?"

Heather let out a gruff chortle. "Yeah, right."

"So, I'm guessing you haven't told him," D replied. "Are you sure?"

"Totally." She shook her head vehemently. "This is all me. I'm on my own."

D nodded. "Your choice."

Heather was still shaking her head. "If they want to take responsibility, totally up to them. I don't need anyone else. I got this."

The teacher in D wanted to correct her pronoun use, but she suppressed it, considering the situation.

"Would you like a ride home?"

"No thanks," Heather said calmly. "I've got my own car."

"Really? Well, congrats. When was your test?"

"Last week." She actually smiled. "Even nailed the parallel parking."

"Awesome. Y'know, I could tell you another story about my test, but..."

"Yeah," Heather teased, "I think one was enough for today. Hopefully, a better ending than the first one, though."

"Not by much, actually," D retorted, hoping to lighten the mood.

"Besides, the match is about to start. I've gotta get going."

D was still a bit concerned about her being alone right now and hastily added, "Cool, could you save me a seat?"

Heather looked a bit confused. "Sorry, but I don't think you can sit with the team."

"Right, right." She hit her head lightly for forgetting. "Well, I'll be a few rows up if you need anything."

Heather nodded and rose to go.

"Wait." D took out her phone. "What's your number?"

Heather gave it to her, and she quickly texted her. "Text me back so I can make it a contact."

Heather did. "Save mine, too."

D made eye contact. "If you need anything, absolutely anything, call me. OK?"

"OK," Heather paused. "And Ms. D, thanks. For everything."

D's heart jumped, her brain telling her — watch out, that could be a goodbye — but her gut told her it was just a thank you.

"Come see me first thing Monday. We'll figure out the doctor's situation."

"Definitely." She seemed truly on board. "Here?"

"No, come to my classroom. My prep is first, so no one else is in that room. We'll have some privacy. Just tell your first-period teacher before class, and I'll send them a pass, ok?"

"Sounds good. See you in the gym?"

"Yeah, I'll be out in five." She tried to smile brightly. But when Heather left, and she was sure no one else was in the locker room, she broke down and cried.

Chapter 48

"I fucking knew it," Marco spit out venomously. "She's been juicing all along. No way a bitch could do this without it, no fucking way."

"Explains how she beat Warton," Juwann agreed. "Sucks that she ruined his senior year like that." He shook his head. "Hey, do you think they'll be able to tell Johnson and my piss are the same?" he switched direction.

"Nah, they don't do DNA tests or anything. No way they can know."

"Good, cuz if that bitch fucks me up, I will fuck her up."

"I'd like to see that, but no way — you're good."

"Actually, it will fuck us all up," he added. "I don't think Johnson's ready for this."

"No doubt. Too bad Andy's not here," Marco continued his tirade. "He'd totally kick ass." His anger was boiling over. "Stupid fucking bitch!"

"But how do you really feel?" Juwann joked.

"Fuck you," Marco half-laughed.

"I bet you say that to all the boys," Juwann responded in a mincing tone. They both laughed as they headed toward the team room.

As they entered the room, there was a buzzing of muted conversations. Most wrestlers were already dressed, Juwann and Marco having lagged behind to dispose of their test-avoidance paraphernalia unobtrusively in more remote school bathrooms. They quickly changed.

Everything stopped as Wolf and Boxwood entered the room. Every eye was on them as everyone instinctively came toward the center of the room. Wolf stood in the center of the circle and clapped his hands as he tried to start out with a positive vibe.

"Ok, gentlemen. I'm sure I don't need to remind you; this is a big match today." He let it sink in for a second as he lightly paced around. "These are two of our biggest competitors, and for many of you, these are some of the wrestlers you'll have to get through if you want to compete at states. So you need to focus and make sure you bring your A-game out in that circle today." He paused and looked around.

Then, he addressed the elephant in the room. "As most of you have already heard, we have a slight adjustment to our lineup today." He stared hard at the group as a few comments were muttered, and then silence followed. "Unfortunately, Prince won't be able to go due to a medical issue." He stared preemptively in the direction of Juwann and Marco. "So Johnson will get his first taste of varsity wrestling today."

A few "All right's" and "You got this, bro" came out, along with some light applause.

"Trial by fire," Wolf added. "Everyone in this room faced that first match, Mr. Johnson." He looked right at him. "And you are ready. You've practiced hard and did everything you could to prepare. Now, you're going out there to do what you've worked so hard to accomplish. Win your match. Support your team," he emphasized. "Be a Scarlet Knight."

A roar came up unbidden from the throng. Without any prompting, they all came in. Juwann barked at the top of his lungs, "One, Two, Three. SCARLET KNIGHTS!" Every hand rose and fell together, and they jogged out in a line for the gym.

Wolf looked at Boxwood and raised his eyebrows. "I think we're going to be all right," he said, half hopefully.

"We'll see," Boxwood added more stoically. "We'll see." They followed the boys out.

Chapter 49

Heather sat on the second row of the bleachers, right behind the starters. She was accompanied by a few of the "program" seniors who weren't wrestling today. They were varsity and would wrestle in enough matches to letter but didn't go in the biggest matches, as the starters were all on board for those. Right next to Heather was Davey Wainwright in his skateboard-induced cast.

"This sucks," he tried to commiserate.

It took her a moment to realize what he was talking about — their shared exclusion from wrestling — then she realized and responded politely. "It truly does."

They both shook their heads for different reasons.

First Willie, then Jon came over to check on her and rail against the messed-up system that was screwing her over. She forced a smile and told them she was fine, just some stupid mix-up. They jogged back toward warmups. She was gazing off into space when a voice interrupted her.

"Hey, you all right?" Her look of surprise hardened quickly when she focused on Jake Adler, leaning over with hands on knees to talk quietly to her.

"Fine," she snapped and looked past him toward the circle.

"I'm sure it's nothing," he tried to console her. "Doc will straighten it out come Monday." He waited. No response. He began again. "Hang in there. We need you back as soon as you can." He tried to smile and whisper. "Johnson can't carry your jockstr—" He chuckled at his faux pas. "Well. You know what I mean."

She half smiled but still made no direct eye contact.

"All right, you hang in there." He lightly touched her shoulder as he turned away, and anyone looking might have mistaken her tensing up as if she were expecting Jake to cuff her shoulder a bit harder. But she felt almost an electric shock of panic and had to quickly regain control of herself. She made herself breathe. In, out. In, out. She was okay, she hoped.

A blaring horn erupted from the overhead speakers, calling the teams to begin. It helped Heather shake herself loose from the moment, and she gave her full attention to the opening match as Willie stepped gingerly into the circle.

She clapped as the ref held up Willie's hand at the end of a well-contested victory. Wolf was thrilled as Willie jogged off, victorious over a well-established Tuscarora senior. Heather felt her teeth clenching as Johnson nervously jogged to the center in what should have been her match. She shook herself. *It's not his fault;* she forced herself to think. "All right, Johnson, you got this!" she shouted in a cheer. Consciously unclenching her jaw, she clapped and watched the match, imagining herself there, thinking how she would have responded to every move.

The horn sounded. Johnson came off, head hanging at the defeat. Wolf clapped him on the back.

"Great job!" he said, and he meant it. "You really battled." And he had. At first, in panic, but then trying to contend. In the end, he actually helped the team — by not getting pinned. That was a small but important victory in itself. Heather clapped politely, thinking to herself, *I would have pinned him. He was way too slow.* The matches continued.

During the break, she grabbed a snack and came back to the stands as the Winslow wrestlers moved into the Knights' spot. She had thought for a moment about joining everyone in the team room but decided she couldn't stand to look at most of them at this moment. She looked in the stands, and true to her word, D was a few rows up, waving to her. Heather headed up.

D scooted over a bit for Heather to sit. She took a handful of the popcorn Heather offered her.

"Pretty good match, huh?" D started casually.

"Not bad," Heather nodded, munching on popcorn. "We won just about everyone we should have." She swallowed and took a drink. "I thought Willie was the best. That was a really good wrestler he beat in the opening match."

"He's only a freshman, right?" D asked, reaching for more popcorn.

"Yeah," Heather nodded. "I definitely think he's gonna be a state champ before he's through."

"Maybe you too," D reminded her. "You've got a lot of time left."

"Hmph," Heather grunted. "We'll see."

The horn blared again as the second pairings began. They watched raptly, Heather explaining along the way like a play-by-play announcer for D's benefit. There were some excellent matches.

It was a long day, and at the end, the Knights squeaked by, barely edging out Winslow. The fact that Johnson had managed not to get pinned in either match may have been just the difference. Heather was glad of that but thoroughly annoyed, as she believed she would have won both matches.

She lingered a bit afterward but couldn't bring herself to go down to the team room. In the end, she waved to a few folks and headed for her car. She sat there in the back of the parking lot, music on low, as she watched the crowd meander away, the buses fill with subdued visitors and drive off, and finally, her teammates, singularly and in cheery small groups, leave.

It wasn't until she saw the coaches coming out the doors of the gym that she finally put her car in gear and drove away. A big sigh escaped her lips as she headed home.

Chapter 50

Heather unlocked the door quietly, as most of the lights were out. She was about to head right up the stairs when she noticed a light shining from the door of her dad's office. She passed through the kitchen and past the dining room table down the hall. Her father sat with only a desk light on, working through a pile of papers. She rapped lightly on the doorjamb. He looked up, glasses hanging low on his nose.

"Hey," he said cheerfully. "You're late today."

"It's only seven," she contended.

"Really? I forget how early it gets dark this time of year." He pushed back his chair. "I left you some dinner in the microwave. I made some pasta. I know you probably don't want any, but there's a salad in the fridge too." He gazed at her for a moment, sensing her mood, his inner father overriding his determination to have nothing to do with her wrestling. "Tough day?"

"Kind of," she responded, unsure of how to proceed. Then she just blurted it out. "Failed a drug test."

"What?" He was taken aback. "How… hydration?"

"Nope," she paused.

"Then what? You haven't…" he half stated, half asked.

"No. Nothing," she shook her head, barely able to contain herself. "Too much estrogen."

"That's ridiculous," his voice rose. "You're female. Of course, it's going to be way high. They can't compare you to guys!" Despite himself, he was getting fired up.

"They used the standards they use for girls' track and field. I was above that."

"Still. That's crazy." He was confused. "Wolf couldn't get you a waiver?"

"They wouldn't budge." He could tell she was on the verge of tears, so he tried to calm his voice.

"Well, Mom comes back Monday," he tried to sound casual. "She'll get you to her doctor. I'll call Doc and get him to fax it over." He tried to reassure her. "It'll get straightened out." She felt an urge to run to him and throw her arms around him, like when she was little, and believed he could fix everything. Everything was about to come spilling out of her when he changed the moment.

"You know, this was one of the things I was afraid of," he started in his lecturing tone. "A girl's body just isn't made for the kind of stress this puts on it."

"But a guy's is?" she retorted, feeling herself hardening in anger.

"No, not all of them. It's hard on anyone."

"Except for the 'special' young men who become Knights?" she fairly barked at him. He was taken aback.

"No, I wasn't…"

"But I am a Knight, Dad." She felt an explosion coming and bit it off. "You know what? I'm tired. I'm going upstairs. Good night," she added in a mock, happy tone as she turned and headed back down the hall. He wanted to follow her, apologize, hug her, and comfort her for the day she just had. But he didn't. Instead, he sighed, shook his head, and turned back to the stack of papers in front of him.

She was almost out of the kitchen when she turned and headed back to the microwave. She grabbed the plate of pasta. Still cold, she pulled a fork from the drawer and jabbed a large bite.

"Fuck it," she surprised herself by saying it out loud. She headed up the stairs, eating on the way.

Chapter 51

Heather knocked lightly on the jamb of the open classroom door. Ms. D looked up from her computer, smiling brightly.

"Hey, there she is. C'mon in," she gestured toward a chair next to her. "Might as well close the door. People just like to pop in and out." She waited as Heather sat down, ostensibly finishing what she'd been doing on the computer. "So, how you feeling this morning?" she added casually.

Heather paused before answering. "OK, I guess. No throwing up, anyway," she half chuckled.

"That's good!" And then D cut to the chase. "So, do you want to see the doctor I have in mind, or did you sit down with your parents yet?"

"No, my mom's still out of town." She hesitated. "And my conversation with my dad didn't get very far. Sooo…"

"All right then." She grabbed her phone and texted Heather an address. "She's really good, and I told her your situation, so she'll keep everything private until you're ready to make a decision." She watched as Heather smirked at the thought of decisions. "How about I meet you there?"

"That would be awesome if you can; I mean…"

"Yeah, I just have a few things to wrap up. See you there at 3?"

Heather turned to leave, then turned back, stuck as to what to say, and finally blurted out, "Thanks," with half a smile.

"No problem." But what D choked back was half a sob as she watched Heather head out into the busy hallway.

Chapter 52

She sat staring at the clipboard, unsure of half the answers. Normally, her mom would have snatched it from her hands and filled everything out in detail, numbers and dates popping out from cards and notebooks in her ubiquitous giant purse. Now, however, she was on her own. She looked up, forcing herself not to cry, and felt as if every eye in the place was on her. Ladies as old as her mom sneak peeks over their magazines. Nurses and receptionists glanced at her as they bustled about the offices.

There were several doctors here, each with their own staff, it seemed. Heather glanced down a corridor, and three young women in scrubs appeared to be looking right at her. While they looked away quickly, one's gaze seemed to linger a second longer. The instant was over as D's cheery voice called out to her.

"Hey, there you are," she said as she plopped down in the seat next to her. "I was worried you'd gone in already. I ended up stuck at the school longer than I planned." She nodded at the clipboard. "Everything OK there?"

"Actually, I'm missing a few things… I don't know the name of my gynecologist or our family doctor," her voice cracked a little. "I don't even have my insurance info."

D gently took the clipboard out of her hands. "Don't worry about that. I've already cleared everything with Dr. Rivera. We'll take care of those other things later." She lightly patted Heather's arm as she headed for the reception desk.

Heather watched as D had a pleasant conversation with the receptionist, who she obviously knew fairly well. Stifling a sob, Heather sank back into her chair.

D returned. "It will only be another minute or two; then they'll call you back."

Heather had a second of panic. "Are you coming with me?" D looked at her evenly.

"That's up to you. Do you want me to?"

"Please?"

"Sure. And like I said before, everything in here is in complete confidence — with me and with Dr. Rivera," D reassured her. "Once you become her patient, everything going forward is completely confidential and under your control. I'll be right there with you, but she'll be talking directly to you, OK?"

Heather nodded assent as D looked up and acknowledged the receptionist, who was waving them in. Heather's heart was beating a mile a minute, and the walk toward the door felt like a death march. She stiffened her shoulders and put one foot in front of the other.

"Here we go," she thought silently.

Chapter 53

Heather stared at the idyllic mountain scene on the ceiling above her. A sniffle escaped as she did her best to hold back the tears that screamed to escape from her. She almost flinched as the snap of plastic gloves being pulled off broke the silence. Dr. Rivera rolled away from Heather's gowned and stirruped legs on her stool. The doctor doubled back with a whirl after disposing of the gloves in a special receptacle and touched a button on the side of the exam table. Heather slowly rose to an incline as the stirrups came down and inward in a smooth, gentle motion. She came to rest in a comfortable sitting position, the gown settling in her lap like a blanket.

D looked up from behind, where she had been sitting, looking unobtrusively away during the exam.

Dr. Rivera looked straight at Heather with a calm smile on her face. "Well. The blood test will be back in a few minutes, but I'm pretty sure it will confirm it." She paused and tilted her head. "Looks like about a month, maybe five weeks. Sound about right?"

Heather could only nod. Speaking would have triggered a huge sob.

"Well, the plus here is that this gives you plenty of time to consider your options."

Heather tried to mouth a thought, but the words wouldn't come. She swallowed and tried again, but Dr. Rivera spared her the effort.

"Try not to let it overwhelm you." She reached out and lightly touched Heather's knee. "There's a lot to consider, but like I said, there's time. So let's just try to absorb this a bit before we move forward."

Heather took a deep breath and found her voice. "What do you mean by options?"

"Okay, if you're ready." She looked over to D, who nodded.

"Well, it is very early, so termination would be a fairly simple procedure at this point." She continued, even though Heather was already shaking her head. "As I said, you'll want to take a little time to think this all through. There's no rush. Our first reaction isn't always our best reaction." She let things calm a bit, even though Heather was still slowly shaking her head. "There's a lot of time, and time should be taken to have some conversations."

Heather finally gave a quick affirmative nod.

Dr. Rivera continued. "One of our biggest obstacles, or hurdles rather, is how much you want your parents to be involved." She watched as Heather's chin fell to her chest, and a stifled sob made her shoulders rise and then fall.

"I know, I know. We often think this is an unbearable and unshareable thing with our parents." She hesitated and nodded gently. "And they often react incredibly strongly. It's never easy, but I've found that once the initial emotions subside, they are often very supportive. Now, of course, that's entirely your decision. But again, take some time to think about it. Whatever you decide, it's going to be a big step in your life, so try to make the best, most carefully thought-out decision you can. Okay?"

She looked closely at Heather, watching for signs, then over at D, who was also watching Heather carefully.

Heather wiped her arm across her face and sniffed back a bit. Surprisingly, she answered. "One way or another, I have to tell them. I can't just lie and hide it." She seemed to begin to steel herself. "Since I'm having it, they'll obviously know sooner or later."

Dr. Rivera bit back the comment to think about it, not wanting to set up a wall that Heather might push away from. "As I said, it's your decision," she paused, "but if afterward you want to involve them, I'll be happy to speak with them."

Heather nodded in acknowledgment.

Dr. Rivera rose. "I'll give you a minute to dress, and then we'll talk some more." She smiled and nodded to D, then left the exam room.

Heather leaned back into the reclined seat, closed her eyes, and quietly cried.

Chapter 54

There was a tick of silence that seemed to last forever as if no one understood the words Heather quietly dropped on the breakfast table. She stared down and waited for the coming explosion.

"How..." her mom stuttered incredulously. That opened the floodgates.

"That's an asinine question," Dad stated in an icy tone, staring at Heather, who would not make eye contact.

"The real question is, 'Who?'" He waited. Heather still refused to look up.

She jumped back a bit when his fist slammed the table, and he thundered, "I asked you a question!"

"Paul..." Mom began after she jumped.

"Don't." He punctuated his steely command with a pointing finger. "This is a direct result of your undermining. So, don't. Even. Start." His finger remained poised as he stared her down, almost daring a response. Mom also stared down at the table, tears beginning to flow.

"Look at me," he demanded, turning his attention to Heather. She looked up, meeting his gaze tentatively. She saw neither comfort nor sympathy—only seething anger.

"Now," he continued, "I asked you a question."

Her eyes locked on his for a moment, and her will steeled as well. She just shook her head slowly and looked back down. He continued his gaze, growing nearly uncontrollably angrier. Heather refused to re-engage. The silence was broken only by a few light sobs from Mom.

Paul Prince regained a modicum of control and began again. "I see. So you obviously don't want our input on this." He paused for a response and got none. "Well, young lady. Childhood is over." Seconds ticked by. Mom cried quietly. Heather continued looking at the table.

"This is a direct result of you deciding to make your own decisions. You wanted to wrestle—against my very clear direction." He took a moment to change direction toward the end of the table. "And you..." He pointed at Mom. "You went behind my back to support her."

Mom almost looked up to respond but didn't. There was a negative smirk on Heather's face, but she also didn't look back at him.

"And look at the results." Dad let it sink in. "Well, now it's time for you to start making some decisions. Adult decisions, not spoiled brat decisions. This is the real world now."

Mom looked up and was about to speak when a fist again thundered down on the table.

"NO!" He leaned forward as if he were about to leap across the table. "You will not run interference for her on this." He pointed back at Heather. "She will get on board this second," he leaned back a bit, "or she can handle things just like she's been doing the last two months. On her own." He added for clarification, "Completely."

Mom was about to ask for clarification, but she already knew the answer. Paul had always been very black or white, in or out, his way or the highway. She knew what he meant.

"Now," he began again, "to my original question. I'm quite sure it's one of the wrestlers—exactly one of the situations I tried my damndest to keep you out of. But no, you..." He looked again at Mom. "...and you knew better. Well, here's the result."

"Oh, don't worry; I don't want to know so I can kill or beat him up." He hoped for some response. Still, he got none.

"So don't worry about me hurting your little boyfriend." He almost lost it when a slight 'hmph' of a sarcastic chuckle came from Heather's downcast stare, but he controlled himself.

"Though I can't speak for his father when he finds out. No. I want to know so I can make sure he takes responsibility for his actions." He shook his head.

"You are—that is, were—an innocent and naive young lady. Maybe that's even partly our fault. We wanted to protect you from things like this. Obviously, I..." He paused and nodded across toward the other end of the table. "...we failed. Now, though, it's time to deal with this. The young man involved here must own up to his part in this. He, quite clearly, took advantage. And he, and his family, have to own this. So, once again. Who?"

The seconds ticked away. Still, no response. Dad let out an annoyed sigh.

"I see." He paused. "So that's how you want to play it." Still nothing.

"Well. I will give you some time to think and reconsider." Another pause. "I'll be in my office all evening and at 7 AM, as usual."

He stood and pushed away from the table. "If you don't come and discuss this and begin to make sensible plans, well..." He held his palms upward by his shoulders. "...then I can only assume that you intend to deal with this on your own."

Stepping away, he added in a faux-calm monotone, "But that means that you can do that somewhere else. Maybe your boyfriend or his family will have this." He leaned on the table for emphasis. "But it won't be here."

With a quick turn, he headed down the hall to his office. Heather stared after him with rising rage. Mom broke into full-on crying. With a conscious effort to keep control, Heather slowly rose and walked away.

Chapter 55

She stood at the bottom of the stairs for a long moment. No one was in the kitchen, but she could smell the morning coffee. Down the hall, she could see the light coming from her father's office door. She believed her mother was still upstairs. Stifling a sniffle, she strode toward and through the front door.

Hardly registering the drive, Heather pulled into the numbered space in the underclassmen's lot. She gathered up her things and took a moment to compose herself. With a deep breath, she stepped out of the car, locked the doors with a beep, and headed up the long, sloping sidewalk toward the school. Thankfully, no one really interacted with her except for a few smiles and nods in passing. She wasn't up to talking with anyone quite yet.

The cacophony exploded as she shouldered her way through the mob that always filled the front lobby before the bell. There were a lot of glances her way, but she kept her head down and angled through the crowd. Things thinned out as she headed down the wing where her locker waited near the end of the hall. Looks followed her, and she was aware of people leaning back into their groups as she passed.

"Well, I guess the news of me not wrestling's already gotten around. Wonder if I'll get another mural," she wondered. She was not disappointed.

Her jaw dropped. There was truly a hush in the crowd as they awaited her reaction. An almost perfect likeness of her stood in black marker. A likeness that included her in a wrestling singlet, with a headgear in one hand. In the drawing, her head was looking down at her other hand, which held a well-rounded, obviously protruding baby bump.

She couldn't breathe. No sound came from her mouth, but as she turned on her heel and strode away, tears began to stream down her face.

Like the wave at a sporting event, the voices rose like a buzz as she passed each throng. She moved faster and faster as the buzz seemed to follow her like a tsunami. The flow of tears seemed to move faster and faster as she picked up speed. She had been on the way out of the building, but as she passed D's room, she turned right into the open door and slammed it shut behind her. Leaning back against the door, a sob burst out like an explosion.

D looked up from her desk, surprised by the sound. Her eyes grew wide, and she leapt from her seat.

"Oh my God," she gasped and rushed toward Heather. "What's wrong?"

"They know," she croaked.

"Who?" D asked incredulously.

"Everyone," Heather whispered.

Chapter 56

D went to Heather and pulled her into a hug, deftly clicking the lock on the door as she pulled her in. Heather basically collapsed into her arms and began an almost silent heave of sobs. D just held her. As they started to subside, D turned and slipped an arm around Heather's shoulders, steering her to the back of the room, out of the sightline of curious passersby gazing in the slit window of the classroom door.

They sat at the back table, where D did one-on-ones with her students. As if out of nowhere, D produced a box of tissues and passed them over to Heather, who had worn no makeup, so she only had tears to wipe from her reddened eyes.

"How could they know?" Heather started with a rasp. "I didn't tell anyone but my parents." The unspoken question hung in the air. D held her hand to her heart.

"I didn't tell a soul. Not a single person," she paused. "Maybe your, ahh…" she paused again, "partner?"

Heather vehemently shook her head. "I didn't tell them."

"Any friends, texts, postings that maybe hinted?"

"No." Heather kept shaking her head as if answering an interrogation. "Nothing. Nothing at all." And as if anticipating, she added, "And my parents, no way. They were blown away." Still shaking her head, "No way they said anything to anyone."

Both sat in silence, considering, dumbstruck.

"Fuck."

D was taken aback more by the vehemence than the word. "What?"

Heather shook her head back and forth, gazing down and gritting her teeth. "The waiting room," she let out a sigh.

"But I didn't see anyone there. We were alone."

"Not the patients," she looked up. "Down the hall, there were some assistants for another doctor. They were looking at me for a second." She closed her eyes, and her shoulders slumped. "I thought they were judging me for being so young."

"And?"

"One of them was Kayla Shelby's sister."

"Are you sure?"

She nodded. "I wasn't thinking about it then, but now that I do, I'm sure."

"She can't do something like that," D started getting hot. "That is totally illegal. She has to know that."

"Probably told Kayla, and now the world knows."

"Well, neither of them are getting away with this."

Heather shrugged. "What's the point? Cat's out of the bag now." She wiped a hand across her face, then followed with a wad of tissues.

"Still," D fumed. And the silence returned.

"Do you mind if I stay here until the halls clear?"

"Absolutely," she waited. "So, are you staying?"

"No, I'm heading home." She paused. "It's just too much."

D nodded, then started tentatively. "So, how did your parents take it?"

Heather let out a "hmmph" that was almost a laugh. "Not well. Not well at all." D let her silence lead the conversation. "Dad totally lost it. Went straight to anger and proclamations," she shook her head. "Mom just cried." She raised her eyebrows. "Apparently, I've let them down in every way possible." Her face was a mask of mock horror.

"Kinda to be expected. They'll come around. But in the meantime, if there is anything I can do, anything at all," she put her hand lightly on Heather's arm. "Call me any time, day or night." She tried to make eye contact. "I'm serious. Absolutely anything."

Heather finally looked up and nodded. Despite her best efforts, the tears started again. Her head fell to the table, and she sobbed into her arms. D came around and put an arm around her shoulders as she knelt next to Heather.

The bell for the first period rang. They waited together.

Chapter 57

Pulling up to park at the curb, Heather turned off the ignition and took a moment to catch her breath. She was hanging on by a thread and steeled herself for another go-round with her parents. They were just going to have to accept the way she wanted to handle this. After all, it was her decision, her body, her life. So, taking a deep breath, she stepped out of the car and headed up the driveway—when the sight stopped her in her tracks.

Neatly piled on the front steps were several suitcases, boxes, and even a few bags, obviously full of her things.

The urge to break down and cry was soon overwhelmed by cold, hardening anger. *So this is how they have my back,* she thought as she stared. *This is what the 'we'll support you in anything you do' mantra really means.* She stood dry-eyed, shaking her head.

"Fuck you, too," she said loudly enough that anyone inside watching, and even the neighbors, could hear. Turning halfway toward the car, she clicked the key fob, and with a beep, the trunk popped open. Striding up to the steps, she snatched the handles of two suitcases and headed back toward the curb. After several trips, she picked up the last bag, hesitated for a brief second, and just as they had turned their backs on her, she turned her back on her parents, refusing to look back—knowing full well that her mother was watching, likely crying, from an upstairs window.

"That's how you want it. That's how we'll do it," she said aloud, half to herself and half to the world. Slamming the car into gear, she unintentionally left some rubber as she spun out of the cul-de-sac into who knew where—just away from here.

Chapter 58

Heather slowed a bit as she reached the main street of town. She was driving aimlessly, her mind consumed by nearly exploding rage. She literally felt as if she could explode. Snapping out of it, she realized that she was unconsciously driving back toward the school. Tapping the brakes lightly, she began to consider a destination.

Ahead, among a strip of stores, she saw the Barnes & Noble she'd often gone to. Making a quick left, she pulled into the lot, thinking a coffee might help calm her jangled mind.

Waiting at the end of the counter, she half smiled as the barista still called out her name and placed the grande with her name written on it down, even though she was the only one in the café area. *Something to be said for routine, I guess,* she thought. She smiled at the bored clerk and headed for one of the comfy seats.

As she sipped, she noticed a local paper on the coffee table nearby and scooped it up. Flipping to the sports page, she had a moment of panic. *Could it?* No, she thought, she wouldn't be in the papers for *that*. The second page did have a story on the weekend's tri-match. It was mostly a fact and stat piece, with some brief mention of Juwan and Jake's pins, and a few of the Tuscarora wrestlers as well.

The concluding paragraph said that the Knights had scored an impressive victory, even though they were short-handed. She smirked at that. At least they hadn't called her out by name. Finally, the article conjectured that the Scarlet Knights would likely regain the number one spot in the state rankings as a result, and with four weeks left in the regular season, they were well on their way to another state title.

Heather sighed.

Putting down the paper, she began to consider her next move. She could try a motel, but if they asked for ID and a credit card... maybe Willie or Gina. But she wasn't ready to face them. And would their parents even go along with it?

Her soccer friends? No, they probably already deleted her from their phones and blocked her from their accounts and stories. That's just how they were.

She looked down at her phone. A dozen messages, but none from her parents. Some, she knew, just wanted "the scoop" so they could talk about it with others. Willie and Gina were both there, but she couldn't respond to them quite yet. One was even Coach Wolf. She almost felt panicked by that.

Finally, the only one she could open was from D. It was simple: "You OK? Call me when you can." She hesitated, sobbed for no good reason, and hit call.

"Okay, just try to relax and catch your breath," D said in her most soothing tone. "I'm the last unit in Building K. Just go around the side, and you'll see a little entryway with a little garden and a white bench. Under the bench is a brick. It's actually a fake brick. Turn it over, and you'll see a little slide door. The key's inside." She waited for a response, only hearing ragged breathing.

"Thank you," Heather croaked out.

"Just go in, relax. Watch some TV, grab something to eat. There are two bedrooms upstairs. Take the one on the right." She laughed to try and lighten the mood. "The one on the left is where I pile all my junk. So watch out if you open that one. I'd have to dig you out when I got home." She got no laugh in reply. "Just put your stuff in there. Make yourself at home." She paused again. "So, I'll see you around four. I have some things to wrap up. Hey," she added quickly before Heather could hang up, "any preferences for dinner?"

"Uhh, I'm good. Don't worry about me."

"Well, you're stuck with whatever I get then," she tried to joke brightly.

"Ok. I'm fine with anything."

"Of course you are, but you may regret saying that when I bring home some slop." She finally got a little chuckle. "All right, see you later."

"Bye. And thanks again."

"No problem. Just go chill." And she clicked off.

Holy shit, she thought. D sat silently in her empty classroom for a moment, thinking. Then, with some resolve, she pushed her chair over to the computer station. Looking through the school's records program, she found what she was looking for.

Steeling herself, she dialed the number. After two rings, she spoke as brightly and calmly as she could. "Hi, Mrs. Prince? This is Dawn Dykstra, Heather's math teacher. Right, Ms. D," she chuckled after Mom added the comment. "I was wondering if you have a moment."

"Is it about her grades?" she hesitated. "She's actually going through some things right now. She... uhhh... might be missing some time..."

"No, her grades are fine. It's—well—it's the things she's going through." She tried to find the best way to phrase it. "I'm not trying to get involved in your privacy or your family decisions. It's just that she's confided in me. A few things."

"I see," Mom responded a bit coldly.

"And, as I said, I understand that much of this is a private family business," she treads as carefully as she could. "And I am in no way trying to insert myself or looking to get others involved. I just wanted to talk to you," she paused, "and maybe act as a kind of... I don't know, kind of a bridge."

Mom softened a bit. "Well," her voice started to sound a bit shaky, "I appreciate that."

"I was worried a bit," she paused. "Did she call you yet?"

"No. I texted her a few times, but she's not responding. What's wrong? Why are you worried?"

D hesitated but then jumped right into the deep end. "It seems that word has gotten out somehow. Things are not so private anymore."

A quick inhale of air. "Oh my God."

"Exactly."

"I have to call her," she was about to hang up.

"Wait," D begged. "One more thing. She, uh, told me she can't go home. Is that her, or..." She half expected to be told to mind her business, but Mom let out a ragged half-sob and took a moment to compose herself.

"No. That's her father," she responded, half angry, half apologetic. "Paul is not handling this well."

"I see."

"He just needs some time." She felt a need to explain. "It's just that it came as such a shock to both of us."

D wanted to say, "But she's still your daughter," but bit her tongue and just said, "I can't even imagine."

Mom sniffed back a tear. "Well. I have to try and reach her."

"I understand. Um, do you think Mr. Prince will let her come back home?" She winced, knowing she had likely just crossed a line.

Mom was silent for a second but then responded. "I'm not sure. I can't even get him to talk about any of it. That is, except for his obsession with 'who's the father.'"

D thought about how to respond, then decided to go for it. "Look, I have a couple of extra bedrooms. My um, husband passed away a few years ago. So..." she let it hang for a few moments.

They both waited in silence.

"I don't know," Mom sniffed again. "But I don't think Paul's ready to give in yet." Then, with a bit of panic, "Do you think she's okay? I mean, with it coming out. Will she…"

"No, I don't think so. I mean, she was more angry than anything. She might punch a hole in something, but I don't think…"

"I have to call her," Mom paused, "but if you're sure, it's no problem. I mean, I'd really appreciate…"

"No problem at all." She then told a little white lie. "I'll start texting and calling, too. If she answers, I'll tell her you need to talk to her. And I'll see if she wants to stay with me a bit."

"Okay." Mom sounded overwhelmed.

"And I'll keep in touch to let you know anything that comes up." Then, trying to be positive, "And as soon as Dad, uh, adjusts to this news, we'll, ahh…"

"Yes. Things will calm down soon, I'm sure." A big, deep breath. "Okay. Okay. Thank you again. I really need to call her now."

"Absolutely," D said to a dial tone. She then quickly dialed Heather.

Chapter 59

Heather sat on the edge of the bed, her one small suitcase standing there with the handle still up. Half of her wanted to grab it and run; the other half wanted to curl up under the covers and cry herself to sleep. She pushed herself up and started pacing. Finally, she decided to go downstairs and get something to drink.

She looked around the impossibly neat living room. The furniture and floors were beautiful, but they hardly looked lived in. She was almost afraid to sit down anywhere; it was so clean and arranged. Strolling into the kitchen, she ran her finger along the clean white countertops and grabbed the handle of a bright stainless steel fridge. Looking inside, she saw a lot of fresh produce, juice, and on one shelf, some containers of yogurt and cans of Diet Pepsi. Grabbing one of each, she slid into a chair at the kitchen table and opened them up.

"Need a spoon, dummy," she said aloud to the empty house. She started opening drawers and finally found the silverware in the last drawer. She glanced into the living room and saw a large framed photo on the wall. It was a much younger Ms. D and some really hot guy. They looked really happy on some beach somewhere. Heather knit her eyebrows, thinking she'd always thought of D one way—as the teacher and coach she'd known the last few years. She'd never thought of her as a person with a whole life lived before then.

Picking up her yogurt, she walked out to the living room, paying attention now to the pictures and photos around the room. Some had family members, but most had the hot guy. Heather stopped and looked at a large one with a gold frame sitting on a side table. It was a wedding photo—D looking young and beaming in a white dress with big upswept hair and a little tiara, the hot guy with a big goofy grin wearing a tux that seemed to be stretched tight against his broad shoulders.

"Holy shit," Heather thought. "I didn't know she was married."

She continued her stroll, seeing several other happy couple photos, stopping at one that showed the hot guy looking tan and rugged in an army uniform, a desert scene behind him. *He looks even hotter there,* Heather thought. She finished her scan of the room. At the end was a glass table, but there were no pictures on that one. About to head back to the kitchen, the glass table caught her eye. There was something inside it, and when she realized what it was, it stopped her in her tracks.

A folded flag was neatly displayed with several medals around it.

"Oh," she said aloud again, and it echoed in the empty room. She tried to sniff back a tear, but the crying came anyway, hard and deep.

Chapter 60

"Hey!" The voice from downstairs snapped her awake. "Hope you like Chinese."

Heather wiped her face, which was still wet, and noticed a damp spot on the comforter she'd been lying on.

"Oh my God," she thought. "How embarrassing," and she tried to wipe it up with the sleeve of her sweatshirt.

"Are you awake?"

"Yeah, be right down," Heather called, surprised at the creak in her voice. She sucked in a deep breath and tried to wipe her face dry, then pushed her hair back with her fingers. *Thank God I'm not wearing any makeup,* she thought. *At least there's no mascara everywhere.* She tried to screw a smile onto her face as she headed downstairs.

D's pristine kitchen was now a bit messy, with several cartons of food, some plates, and a handful of soy packets strewn across the counter.

"I got chow mein, lo mein, General Tso's, and beef and broccoli. You've got to at least like one of them!" D chatted brightly.

"You didn't have to. I'm fine," Heather started to object.

D just waved a hand in dismissal. "I would have got most of them anyway. I like a little bit of everything."

Heather smiled. "Well, General Tso's is my favorite."

"I thought it might be. You definitely have a little spicy in you."

"Me? I'm Miss Bland."

"Yeah, right. You're definitely one of those girls who sits in the back and hopes no one notices her."

"Well, maybe not quite that bad."

D laughed and poured herself a glass of wine. "There are drinks in the fridge. Sorry," she nodded at the wine, "but you're not 21 yet."

Heather nodded. "My mom lets me have some at home, but I don't really like it…" The mention of home made her look down and away.

"Speaking of Mom," D segued as casually as she could. "We had a little chat today."

"What? Why?" Heather felt panic rising in her.

"Well," she tried to sound calming, "I needed to make sure she was okay with this."

"They threw me out. Kinda lost their say, don't you think?"

"Yeah, to some degree, but still, they are your parents." She paused. "And in my position, I have to make sure they're on board." Looking for the right words, she continued. "If she heard it from somewhere else, or if the school thought I didn't have her permission, people might get the wrong idea."

Heather looked at her, confused. "Like what?"

D laughed. "What, you think I don't know what you guys do with my name? Dike-stra?"

"Oh…" The light bulb went off in Heather's brain. "No, I never…"

"No, you probably didn't. And the nice ones don't," she smiled and tilted her head. "But come on. Name like that. 'Ms.' Obviously single. Softball coach. Always involved with the girls?"

"Yeah, some—but they're all assholes!" She stunned herself a bit, cursing in front of D.

"True. Probably the same assholes drawing the pictures on your locker."

"You heard about that?"

"Hard not to," she said as she poured a helping of beef lo mein onto a plate with chopsticks.

"But anyway. You're married. I mean… you were." Heather looked down. "Oh. I… uhh… I'm sorry."

D smiled and waved it away. "Don't be. You're right. I am married." She looked toward the living room. "I mean, in a way, he's still here," she paused, "always will be."

Heather tried to break the silence. "You guys looked really happy." Again, she winced inside, feeling she'd blundered, but D seemed okay.

"Oh, we were. Don't get me wrong, he wasn't perfect. But he was really great." She nodded her head up and down.

The silence grew as they ate, and D finally broke it. "But how are you feeling?"

"Not bad," she replied as she pushed her food around with the chopsticks. "Haven't thrown up at all the last few days. That's a plus." She chuckled. "Other than that, I don't feel bad at all."

"Good, good." D hesitated. "How about the other part? You know, the parents… everyone knowing."

Heather sighed. "Well, the cat's outta the bag, so not much to do except keep on moving." She cocked her head and kind of raised her eyebrows. "I suppose I've kinda been in training for ignoring all the stares and gossip with the wrestling experience."

They both laughed lightly. D responded, "Yeah, I guess you have."

"The 'rents, though…" she paused. "That's a whole different thing." She unexpectedly couldn't speak, and despite her best efforts, tears welled in her eyes.

D fought back the catch in her own voice and reached out, placing her hand on top of Heather's. "They just need a little time. They'll come around."

Heather just nodded in silence as D gave her hand a squeeze.

"Believe me, talking to your mom—the only thing she's worried about is you."

Heather could only respond with a widening of her eyes and a raise of her brow. She knew no sound could come out without a crying explosion. D smiled and patted her hand. They both focused on their chopsticks.

Chapter 61

Heather strode in through the front door, standing tall and looking straight ahead. She didn't bother to look around or respond to a few whispered "Hi's" and "Heys" but headed straight through the throng and toward her locker. She was unsurprised as the ritual of surreptitious watchers waited for her reaction to the ubiquitous drawing on her locker.

She stood facing it, hands on her hips, and looked it over. Her, in a wrestling singlet again—pretty good likeness, she thought. This time, she was pushing a baby carriage. Her brows knit, though, when she saw the baby sitting up in it. It had exaggerated African American features. She shook her head, not liking at all what that implied. Pointing her cell phone at the caricature, she snapped a few photos and pocketed the device. Then she set her backpack on the floor and took out a can of acetone and a roll of paper towels. Quickly wiping away the marker, her locker gleamed brightly in its restored scarlet color.

Opening up the locker, Heather placed the tin and roll on the top shelf, hung up her coat, and grabbed her books. Closing her locker and giving the dial a spin, she turned on her heel and walked back up the hallway. The ogling heads turned like dominoes, acting as if they were dealing with their own lockers. Heather headed for first-period English.

The rustling sound of pre-class chatter softened a bit as she walked into the room. Eyes tried to watch her unobtrusively as she crossed toward her seat against the wall. Mr. Poe was writing a few last-minute things on the board as everyone began to settle in. His name was Poe, like the infamous gothic author (though he claimed no relation). Most students dropped the "Mr." and called him Po-po, as if he were a cop, though his demeanor was far from authoritarian. Most students said he was a "chill dude," and even though he wasn't nearly old enough, they often said he must have been at Woodstock.

Heather generally enjoyed English and usually joined in eagerly, if for nothing else than to spare Po-po from the general indifference the students had to *Of Mice and Men.* Today, however, she just stared down at her notebook, not wanting to deal with the surreptitious stares around her.

"What a slut," Brianna—"Breezy"—said quietly to her little gang of three compatriots: Delin and "Becks."

"That's harsh," Becks laughed and said quietly.

"Sucks to suck," Breezy shrugged her shoulders.

"Hmph," Delin added with a smile, "if she had, she wouldn't be in this mess."

Both girls looked at him with knit brows until the light came on for Breezy.

"You are so disgusting," she sneered jokingly. "It's no wonder you can't keep a girlfriend."

"Oh, I keep 'em long enough," he raised his eyebrows up and down.

"Eww!" Becks added. "Only the skanks and ho's!"

"Hey, a player's gotta play with who's in the game." He shrugged and gestured with his chin toward Heather. "I'd definitely have done her."

"Just when I thought you'd reached the bottom," Breezy shook her head, "you sink even lower."

Delin laughed lightly. "Y'know what they say, don't hate the player…"

Both girls shook their heads.

"But c'mon, she's not a ho…" Becks began a defense.

"But you don't exactly get in that condition being a virgin, do you?" Breezy intoned superiorly.

"Yeah, if it walks like a duck…" Delin lifted his shoulders to complete the thought.

"Would you guys stop?" A hissed whisper interrupted them. Madison Manford chastised them with a glare.

Breezy just gave her a snarky look, but Becks hissed back, "Well, tell them not to listen!"

"C'mon, Becks. You've known her since kindergarten. She's our friend." Becks just shook her head and looked away. Madison looked around. "That could be any of us," she whispered, looking back and forth.

"Not me…" Delin started.

"Shut up," the three girls hissed in harmony.

"Me either," Breezy added caustically. "I'm smart enough to handle my business."

They all stared with their mouths open, but before they could respond, Mr. Poe started his lecture.

"So," he paused to gather attention, "why do you think the guys are so judgmental of Curley's wife? I mean, what has she actually done?" He waited for an answer. When none came, he almost called on his usual savior, Heather, but thought better of it. He turned and continued his lecture. After a long, slow class, the bell finally saved them.

Heather waited a bit, gathering her things as most bolted for the door. Mr. Poe called after them to remember to finish the questions for Chapter 4. Heather rose to leave, books in her arms. Looking up, she saw the young and earnest new assistant principal, Ms. Hughes, in the doorway. Mr. Poe stopped writing on the board, a bit startled.

"Ms. Hughes," he said pleasantly, "to what do we owe this honor?"

"I just need to see Heather here for a moment," she responded and turned her gaze to Heather.

What now?

Chapter 62

Ms. Hughes imparted no information on the walk to the office. The fact that she had to be "escorted" did not bode well as far as Heather was concerned. Of course, she had to wait in an uncomfortable seat outside Mr. "my door's always open" Dale's closed door. Mrs. Calhoun, the receptionist, gave her a perfunctory smile when Heather looked up and found her staring. Heather faux-smiled back, and Mrs. Calhoun returned to some busy work on her computer.

After a few more moments of silence, the intercom buzzed, and Mrs. Calhoun called out, "Mr. Dale will see you now."

"How kind of him," Heather said aloud, continuing her faux smile. She opened the door and headed in.

Sitting behind his desk, hands folded and looking like a giant Cheshire Cat, Principal Dale smiled an even more fake smile than Heather's.

"Thanks for coming. Have a seat," he gestured toward another uncomfortable chair. "I just wanted to verify something. These are yours, are they not?" He gestured to the items on his desk like a game show host displaying a prize. There sat the tin of acetone and the roll of paper towels Heather had used to clean her locker.

"Well. I assume you had security get them from my locker, so I believe they are."

"Yes. Unfortunately, I did have to send security. We like to respect a student's privacy as much as possible, but when a danger to the school presents itself... well, as I said, sometimes we're forced to take action."

Heather took a moment to collect her thoughts. "OK. And how is this a danger to the school?"

"Students may not bring in, nor store, any toxic or flammable substances in their lockers," he said, giving his best serious and concerned look. "I mean, just imagine if this caught fire. It could spread before we even knew what happened."

"But," Heather raised a finger, "isn't this exactly what the janitors have been using to clean my locker?"

"Custodian," he corrected her. "And they are trained professionals. This," he gestured at the offending items, "is stored in a specially made cabinet with a ventilation system and fire retardants nearby."

"I see. Trained professionals. That must be why you pay them so much," her sarcasm got the better of her. "So, let me get this straight." She paused as if wrestling with a deep question. "For the last two months, my locker has been vandalized and graffitied, and you've been unable to get anything on the cameras." She paused. "Yet, you manage to get me on camera, dispatch security to break into my locker, and gather everything to get me down here, all during the first period." She paused again. "Do you notice something unbalanced here?"

"Two totally different things. As unfortunate as these drawings are—and I promise you we continue to investigate—and I might add, taking matters into your own hands actually only makes investigating it more difficult. Regardless," he regained his train of thought, "they do not present an immediate danger to the safety of the building."

"Right. I got it. It's just me. Not that big a deal on your list of priorities."

"Now that's not what I'm saying at all," he tried to backtrack. "I take your situation very seriously, young lady," his offended tone rose a pitch. "Do not put words in my mouth." He visibly calmed himself. "Let's return to the matter at hand."

"Of course," she said, mockingly sharing his serious tone.

"School policy is pretty clear on this. Any banned substances found in the possession of a student calls for a mandatory three-day out-of-school suspension."

Heather's jaw literally dropped. After a few seconds of shocked pause, she repeated, "I'm getting suspended for three days. Three days for cleaning my locker of disgusting and degrading graffiti that you have done absolutely nothing about for two months. How the fuck is that fair?" she exploded.

"And that will be an additional day for directing profanity at an administrator."

Heather threw her hands up in amazement. "Why the fuck not make it a whole fucking week, you fucking asshole!" she bellowed as she leaped to her feet, knocking her chair over backward.

Dale just stared back at her incredulous face and touched the intercom button. "Have security report to my office immediately." He continued, "Now you can either calm down, pick up that chair, and sit back down, or you'll be leaving here in cuffs." He waited as she continued to stare. "So, what's it gonna be?"

She took a deep breath, shook her head, turned and righted the chair, and sat down to await her escort. The silence ticked away as Principal Dale shuffled papers on his desk. Heather just stared, silently fuming. He broke the silence.

"Who can come get you—Mom or Dad?"

"Hrhmpphh," she almost laughed. "Neither. We're not on speaking terms at the moment."

He gazed at her uncomprehendingly for a moment, then remembered the annoying three-way conversation he'd had with the mother and Ms. Dykstra. He'd wanted to squash that immediately, but the superintendent had approved it. He was still wrestling with a direction when Safety Officer Barnes stepped in.

"You know what, you can cool yourself down a little in ISS, young lady. You'll stay there the rest of the day." He signed a form with finality and slapped it into his outbox. "And your five days start tomorrow."

Giving Barnes a dismissing nod, Dale turned to pick up his phone as if to make a call. He indicated with his head that Heather should leave.

"And I still have to notify your parents," he added.

"Knock yourself out," she mocked as she turned to leave.

Barnes smiled at her as he started to step out next to her, but Heather had no smiles left to return.

She sat staring at the wall, casually reading the graffiti on it and on the separators surrounding her desk. There were approximately ten such cubicles in the ISS room. Like Heather, they all faced the wall and were reminded of a laminated poster directly in front of them:

NO TALKING
NO SLEEPING
NO CELL PHONES
(and, hilariously)
NO GRAFFITI

It had only been about a half hour, but she just couldn't take it anymore. She leaned her chair back and stared at the annoying young gym teacher, who sat reading the sports page, ready to bark out, "No talking!" in his best coach voice at any disturbance.

"Excuse me," Heather started semi-politely.

He looked up, ready to shout his mantra, but paused when he saw Heather (he rarely yelled at the pretty ones). Heather gave him her best smile.

"Can I use the restroom?"

He put down his paper momentarily. "You just got here," he responded. "And you only get one pass per day. Sure you wanna use it now?"

"Sorry. I just really need to go," she paused for effect. "It's a, uuhhh, girl thing."

He waved her out quickly. "OK, go."

She sprang up and grabbed her backpack.

"Leave your bag," he tried to speak sternly.

Heather tried to look embarrassed. "But it, I... but..." she looked down at the ground. "It has the, uhhh, things I need."

His eyes got big, unsure of what to do, then he just gave up. "Y'know what, go ahead. Go."

He followed her out and stood at the open door. He had to watch to make sure they went to the restrooms right down the hall.

"Shoot," she thought, realizing he'd come out too. As he watched, she turned right and entered, trying to come up with a plan B. Stepping into a stall, she sat and thought for a moment.

A new plan entered her mind as she heard a gaggle of chattering freshmen enter the girls' room. None bothered to actually use the facilities. They just ran the water, giggled, and gossiped while one grabbed a quick smoke to show off.

As they gathered to leave, Heather stepped out and rinsed her hands. They all stared, realizing who she was. Heather just smiled. They broke the stares and started mindlessly chatting, the smoker quickly extinguishing her half-smoked butt and discarding it. They moved as a flock toward the door, and she moved with them. Stepping past the one holding the door, she blended in with the others as they exited.

Stealing a furtive glance toward the ISS door, she shook her head and smiled. The young gym teacher only slightly glanced at the pack of freshmen girls heading down the hall. He was quite busy at the moment, chatting up two senior girls.

At the end of the hall, the freshmen turned right, and Heather turned left, heading for the parking lot.

Chapter 63

Throughout the day, Principal Dale couldn't quite shake the feeling of annoyance and frustration that dealing with Heather Prince had left him with. There had been nothing but one problem after another since she'd started this wrestling nonsense. He half wished he'd put his foot down, as Boxwood had suggested. All these ridiculous regulations were making his job nearly undoable. He half wanted to go back to teaching. The extra money was definitely not worth all this aggravation.

In this mood, he snapped when he heard a click and looked up to see Mrs. Calhoun standing with her back against his closed door.

"What now?" he nearly bit her head off.

She hesitated. "Uhh, two things. One, Heather Prince, slipped out of ISS and hasn't returned…"

"Son of a bitch!" he slammed his fist on the desk so loudly that Mrs. Calhoun flinched. "How fucking hard is it to watch a half dozen kids?" He grabbed the edge of his desk and lowered his head, trying to regain his composure. "Okay. OK," he restarted. "Sorry about that. Didn't mean to curse like that. It's not your fault. All right, let's have security check all the likely spots and have Harry see if her car's gone."

Mrs. Calhoun nodded and waited. Dale looked at her and said, "Right. Number two. What else?"

Her eyes widened in exasperation. "He's here again. Your friend."

"My friend?" he was perplexed. "Who?"

"The big guy. The lawyer."

He hung his head again. "You gotta be fucking kidding me." He added again, "My apologies."

Drawing a deep breath, he smoothed his jacket and tie as he rose, then nodded and stepped past Mrs. Calhoun through the door and out into the reception area. Plastering a politician's smile on his face, he stepped forward and greeted Bryan Finnerty.

"Bryan," he said, sticking out his hand. "Good to see you."

"Bullshit," Finnerty laughed, rising and taking the offered hand. "I bet you're sick of seeing me."

Dale shook his head. "No, always glad to see you on a personal level. But..." he dragged out the word, "professionally, I've been advised to always have the board counsel here if any lawyer comes into the school." He nodded for emphasis. "I kinda got reamed when I told them about our last meeting."

"Yeah, I heard. Eddie called me after that one and emphasized, 'no more ambushing,' he called it."

"So, as you can tell…" Dale shrugged as if to say it was out of his hands.

"Oh, I know. I know. You don't need to tell me twice." He sat back down. "That's why I called Eddie. He should be on the way." He looked from Dale to Mrs. Calhoun.

Dale turned to her.

"I just got back from my lunch break," she replied tremulously. "The front office girls were supposed to take your messages," she added meekly. "They didn't buzz you?"

"I'm sure they did," Dale said diplomatically. "I missed a few buzzes when I was already on the phone. Well, okay then," he said randomly. "If you'll excuse me a moment, I need to make a quick call." He nodded to Finnerty and turned back into the office, closing the door on an aghast Mrs. Calhoun and a smiling Bryan Finnerty.

"What the fuck, Eddie?" he tried to ask quietly into the phone. "I can't do my job if I've got a goddamn lawyer on my ass every time I suspend a kid!" Dale's teeth were nearly grinding to dust as he hissed into the phone. He leaned back and sighed. "This is insane."

"I know, I know," Ed tried to calm the situation. "But I spoke with a few board members and the superintendent. They all agree that it's in our best interest to try and calm this down," he paused, seemingly searching for the right phrasing, "in light of her 'situation' and the potential PR backlash."

Dale's exhale was audible as he leaned back in his chair.

Ed continued. "I went over the notes in Genesis," he gathered himself, "and compared to some other incidents, it seems, I don't know... a bit heavy-handed. I mean, we've had kids with drugs in their lockers getting less."

Principal Dale's jaw dropped. He stared at the phone in silence, thinking to himself, *Really? Really? You wanna come do this fucking job?* But he regained control and responded.

"It probably would have been a lot less if she hadn't gone off on a profanity-laced tirade," he added, "and then threw her chair across the room. Believe me, I don't call security up here lightly." He threw his hands up. "She was totally out of control."

"Oh no, Jim, I don't doubt you. And I've totally got your back here," Ed said, switching to a friendly, supportive tone. "It's just that the board wants this to calm down, especially since Finnerty's involved." He laughed lightly. "I'm sure I don't need to tell you. He can be a real pain in the ass."

Dale let out a harrumph in response.

"All right, I'm pulling into the lot. Be up in a sec," Ed said, then disconnected abruptly.

Principal Dale gazed at his door, knowing Finnerty was out there plotting. He grabbed the stress ball off his desk and nearly tore it in half as he tried to compose himself.

He had a big smile on his face by the time a light rap came on the door.

"Come on in," he said as brightly as possible, rising and rounding his desk, extending his arm to shake both men's hands as they entered. "Have a seat," Dale gestured to two chairs. He then sat back behind his desk, sitting tall and calm.

"So, I assume this is about Ms. Prince again…" he started.

"Bingo," Finerty bellowed out with a smile. "You nailed it, Jimbo. I'm here AGAIN because your school insists on harassing my client." He rose fully out of his chair, emphasizing his intimidating grizzly bear size. All smiles were gone.

Ed leaned back calmly, smoothing his jacket and crossing his legs. "Now that's a bit of a reach, don't you think, Bryan?"

Finerty turned toward the board attorney, the smile returning, his voice a serious, concerned tone. "No, Ed, I don't believe it is. In fact, I believe this is simply another part of the ongoing GARBAGE," his tone rose gradually, "she's had to endure simply because she challenged your little boys' club."

"Now that's just ridiculous…" Principal Dale interrupted. He almost physically recoiled as Finerty turned to him again, his florid face seeming to seethe with rage. And just as quickly, the smile returned.

"Oh, I see, I see," he nodded his head. "Perhaps I'm overreacting." He turned as if he was going to sit back down but hesitated as he saw the items on Dale's desk. "Is that what she had?" He paused before touching the can. "May I?"

Dale nodded assent. Finerty glanced at the can for a second, returned it to the desk, pivoted, and left the room. The principal and the board attorney looked at each other, hoping there was some explanation. Both shrugged.

Finerty stopped at a shocked Mrs. Calhoun's desk. She stared up at his impressive size, glad he was smiling.

"Mrs. Calhoun, I couldn't help but notice that you'd had your nails done. They look awesome." He flashed his perfect teeth. "My wife gets hers done every week. Where do you go?"

"Oh, well, actually, she's an ex-student who does it out of her garage—she's just a few blocks away—and she really gives me a break," she smiled meekly, "you know, because…"

Finnerty winked. "I bet you gave her a few breaks when she was here. Especially with…" He conspiratorially nodded his head back towards Dale's office. Mrs. Calhoun just let her eyes grow big in silent acknowledgment.

"But actually, maybe you can help me out. Do you have any nail polish remover, by any chance?" he asked in a friendly tone. "I have a little mess I need to clean up."

"I think so." She dutifully rifled through her desk drawer. "Yes, here it is." She passed him a nearly full, fairly large bottle of the pinkish liquid. "Will this work?"

"Perfect." Finnerty beamed as he took the proffered item. "You are an absolute peach, Mrs. Calhoun." He nodded thanks and headed back into the principal's office.

He smiled at the two confused and waiting men, placed the nail polish remover on Dale's desk next to the can of acetone, and sat back down. They all sat in silence for a second, confused. Brian Finerty looked around the room, then at the items on the desk, and then around the room again. Both men just stared at him.

Leaning forward, he picked up the tin and started to search his pockets dramatically. "Now, where did I put them... Ah, here they are," and he pulled some glasses out of his jacket pocket with a flourish. Slipping them on in an exaggerated fashion, he leaned in and started reading.

"Let's see... Hmm, there it is—active ingredient: 45% acetone. Yep, yep." He nodded to Principal Dale. "That is some pretty strong stuff." Replacing the tin on the desk, he turned the nail polish remover around and read the back.

"They make this stuff so small, you can hardly read it. Ok, here we go. Emulsifiers, skin softeners, aloe, dyes, and there it is—active ingredient: acetone," he let it sink in. "Forty-five percent." He replaced the bottle on the desk with a thunk.

Dale started shaking his head in disgust and was about to retort when a look from the board lawyer stifled him.

"You've got, what, sixteen hundred students here, give or take, right?" Finnerty didn't wait for a response. "So about eight hundred girls, and I'd guess at least half of them get their nails done." He paused for emphasis. "And I'd wager the majority of them, just like your intrepid assistant, have this very product in their locker, or heaven forbid, in their purse—in class, right now." Dale was shaking his head back and forth.

"So I was wondering if I could see the suspension slips for them. Hell, just show me the top ten offenders."

"Totally different situations," Dale started.

Finerty laughed. "What, do you think that the 'aloe' makes them somehow less toxic? It's the exact same fucking thing, Jim. With a little pink dye to make it pretty. So again, show me even one person you've suspended or even confiscated this from."

"Ok, ok. You've made your point, Bryan. In your typical dramatic fashion," Ed interjected. "In Jim's defense, the optics of the industrial-style canister do make the appearance a bit of a problem. It could cause some alarm among other students."

"Oh, the optics. I see. That's in your guidelines for discipline...?"

"No, it's a common-sense judgment call," Ed added. "Let's take a breath here. If Ms. Prince had remained calm, this likely could have been sorted out, but she went ballistic. And that rarely goes well." He looked down at his notes. "I mean, she threw a chair across the room."

Finnerty looked concerned. "I see. I was under the impression that she stood up quickly, and the chair shot away and tumbled. I didn't realize she picked it up and flung it."

Dale looked a bit uncomfortable. "Well, she jumped up like she was going to come over the desk at me, and it went flying behind her."

"I see. She wrestles what, 115 or something? You're 190 or so, and you hit the gym pretty regularly. I can't blame you. Must have been in fear for your life."

"Let's not get carried away," Ed tried to redirect while casting Dale an annoyed glance. "I'm sure Principal Dale is willing to try and help Miss Prince out here." His quick look told the principal to shut the hell up. "I think we can agree that, after considering the contents of the tin, maybe we can roll that part back a bit, but the profanity—well, we do have to draw a line somewhere."

Finnerty raised his hands in a conciliatory gesture. "I get it, I get it. But you also need to take her frustration level into account."

"C'mon, Bryan. Every student who gets disciplined has a 'frustration level.' It doesn't excuse their outbursts."

"True, true," he nodded in response. "But her case is a little different. I mean, come on, let's just take a look at the HIB reports." He looked directly at Dale, who seemed very surprised.

The board attorney shot daggers with his eyes at Dale. "HIB reports. I'm not sure we can discuss anything like that at this time."

"Sure you can. Students, parents, and legal representatives are entitled to a full accounting and access to all reports. Hell, you've got to report them to the state and review them with your HIB committee, right?" Finnerty sat back in his chair again, his considerable bulk causing it to creak in response. It could be clearly heard in the silence of the room.

He started up again. "I mean, what are there, twelve? More? Or have you treated it as one ongoing case?" He waited. Nothing. "Do you have the files here, or should we have Mrs. Calhoun fetch them?"

"Let's schedule that for another meeting," Ed tried to calm it down.

"No!" Finerty roared, leaning forward and slamming a meaty hand on Dale's desk. "This is the heart of the problem here. An ongoing campaign of harassment and bullying by both students and staff has been waged against this sixteen-year-old girl. And nothing, not a fucking thing, has been done about it. And this—this ridiculous bullshit—is a part of the problem."

"Bryan, you need to calm down. This is a school..." Ed tried to sound stern.

"You're right. It is a school. And as such, you have certain legal responsibilities to protect, not harass, your students."

"Come on, Bryan. This isn't a courtroom. You don't need the histrionics. Let's take it down a notch."

"Really? If it was your daughter? You'd accept months of harassment with no response? I mean, you have seen the pictures, right? You'd be all over this."

Both attorneys turned toward Principal Dale—one in challenge, the other in shock.

"So, you haven't seen them. I bet you haven't seen any HIB reports either. Because neither have I. Nor has my client been invited to any such meeting." He let it sink in. Dale sat dumbfounded.

"Not to worry, though. I have photos of the locker drawings right here," he started to thumb through his phone. "A number of them do portray our girl in sexual situations. That actually adds an additional element to it, I believe. Wouldn't you agree, Ed?"

"As I said earlier, this is going to require an entirely separate meeting," Ed spoke evenly and seriously. "We need to gather all of the appropriate materials and information so we can discuss a solid plan going forward." He shot Dale a withering look. "But back to today's issue, after reviewing everything, and in light of the fact that Miss Prince is obviously under a great deal of pressure, we"—he emphasized with a stern glance at Principal Dale—"have decided to rescind the suspension. However, in light of her just leaving yesterday, perhaps it's best if she just takes another day off— unofficially and voluntarily, of course. Just to let things calm down."

"All right, I think I can suggest that to her." He kept looking at his phone. "Oh, and just so you can get a quick look at the drawings, Ed, I'm sending you a link." Ed's phone dinged. "Apparently, some joker called 'WrestlemaniaPrince69' has compiled them and added some music. Convenient but inappropriate. I will have it taken down soon, so grab a quick look."

The two school representatives started to move as if the meeting was over, but Finnerty wasn't done. "My biggest concern, though, is the current incident. What are you doing about this? I guess it's number thirteen." Finnerty waited.

"Well, I was unaware that there were any additional drawings..." Dale started.

"No, no. I mean the releasing of her information on her 'condition.' That's clear-cut harassment and a HIPAA violation to boot."

Dale looked shocked. "I hope you're not implying that I had anything to do with that!"

"Of course not. I'm asking what you are doing about it." Ed jumped in. "There has been no indication that it came from the school. I don't believe any school official had prior knowledge."

"Ah, so again, you are doing nothing," he nodded with disdain. "Well. Let me help you do your job, gentlemen." He glanced at his phone. "A young lady named Carla Enders, a classmate of Miss Prince has an older sister who works in an OB-GYN office. The very one Miss Prince went to. Apparently, the older sister shared the information with Carla—needless to say, she's about to have some serious job issues—who then shared this information with a number of others via electronic means, which then became, as the kids like to say, 'viral.'" He sat back and looked at the dropped jaws. "It would be in your best interest to aggressively investigate this. At least then, you'd have one properly addressed HIB case working. Maybe that will ease things when I bring up the myriad ones you've ignored over the last two months."

Bryan Finnerty arose, put his phone in his jacket pocket, and nodded. "Good day, gentlemen." He turned to leave. Over his shoulder, he called back, "Let me know when you're ready for that meeting. Ed." He smiled to himself as he pulled the office door closed.

Chapter 64

"So I can go back tomorrow?"

"Well, you're no longer suspended," D replied. "But it was suggested that you take an extra day. To kinda let things cool off." She chuckled. "You know, kind of a Ferris Bueller day."

"Hmm, not sure how much shenanigans I can get in." "Maybe a bit of shopping. I hear there are all kinds of sales going on at the Red Brick Outlet Mall."

Heather tilted her head back and forth as she pushed her food around her plate with her fork. She'd taken a stab at making lasagna, and at the moment, it was nauseating her.

"Not really in a shopping mood. Kinda not so worried about fashion at the moment." She tried to smile, but the smell of food was starting to get to her, and she leaned back in her chair a bit.

D pointed a noodle-covered fork at her. "Ah, but I bet you're wearing your loosest sweats pretty regularly now, aren't you?" she teased.

Heather reddened a little in reply. "There's just no way around it." D chuckled as she put in the bite of lasagna.

"Sorry, bad pun." After chewing a bit, she continued. "Seriously though, the changes are coming really quickly now to your body. I'm not saying you should hit the maternity department quite yet, but you should probably consider a few things."

D sat back and pushed away from the table as she rose. "Let me show you something."

She came around to Heather's side of the table. She stood next to Heather and pulled up her loose fighting blouse a little.

"Check it out." She pulled at the side of the waistband of her jeans, revealing a sliding of the band at her hip.

"You can't even tell, but it sure is more comfortable. Kind of like sweats," she emphasized. Heather laughed. "You don't even need them!"

"Oh yeah?" She snapped her waistband. "I wouldn't even be able to sit down after all that lasagna with regular ones! Seriously though, they're pretty comfortable." She sashayed back toward her chair, hand on one hip in mock modeling.

"So a couple of pairs like these will give you a few months. And it will give your sweats a break."

"Okay, okay," Heather actually had a smile on her face. "I'll grab a few."

"Oh," D stopped in mid food-stab, pointing again with her fork. "And you'll definitely want some padded bras." Heather began to redden again.

"Uhh, I'm more of a sports bra kinda girl. Not a lot there, you know what I'm saying."

"Hmph. I'm sure they're already feeling a bit tight. And surprise, surprise, they're gonna practically explode over the next few months."

Heather looked down at herself for a second, brow knitting. They actually were feeling tighter.

"You'll want a few that have a bit of room to grow, and you definitely want padding—or the freshman boys will be staring all day. Sorry, the nips are gonna be really popping out in a sports bra."

Heather's flush turned fully crimson. D tried not to laugh. "Just sharing some of my years of wisdom."

Heather squirmed a little. "I guess you're right. Never thought of that."

She half grinned, half grimaced. "Maybe a bit of shopping tomorrow is a good idea." She picked up her fork again, pointing back at D.

"But I'm definitely getting Cinnabons!" she added seriously.

"Bring some home," D demanded. "I've got some extra room right here," grabbing her sliding waistband.

They both enjoyed a good laugh.

Chapter 65

Heather's day of return to school had, so far, been uneventful. Not many people had spoken to her, which was just fine as far as she was concerned, and most of the stares had quickly broken eye contact when she stared back. Taking her tray in one hand, she exited the lunch line and headed into the throng that was fifth-period lunch. She almost stopped in mid-stride as she looked up. Her "table" sat waiting for her, completely empty. She nearly turned and left, barely suppressing a tear, when she realized that every eye in the room was on her. Steeling herself, she strode forward and calmly set her tray down in the middle of the table and sat.

There was nothing to be done about the reddening of her light skin, so she busied herself by putting in her AirPods and finding some music on her phone. With a deep breath, she was about to try to nibble on some lunch when a soft hip bumped against hers.

"Hey, girl! What's up? You don't answer texts anymore?" Gina's beautiful smile looked her right in the face.

"Sorry," Heather replied as she paused her music and pulled out one of the AirPods. "Been kinda busy."

"I heard you threw a chair at Dale! I'm surprised they let you back so soon."

Heather chuckled. "Slightly exaggerated. I stood up really fast, and the chair fell back. A little less dramatic." Gina nodded. "But I did call him a fucking asshole. So..."

"No, you didn't!" Gina said in mock surprise.

"He deserved it. He is an asshole." They both laughed.

"Seriously though, Gina," she said lightly. "You don't have to sit here. I'm good."

Gina looked at her as if horrified, flicking a bit of fruit cup at her. "Oh my God! Gretchen Wieners, are you trying to kick me off the cool table?"

Heather had to smile. "No. I suppose you can stay if you want. There is enough room."

Gina playfully punched her in the arm. "Want some fruit cup?"

Both girls left the lunchroom a bit early; Gina to her locker, and Heather to Wolf's classroom. She stopped at the frame of the open door and rapped lightly on the jamb. Sitting at his desk, he looked up from some paperwork.

"Hey, Prince," he smiled and rose from his chair. "You're back! Come in, come in." She half-smiled and entered, standing a bit awkwardly with an armful of books.

"Hi."

"Grab a seat," he gestured and settled back down into his own. "So what's up? You look none the worse for wear after your brawl with Mr. Dale."

She reddened. "I didn't really do anything..."

"Just kidding. Seriously though, how you feeling?"

"Pretty good, actually." She hesitated. "I was wondering. Since we, uh, figured out what was wrong... well, when can I come back to practice?"

Coach Wolf bit his lip a bit and slightly shook his head. "I knew you'd be ready to jump right back in." He drew it out a bit. "So... I checked with Principal Dale, the athletic director, Doc, the board—who made me talk to the board attorney—and the state wrestling commission. And it was unanimous." He paused. "Sorry. Not a chance."

Anger started to well up in her. "That's totally unfair!"

"I know it seems that way, but really, they're all just looking out for you and your..." He let it hang. He waited, expecting an explosion.

"So that's it?" she asked calmly. "I don't get a hearing? No say, no appeal?"

He felt genuinely bad for her. "Look, of course, you can try to talk to Dale. But it won't do any good. The board attorney checked some similar situations. They went all the way to the state level." He shook his head. "And the answer's a clear-cut no way. They just won't allow the risk to the..."

"The baby." She tersely finished for him. "What about me, though? Don't I have any rights? Don't I have any say in what I want to do?" Her voice started to rise.

"Look. I'm not saying you're not still part of the team. You can still do light conditioning, attend practice and home meet, and come to every meeting. It's just..." He paused. "No contact, no actual wrestling. At least until..." He stopped again, unsure of how to finish.

She stood, caught between bursting out in tears or fury. Finally, she snapped out of it and turned to leave.

"This is total bullshit," she threw over her shoulder as she stormed out.

For one of the few times in his career, Wolf was at a total loss for words.

Chapter 66

Boxwood looked at Wolf, raised his eyebrows, and blew his lips out in frustration. He wasn't sure how to, or if he even should, respond to one of the worst and most distracted practices he had ever been a part of. Wolf shook his head in agreement but said nothing.

Every wrestler couldn't help but glance over, surreptitiously stare, or outright shake their head in wonder or annoyance at the young woman riding the stationary bike. As if impervious to the attention, she kept up a good pace, pedaling hard in her practice attire and working up a good sweat. No matter what the coaches did to refocus the wrestlers' attention, it remained a good old-fashioned mess. And with an important meeting tomorrow, it couldn't have come at a worse time.

Boxwood sidled over to whisper something to Wolf and was surprised when Wolf hissed through gritted teeth, "If you say 'I told you so,' I will take you down and pin you in front of this whole fucking team."

Box smiled in reply. "I was just gonna suggest we send them on a run and call it a day. But if you really want to wrestle..." he chuckled.

"Fuck you," Wolf whispered but smiled. He put his whistle to his lips and let out a shrill blast. "All right, gentlemen. Time for a good run." He ignored the mild groans from around the room.

As the wrestlers shuffled off to grab their running shoes, Box and Wolf exchanged a startled glance upon seeing Heather hop off the bike and start a jog toward the girls' locker room.

Wolf quickly called out, "Prince, hang back a sec." She stopped, brows knitting, and changed direction.

Wolf yelled at a few wrestlers to pick up the pace. When Prince arrived and stood in front of him, he smiled and put on a concerned look.

"Heather, need you to do me a favor. Instead of running, could you head over and find Doc?" Before she could get out a response, he continued. "I just need a detailed list of exactly which activities you can participate in."

"I don't see how running is any different than the bike..." she started.

"Yeah, you're probably right. But I'd rather err on the side of caution."

Boxwood jumped in. "I'll meet you over there in a minute; just let me make sure these guys get started."

Heather looked like she was going to argue but just shook her head and turned away.

"Okay," was all she said.

Chapter 67

The worst practice of the year turned into the worst meet of the year. It started with Willie nearly getting pinned in a loss and ended with a very lackadaisical, far too-close victory by Jon Martin. In between were some of the most unfocused and tentative matches most of the boys had wrestled all year. They squeaked out a victory over a team that Wolf had thought they might actually shut out.

As they shuffled around, gathering their things after the match, the wrestlers kept glancing at the coaches, half expecting an explosion. Wolf was surprisingly quiet, simply mouthing a short "shower up" as he walked away toward his office. He couldn't help but notice one person sitting alone in the middle of the row, right behind the wrestlers. There sat Heather Prince, looking almost as disgusted as he felt. He shook his head and thought to himself, *What a shit show.*

The gym emptied, many parents and spectators shuffling out amid a soft murmur. No one was very impressed with that effort. Heather was one of the last ones to leave. She made a quick stop in the girls' locker room, grabbed her coat and backpack, and headed across a mostly darkened hallway. As she was about to enter the still-lit lobby, she heard two of the younger wrestlers, JV's, walking by the vending machines. She paused and listened.

"Did you hear Andy?"

"I know, right? Man, was he pissed."

"Can't blame him," he said, pausing as he scooped his Gatorade out of the machine. "Like he said, how the fuck are they supposed to focus on wrestling with her sittin' right there, staring them down the whole time?"

Heather almost gasped but wanted to hear more.

"I don't know why she just doesn't stay the fuck home." One laughed. "I mean, who the hell wants to see that shit when you're trying to wrestle?"

"Well, she's still pretty hot…"

"I guess, but kinda damaged goods, know what I mean?" They both chuckled.

"At least you wouldn't have to worry about her getting knocked up…"

"Yeah. Like you'd have a chance!" one teased.

"More chance than you," the other shot back, and their footsteps receded as they headed toward the door.

Heather tried to fight the tightness in her chest as she leaned against a locker in the darkened hallway. *Breathe,* she told herself. *Deep breaths.* Gradually, the feeling of panic subsided, replaced with a growing anger.

"Assholes," she said aloud softly and turned back down the hallway toward the gym.

Upon arriving at the team room door, she nearly kicked it in. A loud bang followed as a chair was knocked flying by the swinging door, making everyone jump. Seconds later, wrestlers quickly yanked up pants and shorts, and even a few quickly wrapped towels around naked torsos.

"What the fuck…" one voice muttered, but every person stared as Heather Prince glared at them, hands on hips, daring someone to say something.

"So I hear you boys don't like me sitting right where you've gotta look at me all meet long," she said, pausing and again daring a reply. "Poor babies. What's the matter, feeling a little guilty?"

Andy Martino, the boy she had beaten to make the team and who had recently been restored, piped up. "Why don't you just go the fuck home? Nobody wants you around here."

She started to step toward him, a terrible resolve on her face when Juwann jumped up and stepped in between. He placed a hand on Andy's shoulder, pushing him back onto the bench he had started to rise from.

"Whoa, whoa. Let's all just chill."

Heather's hard gaze shifted to Juwann. "You know, if you guys have a problem with me, maybe we need to talk it out." She nodded slowly. "Yeah, that's it. Let's get Wolf in here and have a nice long discussion about why I'm such a big fucking distraction." She looked around. "What do you say, guys? How about it? Should we air our grievances?"

She looked to the far right. "Willie," she asked calmly, "wanna go get the coaches for us?"

Willie started to rise when Juwann jumped into the middle of the room.

"Yo, ginger, sit down, bro. We cool. We cool." He held both hands up and turned, surveying the room. "There's no problem, Prince. It's all good." He tried to sound calm and collected. "Andy just got back. He doesn't know what the fuck he's talking about." He stared down Martino to cut off any comment.

"You're still a big part of the team. Everybody wants you here." He looked around again. "Don't we, boys?"

A muted chorus of "yeahs," "uh-huhs," and "definitely" floated in the air.

"It's all good," he continued. "Hell," he said, trying to appeal to her ego, "you're one of the only three undefeated Knights in this room. Anybody got a problem with that needs to shut the fuck up and take care of their own shit." He paused for effect. "Hey, once a Knight, always a Knight." He began to strut around the room. "We got each other's back. Always. Anybody got a problem with that, got a problem with me." He looked around with his fiercest game face.

A single clap echoed through the room. Heather gradually let off her slapping palms. "Nice show. But I don't need your help." She looked around. "At least Andy has the balls to say what he thinks." Her head shook back and forth. "The rest of you…" She let it hang. "If you got something to say, then come on, now's the time."

In reply, nothing but crickets. Heather waited a few beats.

"Any time you wanna go there, I'm good. Otherwise, shut your fucking mouths, get your heads out of your asses, and start wrestling." One last sweep of the room. "Don't you dare try to use me as an excuse for your shit efforts. Man. The. Fuck. Up."

She turned on her heel and left, the room silent behind her. Everyone turned and busied themselves with something—dressing, toweling off, fiddling in his locker.

Juwann sat next to Marco and hissed, "Man, you need to set your boy Andy straight. We can't have this shit right now."

Marco nodded in reply. "I feel you." Then he gestured with his head toward Willie, who had tears streaming down his face. "But I think that's a bigger problem."

"Fuck," Juwann uttered quietly but regained his hard game face. "Let me deal with that." They both nodded in thought as the room kept an awkward silence.

As Heather stormed toward the lobby with her head down, she nearly collided with Wolf and Boxwood.

"Sorry, Coach," she quickly apologized, noting their curious looks that she was just leaving the team room. "Just giving the boys a piece of my mind." She paused. "They kinda sucked tonight."

"They did indeed," Wolf echoed.

A thought flew into Heather's mind. "I'm glad I caught you, though." She searched for the right words. "I was wondering, any chance I could travel with the team to the away meets? I'd really like to see the whole season through." She almost smiled at the panic in both coaches' eyes. She waited in the pregnant pause for the excuses to begin.

"Well…" Wolf dragged out. "I don't know. Our policy has always been that injured wrestlers attend home meets but don't travel." He quickly scrambled. "I know your situation's a bit different, but… if I make an exception here, well, it kind of sets a precedent. You know what I mean?"

She was about to make a veiled threat about talking to Principal Dale and the athletic director when Boxwood surprised them both.

"That's not a bad idea." Both turned and gawked.

"It would be good to see it through. But maybe you could help us out at the same time." They waited.

"I know you said you didn't want any part of it at the beginning of the year, but things have, uh, changed. So," he finally spit it out, "Gina is totally overwhelmed. I mean, we usually have two managers, but this year, she's been doing it all by herself." He caught a breath. "Don't get me wrong—she's great—but she could really use some help, both home and away."

Both Heather's and Wolf's brows knit identically at this unexpected request. Heather made a quick decision.

"Sure, I'd be glad to help Gina."

"All right. It's settled then," Boxwood clapped his hands together. "Thanks, Prince. I know it's not perfect," he put on a big smile, "but hey, two birds with one stone, right?"

"Yeah, that's great," Wolf added. "Really appreciate it."

"OK, well, thanks, Coach—coaches, that is." Heather half smiled and turned to leave. "See you at practice."

"Absolutely, see you tomorrow." Wolf waved slightly, then turned to Boxwood.

"What the hell was that?"

"You're welcome." He cuffed Wolf on the shoulder. "One, I headed off a whole bunch of angry meetings with the brass because you know damn well she wasn't gonna take no for an answer. And two," he continued, "this gets her out of front and center of everyone's view. It moves her over to huddle with the other girl managers by the scorer's table, where hardly anyone will notice her. So again, you're welcome."

Wolf shook his head in exasperation as they headed toward the team room.

"One more thing," Boxwood added casually. "Told you so." He laughed lightly as Wolf half-jokingly raised his hands as if to strangle him and half smiled in reply.

Chapter 68

Two days later, the bus was humming with joking, teasing, and relaxed pre-match banter. Wolf and Boxwood entered, tossed their gear in one of the front-row seats, and moved in to sit in the other.

"All right," Box shouted, "cut the grab-ass! Everybody in a seat." He waited for a beat as they generally settled. "Time to get serious, boys. Today's the last day to qualify for states." He let that sink in, and the group settled a little more. "Most of you are in good shape." He paused again. "But for a few of you, today's make or break. So let's get focused." He gazed around the quieting throng of wrestlers. "Gabiche?"

The sound started back up, more of a murmur now. Several boys looked up to see Gina walking toward her usual seat behind the coaches, but silence reigned again as they saw who was walking behind her. Gina slid into the bench seat, but before her companion sat down, she turned and smiled, waving to the crowd.

"Hey guys!" Heather called. "Didja miss me?" She gave a big smile and slid in next to Gina.

Marco turned to Juwann and whispered, "You gotta be fucking kidding me."

Juwann just shook his head and whispered back, "What a bitch."

Leaning over from the seat behind them, Jake hissed, "Gentlemen, shut the fuck up."

It was a quiet ride.

The ride home was humming, though. As a group, they had wrestled well. Everyone who had a chance to qualify for states did. The only disgruntled wrestler was Andy Martino, despite a vicious, quick pin of his opponent. He was still crying about the fact that he lacked enough matches to qualify.

"If it wasn't for that bitch…" he'd started several times, surprised at how quickly his supposed bros shut him down on the topic.

"Fuck them too," he thought to himself.

Wolf and Boxwood ignored the noise behind them and fell into their own conversation.

"Nine!" Wolf said. "The most ever!"

"Tied," Box corrected him. "The '89 and 2013 teams also had nine." He quietly added, "Coulda been ten."

"Yeah," Wolf mused. "Hell, either of them would've made it if they'd had a full season."

"Hrrmpph," Box chuckled. "I think Martino took it out on that poor kid tonight. About broke his back on the takedown."

Wolf looked quickly over his shoulder and saw that Heather and Gina were deep in their own conversation. "Yeah, he was bitching about it a little. Had to tell him to drop it."

"I get it, though," Box commiserated. "But he had his shot and totally blew it. He should actually be thankful we let him back on. This way, he still may get some college play. He is a good wrestler."

"Yeah, but too much of a hothead. Not sure how he'd take to college coaching."

"True, true."

"Still," Wolf whistled lightly, "ten, that would've been something."

"Indeed." They sat back and enjoyed the noise of a victorious group.

Chapter 69

The Bible Club met on Tuesday and Thursday afternoons. It was run by Mrs. Piatkowski. Tall, in her forties, and likely considered attractive if not for her very harsh demeanor. Not many things pleased her. Her greatest displeasure was the behavior and attitudes of the vast majority of the students. One thing that greatly upset her, and which she often communicated to her minions, was that the school allowed known and obviously pregnant teens to walk around the building as if nothing was wrong. She had always felt that shows like *15 and Pregnant* only glorified sinful behavior and encouraged the worst of youthful desires.

Chapter 70

Wolf looked around, taking in the noise and excitement. Hands-on hips, shoulders back, he reveled inwardly. *This is what I live for*, he thought. Seven wrestlers in the state finals, a truly monumental feat, especially considering the trials of this season. *It might be the biggest crowd I've ever seen for a high school match.* Nodding his head up and down, he smiled. He looked over at his boys. They looked ready; he felt ready. It was going to be a glorious day.

A horn blared, and the first wrestlers stepped to the edge of the circle. Willie bounced back and forth on his toes, shaking out his arms and glancing across at his opponent. Dark and swarthy, the Tuscarora captain stared him down. Already a two-time state champion, Ahmed Reatup merely cracked his neck and rolled his steel-spring shoulders. His eyes followed Willie like a mongoose poised across from a cobra, no wasted motion, just a coiled spring ready to pounce. Word had it that he intended to wrestle for Turkey in the next Olympics, as he had immigrated here as a child and still traveled between the two countries. Willie's eyes were big as saucers as he continued to bounce and shake to get loose.

As the ref went over a few things with a match official, Wolf walked over and put a vise-like grip on Willie's slim shoulder.

"Hey, you got this," he said encouragingly. "Just go out and wrestle like you have all year." *Just don't get pinned,* is what he was really thinking. "You've already had an amazing year. State finals as a freshman—just fantastic. Be strong. Just go for it." He squeezed the shoulder. "This is just gravy. Relax and have some fun. You're gonna do great."

One last squeeze.

Yeah, right, ran through the freshman's brain.

Willie glanced back at his teammates, all standing and cheering him on. Looking further down, he saw Heather, also on her feet, clapping.

"You got this, Willie! You got this!" she yelled in encouragement.

He gave her a twisted smile.

A short whistle blast called the wrestlers forward as the ref held his right hand up in the center of the circle. Reatup settled into a still crouch, poised and waiting. Willie continued his frantic bouncing. The hand came down. Willie burst forward like a frightened cat. Reatup gracefully slipped back from each of Willie's failed swipes. Willie scuttled back out of reach each time, surprised that Reatup had not pounced as he overshot.

Willie calmed and endeavored to feint left, then drive right, but he never got past the feint. With lightning speed, Reatup drove into Willie just as he began to move out of the feint. It was the quickest move Willie had ever seen, and before he could even process it, he felt his face and shoulder being driven into the mat. Willie scrambled and spun in a panic. *This guy's too strong*, his inner fear screamed. His body kept fighting as he felt himself being controlled and driven. He knew he was done, already down at least three points; he just didn't want to be pinned.

His right hand was only six inches from the line. *If I could only...* But Reatup could sense it and planted a foot crosswise, driving right into Willie's attempted reach, pushing all his weight toward Willie's right shoulder, which was firmly pressed against the mat. In a panic, Willie tried to arch his back and bridge his neck to keep his left shoulder up. He strained with every inch of his strength, seeing out of the corner of his eye that the ref had dropped to all fours, watching that inch between Willie's left shoulder and the mat.

He's too strong. He's too strong. Willie nearly cried aloud as he felt his core and neck giving way. There was no stopping it.

He heard the slap on the mat and the whistle.

Reatup leaped up with a fist raised into the air. The ref sprang back to his feet, and Willie rolled over to his hands and knees, ignominiously rising. The ref held onto Reatup's already raised hand, declaring him the winner. Willie turned, head down, to leave when Reatup grabbed him in one last vise-like embrace.

"Great match, Ginger. Great match!" he shouted above the roaring crowd, then finished off with a resounding slap on Willie's ass.

Willie turned crimson and pulled away.

30 seconds was all he thought.

A big wall stood in his path as he tried to slink away. Wolf grabbed both shoulders firmly. "Hey, hey. Head up." He got Willie to make eye contact. "Great job. You fought like a warrior!" This time, he grabbed Willie's chin as his head dropped again. "That guy is going to be an Olympic wrestler, possibly a world champion, and you went right at him. Hell of a job, hell of a job!" Wolf threw an arm around his shoulders and steered him back to the bench. Willie saw his teammates standing and clapping, but he also saw their tight smiles. He knew they had all sobered up quickly from their excitement after his thirty-second pin. He weakly stuck his hand out for some slaps and comforting words. Finally reaching the end of the bench, he sat down and grabbed a towel.

The straw that broke the camel's back was Heather's look. She smiled and gave him a head nod as if trying to say, "It's okay," but he felt as if there was pity behind that smile, and he broke down, burying his face in the towel to hide the tears. People watched for a moment but quickly looked away, allowing him to wallow in his defeat.

They barely watched the next match, which could have been Heather's. Lots of whispering and encouragement as Marco got his game face on. Andy Martino screamed in his face. "You got this! It's all you, it's all you!" He nodded and turned just as Juwann firmly chest-bumped him.

"Finish this," Juwann demanded. Marco nodded. Turning, he saw Prince staring at him with a look of disgust. He almost gave her the finger, but instead, he let the anger and hatred for her build up like rocket fuel for takeoff.

"Let's go," Wolf instructed as the ref blew a short blast for the wrestlers to approach. Marco brought all of his emotions into laser focus as the ref dropped his hand and danced backwards. Both wrestlers mirrored each other as they moved gracefully in a circle. Then, like two cats in an alley, they sprang at each other, whirling like twin dervishes. The ref had a hard time keeping up as the two evenly matched-opponents countered and attacked with lightning speed.

Soon, it was 4 to 4 as the final seconds approached. Castaglia had just escaped, tying it up. Both circled, waiting for an opening. Marco's opponent made the fatal mistake of diving in for a leg sweep. He went a little too far. That momentary loss of balance was all it took. Marco struck and drove right into the wobble, and they went down in a tumble. Managing to gain control, Marco Castaglia heard the ref call the points amid the crowd's roar, and he knew he had just become state champ. His adrenaline allowed him to ride the boy out easily.

As the whistle signaled the end, Marco leapt into the air, punching with ferocity as he rose high. The dejected loser lay on the mat for a second, exhausted. The whistle screamed in short blasts as the

Knights mobbed Marco. Juwann grabbed him in a tight hug and held him up high.

"All right, all right, put him down," Wolf commanded. The team stepped back outside the circle, clapping and cheering as Marco jogged back to the center. The ref raised his hand to another round of cheers from the crowd. The victor leapt into the air one more time. The defeated walked away dejectedly.

"That's ONE!" Wolf shouted as he high-fived Boxwood.

"Here we go," Box agreed.

Marco bounced along the gauntlet of teammates, exchanging slaps and hugs, reveling in his moment. As he reached the end, he glanced at Heather, hoping to rub it in a little, but she totally ignored him, busying herself with some work in "The Book."

"Screw her anyway," he thought and grabbed a seat and a towel. He couldn't stop smiling and yelled in general, "All right, let's go, let's go, guys. Lotta work to do. Lotta work." He let out a final whoop as the next match began.

After several matches where they had no contestants, the Scarlet Knights got a pleasant surprise. Warren Coates, a freshman like Willie, headed out nervously. He half expected the same fate and was half preparing himself for the same "Hey, you had a great season," when a twist surprised everyone. As he nervously circled, the other wrestler charged in and essentially tackled him, sending him flying through the air. Warren landed with a giant "Oommpphh!!" as he hit the mat, the wind knocked out of him.

The whistle screamed like a traffic cop blasting to get a motorist's attention as the official physically pulled the offending wrestler off Warren. With a hand firmly on his chest, the ref pushed him back to center and held up one finger for a penalty point. He also called out,

"Final warning, next is a DQ," and he stared down the wrestler, who looked away with a sneer.

Warren had regained his breath, and his doubt was replaced with anger. He stared down his opponent as they returned to the referee's position, with Warren in the advantage on top.

"You're going down, fucker," Warren whispered as the ref stepped back.

The wrestler on the bottom just laughed.

It was a hard-fought and vicious back-and-forth, but Warren managed an escape with seconds to go, making it 6–5. He held the lead as the crowd counted down the final ten seconds. With three seconds left, the other wrestler tried another wild tackle, but Warren saw it coming. He slid to the side like a bullfighter and followed his opponent's weight down, waiting out the mad scramble. The ref separated them as the horn blew.

Warren stepped back as the loser frantically pushed at the ref, cursing and spitting fury. The ref once again placed a firm hand on his chest and held him back. Eventually, the wrestler regained his composure. Warren hardly heard the roar of the crowd or the cheers of his teammates as the ref held up his hand. He was almost in shock as he headed toward the mob that swallowed him up.

"Holy shit," he thought to himself amid hugs and back slaps. "I'm State Champ." He kept repeating it to himself as if he couldn't quite believe it.

Wolf was the final congratulator, squeezing both shoulders in his vise-like paws. "Fantastic effort! What a comeback!" he screamed in Warren's face. "Way to go, CHAMP!" Warren just smiled goofily, still in shock. Box gave him a final backslap as he walked toward a seat.

"Damn," Box called in Wolf's ear. "Wasn't expecting that one."

Wolf looked him in the eye. "We're gonna do this. It's happening."

"I think you're right," Box added as he looked down the bench. They looked ready.

Juwann certainly was. He approached in a confident, casual stroll—the Ali of high school wrestlers. There was simply no question in his mind that he was going to win, nor any doubt in his opponent's eyes that he was going to lose.

Juwann wove a graceful, panther-like sway back and forth, his opponent skittering nervously, trying to keep away. Juwann made a quick twitch toward him, causing the boy to leap back in a scramble, stepping outside the circle.

A whistle blast stopped the action. The ref gave the boy a warning. Juwann smiled, hands on hips, while his opponent reddened and slinked back to the center. The ref re-centered them, dropped his hand, whistled, and stepped back.

With a subtle move of his head and shoulders to the right, Juwann baited the boy into diving left—right into his trap. Juwann was waiting for him, easily taking him down. Like a rodeo calf roper, Juwann had the boy wrapped and pinned before the crowd could even begin to lift its roar. As the ref slapped the mat, Juwann popped up, grabbed the loser's hand, helped him up, and gave him a slap on the bottom as he rose.

The ref separated their hands and raised Juwann Davies—three-time state champ. Walking with a casual stroll off the mat, Juwann looked up and waved to the crowd, most of whom were on their feet. He paused to enjoy the adulation. His teammates waited patiently as he approached in magisterial splendor, their greeting befitting wrestling royalty. The win had been fully expected. Heather didn't look at him or acknowledge his victory, and he didn't bother to look her way. She wasn't worth it.

Jake was focused in a completely different way. He was a machine, a Terminator, totally locked in with laser-like precision. He did not hear, see, or acknowledge anything outside of his target. His prey couldn't help but feel the intensity and tried to fight the rising panic—to no avail.

This match felt silent, almost sterile compared to Juwann's show, but the result was nearly identical. The Tuscarora wrestler had faced Jake four times over the last two years and had yet to escape a pin. Today was no different. Within thirty seconds, the boy was down and in Jake's vise-like grip. He valiantly tried to escape but seemed almost relieved when he heard the slap that ended his torture.

Jake stood straight up and waited for the ref to raise his hand. Giving a slight nod to his beleaguered opponent, Jake turned and lightly jogged out of the circle. A satisfied grin covered his face, but he hardly made eye contact with any of his fellow celebrants. His gaze was fixed on the end of the bench near the scorer's table, but she wouldn't look back. In fact, she turned her back to him completely, and his victory felt like a defeat.

Over the next three matches, the Scarlet Knights gained one more victory by points. Wolf turned to Box. "What are we looking at?"

Box didn't have to look at notes or check with Gina or the official scorer. "We're at 21, and we still have Jon Martin."

"And…" Wolf asked impatiently.

Box's eyebrows rose, almost afraid to say it out loud. "Tuscarora's next. They're at 16."

Wolf nodded as Box confirmed his internal count. A barely perceptible smile started to creep onto his face, which he forced back so as not to taunt the gods of fate. Up by five, with a head-to-head match between the Scarlet Knights and Tuscarora. Any win or draw would seal it for the Knights. Tuscarora's only chance was a victory by a pin, and the Scarlet Knights were sending out their best heavyweight in years—Jon Martin.

His opponent was a strong but slightly flabby wrestler who had already lost to Jon three times, twice by pin. Wolf couldn't jinx it by saying anything out loud, but his gaze told Boxwood exactly what he was thinking: we've got this in the bag. Box tried not to even think about it, but it was in his head. The tenth state championship was theirs for the taking.

The ref stood at the scorer's table, checking a few things before calling out the final contestants of the season. Jon slowly walked toward the circle to wait, a slightly dazed look on his face. Coach Wolf stepped in front of him.

"Hey, hey…" he called Jon's gaze to him and gave a light, almost playful slap to his cheek. "Focus, Jon. Complete focus."

Jon seemed to snap out of it and returned the stare.

"All you need to do is go out there and be Jon Martin. It's just another match, just like the hundreds you've won over the years."

Jon nodded, looking past Wolf into the circle.

Wolf continued, "Wrestle smart. In control and strong, and it's all yours."

Jon nodded absently. Wolf reached over and snapped up Jon's headgear.

"It's all you, Jon. You've got this," he said as he cuffed the beefy shoulders. "You've been preparing for this your whole life. Now get out there and take it!"

He nearly shouted the last part. Jon nodded again, stepped around Wolf, and started a slow stroll to wait at the edge of the circle.

The ref was still chatting away at the scorer's table as Jon rolled his tensed shoulders. He looked up into the crowd to where his mom and little sisters sat. To his surprise, his dad had made it—sitting there with a windbreaker over his State Trooper Captain's uniform and a ball cap instead of his usual visored brim. A small smile curled Jon's lip as the old man gave him a subtle clenched fist of encouragement.

He gazed back at the bench, where all of his teammates were standing, clapping and practically slapping each other's backs as if the state championship was already theirs. A feeling of anger and resentment started to well up in him as his eyes passed over Heather Prince, huddled over the book with Gina.

Looking up one last time at his family, a sob almost escaped from his throat. His sisters had made a sign and were waving it for him to see. It read: "MAKE US PROUD JON." His mom was clapping in her controlled way, and his dad gave him that nod of encouragement that said everything and spoke to his total belief in him.

If not for the noise of the crowd, they could have heard—even from that distance—the sob that now actually exploded out of Jon's throat. He felt anything but proud.

Taking another look at Heather, their eyes met. She looked at him with a Mona Lisa smile and gave the same nod as his dad. He had to look away.

One last look toward the bench, the cheering and exuberant joy, and his expression changed to one of anger and resolve. He practically stared them down.

Wolf watched the look. "There it is," he said as he slapped Boxwood's shoulder. "Look at the determination. Now that's a game face."

He nodded his head up and down.

"Box, we've got this," he dared to say aloud.

Box wanted to shush him, but by the look on Jon Martin's face, Wolf was right. He had to agree.

The ref finally entered the circle and gave a short blast to call the wrestlers forward. Here it was—the whole season down to one last match, one final toss of the dice. Dice that clearly favored the Scarlet Knights.

The Tuscarora wrestler was a bit tentative in his approach, having faced and lost to Jon Martin three times before. The fierceness of the Knights' winners had him a little worried, and the look on Jon's face almost made him want to give up before they even started. He knew it—an ass whooping was coming his way.

The ref held his hand up, and with a quick blast, it came down as he skipped gracefully back and away. No quitting now, the Tuscarora heavyweight thought.

Jon circled with little extra movement, watching his opponent carefully. The Tuscarora coach yelled to his wrestler, "Be aggressive! Don't   wait!"
"Get it over with, you mean," is what the wrestler was actually hearing.

With a deep breath, like a swimmer at a cold lake, he dove in. Much to his surprise, he made full, solid contact with Jon. There was no feint or counter—it was like two sumos crashing into one another. Instinct took over, and his hand slipped behind Jon's knee. With one good pull and a push of his weight, they went down.

The gym floor actually shook under the mat as over 500 pounds slammed into it.

"Takedown," the ref shouted. "Points to Tuscarora."

Wolf and Box were shocked—Jon was on his back.

He fought back, but the Tuscarora heavyweight was taking his shot, driving and grabbing with every inch of his strength.

"Escape!" Box and Wolf screamed at Jon simultaneously.

The crowd was hushed.

Part of Jon fought lightly, but he stayed on his back, seemingly making no effort to escape. The opponent reached to get a strong arm behind Jon's knee, and Jon let him.

Even though the muscle memory from ten years of wrestling resisted to some degree, the resolve in Jon Martin's heart let his shoulders touch the mat. He did not call his neck or core to resist, and he remained under the weight of his opponent. The strong arm pulled his knee into the tuck, and Jon fairly rolled back to allow it.

"Get out, get out!" Wolf screamed.

Jon refused.

The ref was on all fours, and even though he saw no space between Jon Martin's shoulders and the mat, he held his count a few extra beats, not quite believing what he was seeing. Finally, he slapped the mat and blew his whistle.

The Tuscarora wrestler let go as if he couldn't believe what he'd just done. He stood up, almost oblivious to the roar of the crowd. He snapped out of it as the Tuscarora team stormed the circle and mobbed him. The ref reached into the pile and hoisted his arm up.

"Victory by a pin," he called out and stepped away, shaking his head.

The loudspeaker blared like an MMA ring announcer, "This year's State wrestling champions… the Tuscarora Warriors!" and the crowd went wild.

Wolf and Box stood with their mouths open.

The team stood, a few with tears already on their faces, in total shock.

As Jon began to leave the circle, Wolf took a half step toward him.

Jon did not walk toward the bench. He walked straight toward the stands and the exit.

Reaching the edge of the circle, he unsnapped his headgear and dropped it. He never looked toward Wolf or the bench but moved straight toward the exit.

His eyes were focused straight ahead, tears streaming down his face. He took one glance toward Heather, who met his eyes and matched his tears.

"Oh, Jon," she said aloud, the sound lost in the cacophony of the arena.

Eyes returning ahead, he strode forward, oblivious to the shouts behind him. Wolf's "Martin, get back here!" command went unheeded. In the stands, Jon's father leaned toward his wife, asking her to take the shocked, crying girls home. Slipping to the end of the bleachers, he dropped to the floor and jogged toward Jon. Throwing an arm around him, he pulled him close. Jon fell into the hug like a young boy and wept bitterly, yet they were not tears of defeat. The Martin men left as one.

They all watched in total shock as Jon left. Wolf stood, hands on hips, staring daggers.

"He fucking quit," he said so only Box could hear. "He fucking quit on us," he swore in disbelief.

"No, I don't believe that," Box replied. "He wouldn't. It's just..." His thoughts trailed off, unable to come up with an explanation.

"He fucking quit," Wolf repeated. With a conscious effort, he regained some semblance of self-control. Looking back at his crushed team, he walked toward them.

"All right, grab a seat."

They obeyed robotically, and Wolf took a knee in front of them. He looked left and right. Some faces were totally shocked, others full of anger. He spoke firmly, a touch of emotion in his voice.

"As a team, that may be the most difficult defeat some of us have ever known." He let it sink in. "But as individuals, everyone here," he emphasized, "fought like warriors. And you four State Champs—get your heads up. You should be proud. Don't let this take anything away from what you've done."

Nods and "hell yeahs" bubbled up as he looked them up and down.

"Now, let's get ourselves together. We have individual awards and a runner-up trophy to stand for. And we are going to do it the right way. Head held high, strong as a team."

He looked them up and down again, tears disappearing, replaced with resolve. He put his hand in. All the other hands went on top.

"Knights," he called.

"Knights!" they roared in answer.

He stood and backed away, turning to Box. He was momentarily surprised as the fans and parents gave them a quick round of cheers. With a half smile and a wave, he thanked them.

"Willie's gone, too," Box advised him as the wrestlers gathered their things.

"Yeah, well fuck him, too. Let the losers run away. We only want winners around here." He strode off.

Box watched him leave and noticed the murderous glare that Wolf threw to his right for an instant. He wasn't surprised that the target was Heather Prince. What was surprising was that she returned the look with equal vehemence. Box shook his head and gathered his things.

"Let's go, boys," he said evenly. "Pick up the pace."

They gathered their things and moved toward the locker room.

Gina's face was covered with mascara-smeared tears as she entered the last item of the year—the shocking defeat of Jon—into the Book.

"I just can't believe it," she sobbed. "How could he lose?"

Heather, dry-eyed, shook her head and sighed. "No. Any way you look at it, Jon's a winner."

"I know, I know, I didn't mean anything bad. I was just so sure," she sniffed back some final tears. "I mean, we were so close... we could've..." She paused. "And maybe if you were there..."

Heather harrumphed in reply. "Yeah, right." She continued. "They didn't want me there anyway, so just as well they got their wish."

Gina regretted her comment, knowing she'd struck a nerve.

"I'm sorry. I didn't mean it like that," she pushed. "I just meant—I think you would have won, and the last one wouldn't have mattered."

Rolling her eyes, Heather responded, "Well, we'll never know. And like Coach Wolf always says, 'You get what you earn.' They earned it."

Gina wasn't sure how to respond to that and turned to gather up all her things. Heather did likewise and scanned the crowd, thankfully seeing D still sitting in the stands. Catching her attention, Heather waved and held up a finger. D acknowledged with a nod that she'd wait for her.

"You know what, G? I think I'm gonna pass on the bus ride." She squeezed Gina's shoulder. "I'll catch up with you later."

"Coach'll be mad. He says if you come on the bus, you go home on the bus."

"Yeah, I know. But I don't think they'll mind me not being there today."

"Yeah, I kinda don't wanna be there either," she added. "My mom's probably here with my brothers. I think I'll ask Coach if it's okay if I go home with her."

"Fuck him. Do what you wanna do."

"OK, Miss Potty Mouth," she laughed and wiped her face, smearing some of the mascara around. Heather laughed a little, too, and, licking her thumb, reached over and wiped away the smear.

"OOOHH, gross," Gina squealed. "I can't believe you just did that," punching Heather's shoulder lightly.

"Yeah, well, get some tissues. You look like a zombie." Gina surprised Heather by almost jumping on her with a giant hug.

“This sucks so much,” Gina whispered.

“Like you wouldn’t believe.” They squeezed each other briefly and parted.

Chapter 71

Heather sat on her bed with a bowl of popcorn, watching the movie *Stick It!*. It had been her favorite when she was a tween and a hopeful gymnast. She had watched it so many times she knew every word and even each character's tone. She was thankful that D had gone out for the evening, as she just wanted to veg and not think about today's (and actually the whole season's) events. Today had been mentally and emotionally exhausting yet oddly satisfying in a way. Part of her had wanted a win, but a bigger part had been glad to see them fall short.

She was still trying to process Jon's actions. She was sure it was intentional, but she was still sorting out his motivations in her head. A buzz under the covers burst her thought bubble. Searching around, she dug out her phone and saw a text from Gina.

"Party at Marco's - Interested?"

She typed back: "Maybe after I poke myself in the eye with a knitting needle and pour salt in it." Then followed with: "No F'n way."

"Figured - but thought I'd ask! Gotta take my brothers. Some of the freshmen told them they should come and meet some of the guys for next year. Mom says I gotta go for them to go."

"Sucks to be you." Then: "Wow, they're 8th graders already?"

"Yup. Can't wait to be 'Knights.'"

Heather wanted to say something snide, but Gina was always nice to her, so she wrote: "Have fun. Try to keep them away from the major a-holes."

"Hmm. Tough to do. They're pretty much all... DID I SAY THAT???"

Heather laughed aloud.

"Seriously, have a good time." Smiley emoji.

She went back to the movie and spit out popcorn as the coach was asked if he "broke his weenus." It got her every time.

Another buzz.

"Marco has 'accidentally' bumped my ASS 3 times!!!!!"

Heather actually felt a surge of panic.

"LEAVE. NOW."

"I am. Gotta get my bros out. They already have them doing funnels."

"Seriously. Get out."

"I'm going, I'm going."

Heather was relieved. Gina had her brothers. If she had stayed longer, who knew what would've happened, she thought, growing angrier the more she considered it.

"Fucking assholes," she said aloud to the empty room as she tossed the phone on the bed. No sooner had she hit the remote when another buzz came through. She was about to grab it and text, "Just kick Marco in the..." when she saw that it was actually from Willie.

"Just not strong enough," was all it said.

She shook her head and texted back:

"Don't be like that. You were one of the toughest ones out there."

She waited for a reply. After a long stretch, she turned the movie back on. He didn't reply.

"Willie, the guy's gonna be an Olympian. You fought it out with an Olympian in the State Finals as a freshman! It doesn't get stronger than that!"

She waited again, but nothing, back to the movie. Despite the laughs, she nodded off and woke to the credits. Clicking off the screen, she checked her phone again. A few jokes from Gina about her drunk little brothers. Nothing from Willie.

She shook her head and sighed, then typed:

"Good night."

Chapter 72

"Shit, shit, shit!" she exclaimed as she jumped out of bed. A quick glance at her phone showed that it had died, so no alarm. Her brows knit. It was plugged in. But as she followed the cord back, she saw that it had come out of the wall socket. Touching the screen on her Mac, she saw it was already 8:30. She was over an hour late.

"Shit!" she cursed again. If she hurried, she might make it in time for the third. Third was physics, the only class she wasn't sure of an "A" in—and today was a major test. Pulling on some sweats, she dashed to the bathroom for a quick brush of her teeth, a wash of her face, and a ponytail. Good to go. Heather shoved her computer into her backpack, scooped up her keys, and rushed for the door.

She almost took out the garbage cans as she quickly backed out. "Whoops!" she said aloud as she floored it and peeled out of the neighborhood. Slowing at a stop sign, she reached for her phone, only to realize it was still on the bed, uncharged.

"Great," she thought. "It's gonna be one of those days." A wave of nausea suddenly hit her, and she slowed, almost pulling over. It passed, and she sped up again.

"Just. Fucking. Great," she intoned, passing a slow-moving minivan. "AAARRRGHH," she barked aloud.

"C'mon!!" she said as she circled the student lot. Being a sophomore, she didn't have a pre-assigned spot, so it was first come, first served—and today, she was last. Finally, she saw someone pulling out in the far corner. Speeding up, she swooped in just before some other late arrival. Heather quickly shut off her car and hopped out, speed-walking to the front door.

A substitute teacher was coming out one of the side doors, likely heading to Wawa to grab a coffee. Heather made eye contact and smiled. Young and dumb, he couldn't resist being nice, so he held the door for her.

"Thanks so much," she gushed as she slipped in, avoiding the front desk and sign-in. There was just enough time if she went straight to class. Power walking down the hallway, she was surprised to see a freshman girl pop out of a classroom, crying. The girl stopped, stared at Heather, then burst into another round of tears and quickly moved down the hall.

Weird, Heather thought.

Thankfully, the classroom door wasn't locked, so Heather slipped in casually, just a bit late. Her brow was knit as she looked around. No test for some reason. Students were whispering and chatting and suddenly got quiet as she strolled in, some even staring.

God, get over it, she thought. Never seen a pregnant girl before?

"Heather," Mr. Vargas spoke quickly as if surprised.

"No test?" Heather smiled and stood there, hoping he'd forgo the late lecture.

"No... uhhh..." he stammered. "In light of events, I thought it best," he said, letting the sentence hang as he stared at her.

"Ok," she replied. Creeper, she thought. Turning to face the stares again, she was about to just go to her seat when she noticed Gina sitting in the back with her head down on her desk. There was an empty seat next to her, so Heather headed that way, hoping Vargas wouldn't tell her to go to her assigned seat.

When she was almost there, Gina picked her head up, mascara and tears streaking her face. Heather hesitated. What the...? Then Gina leaped out of her seat and grabbed Heather in a bear hug, sobbing deeply. Lightly hugging back, Heather held her.

"Gina, what's wrong?"

"I can't believe he's dead."

Heather was confused. Dead? Who? she thought as Gina practically crushed her in her hug. All around her, they stared. Mr. Vargas was moving toward them. Heather put her hands on Gina's shoulders and pushed her back a bit.

"Gina," she said softly. "Who? Who is dead?"

Gina sniffed and rubbed a hand across her streaked face. "Oh my God. You don't know!"

Gina's voice came out in a strangled sob. "It's Willie. Willie's dead."

"What?" She thought Gina must be kidding or drunk. "Willie? No, I just..." she was about to say "I just spoke to him," but realized that was yesterday.

"No," she said, pulling away. "That's not true. He's fine. Why would you say that?"

Gina just buried her face in her hands and fell into another round of uncontrollable sobs. As she backed away, Heather felt a hand touch her shoulder. She spun and knocked it away. Mr. Vargas stood there with this stupid look on his face.

"Heather..." he started to say something, but she pushed past him and practically ran from the room. The door slammed against the wall as she flew through it.

Principal Dale, walkie-talkie in hand, was striding down the hallway as she came out.

"Young lady!" he shouted as she strode by him. "Stop right there!"

Heather was oblivious to his shouting and stormed toward the same door she had come in just minutes before.

"I said stop right there!" he repeated, to no avail, as Heather flung another door open with a resounding crash. Dale took several steps after her, then gave up and spoke into his walkie.

"Security..."

Practically sprinting toward her car, Heather noticed the little white pickup that Gary, the outside security guard, tooled around in, making a K-turn at the far end of the teacher's lot. She hopped in and backed out before he completed the turn. The Toyota practically flew in the air as she sped over the speed bump in the exit lane. She ignored the metallic thump and scrape of her undercarriage as she floored it. Ignoring the stop sign, she sped aimlessly down the side streets outside the school.

On a short straightaway, she pounded the steering wheel with both hands, and a rasping sob coughed out, "No! No! No!" in rhythm to the pounding. Tears poured down her face as some sort of realization sank in. He was dead. Willie was dead. How? Was his last text a goodbye, a statement? Did he...? No—no way. He wouldn't.

A deep, heart-rending scream erupted from her throat. She pulled over for a moment as staccato sobs racked her body. Resting her head and hands on the wheel, she cried herself out.

When the sobs had subsided, she wiped her face with her sleeve, glanced in the mirror, and pulled back onto the road. She drove aimlessly, almost unable to think. Without thought, she made the next left and suddenly realized she was on Willie's street. The last few weeks, she had been driving him home after practice and matches. A half chuckle, half sob escaped her throat. Subconsciously, she must have just headed this way.

She was about to turn off the street when she noticed a lot of vehicles in front of Willie's house. She kept going straight. Several vans with local news station decals were in front of his house. A woman with a microphone was quickly trailed by a guy with a camera. Walking briskly away from them, with a cigarette streaming in her hand, was Willie's mom. Tight black stretch pants, a loose T-shirt, and still in her slippers, she threw a middle finger up with her free hand. Heather slowed and watched the sordid scene.

Mascara had smeared down her puffy eyes. Her bleach-blonde hair was pulled back in a ponytail that showed her dark roots. She spun back toward them, ready to explode. Then she looked over at the car and recognized Heather. Spinning quickly, she strode up, grabbed the door handle, and jumped in just as Heather braked.

"Drive!" she croaked in a broken voice. Heather floored it as she took a deep drag off of her cigarette. Heather was about to ask, "Where to?" but the half-cry, half-wail that came out with the exhaled smoke choked back her voice.

"Fucking vultures!" Willie's mom wheezed and punched the dashboard. Heather's eyes bulged as she watched the road and the seething woman next to her.

"Motherfuckers," she added and drew deep once again, holding the smoke for a long pause. When she finally exhaled, she seemed to have regained some composure.

"Thanks."

"No problem." She paused. "Are you... OK?"

"Hrrmph." She almost laughed. "Far fucking from it, kiddo. Far fucking from it," she replied, shaking her head and taking another drag. "Shit. I'm sorry," she started, looking for the window button. "I shouldn't be smoking in your car."

"No, don't worry about it. It's fine, really."

She found the button, lowered it, and tossed the butt out. "No smokes. No good for the ba—"

She paused. "Fuck, sorry, I... you know…"

Heather let out a little laugh. "That's ok. It's common knowledge. And pretty obvious," she added, glancing down at her baby bump. Willie's mom gazed out of the window. Another sob and sigh escaped in the silence. She turned and looked at Heather.

"He loved you, you know." It was Heather's turn to choke back a sob. "He thought you hung the moon." Reaching out, she lightly touched Heather's arm. "I know he was just a friend to you, not your... well, you know."

She nodded and smiled.

"But you were great for him. One of the few good ones." Her anger seemed to return. "Not like the rest of them fucking wrestling assholes. And those useless fucking coaches." She shook her head vehemently. "He tried to downplay it. But they bullied him relentlessly. I could see it in him."

She paused again, unconsciously pulling out another cigarette, holding it unlit.

"He kept saying it was fine, he could 'handle it.' I talked to the coaches; I talked to that useless piece of shit, Principal. 'Can you give us an example?' 'Do you have any proof?' 'Any witnesses?' Yeah, I can prove that my fucking kid is coming home miserable every day from your fucking school. How's that for proof, you dumb-ass motherfucker?"

Heather reached to the dashboard and pushed in the thing she thought was a cigarette lighter. Willie's mom smiled and waited for it to pop. A half-smile crept onto her face as she lit up again, cracking the window a bit.

"I think you were the only thing that made it bearable for him." She patted Heather's arm again. "Thank you." She gestured with her cigarette. "Turn right up here."

Heather turned and hoped the news vans didn't want to keep following.

"And another quick right." Heather complied.

"And I hear they're trying to say it was a suicide. Motherfucker," she seethed again. "Did you hear that?"

"No… I… just left. I couldn't stay."

"Well, everybody's texting me, and apparently it's all over Twitter and all that shit," she puffed angrily. "Well, that asshole principal better straighten that shit out. I called that lawyer, Mr. Finnerty. He said he'd set things straight." She shook her head vehemently, the smoke jetting like a dragon's breath. "He wouldn't, not ever," she jabbed with her cigarette, "no matter how much shit they gave him."

She sighed another exhale. "Pull over here." She waited and looked. They were directly behind her house, one street over. "There's a gate between our yards. Mind if I wait, make sure those fuckers are gone?"

"Sure, no problem." Heather put the car in park and sat back. Willie's mom stared vacantly through the windshield.

"It's actually my fault."

"No. You're an awesome mom. He adored you," Heather argued.

Shaking her head lightly in disagreement, she said, "Nahh, I'm kind of a fuck-up. Had him when I was just seventeen. Dumb kid. Hell, he was kinda the parent half the time, always taking care of me." Tears streamed freely down her face. "I shoulda never told him."

Heather was confused but held back from asking a question.

"I actually thought it was kinda funny, y'know, like, 'Hey kid, your mom's still got it.' But he freaked out about it, wanting a description and asking all kinds of questions. I told him, 'Jeez, Willie, calm the fuck down. I'm a waitress; guys stare at my ass all the time. I can take care of myself.' But that's when he dug out the gun." She looked over at Heather's confused face, then waved forward with her nearly done smoke.

"Like I said, I thought it was kinda a joke. I was leaving work a couple of weeks ago, and I was bending over and putting some stuff in my trunk. And I kinda felt like someone was watching me. Waitress a while, and you can almost feel it when someone's checking out your ass. So these two guys are across the street, and I look over my shoulder, and one of 'em's taking a picture. So I stand up and say, 'Did you get a good shot? Take a picture of this,' and I gave them the finger."

A terrible thought crossed Heather's mind. "What did they look like?"

She shrugged. "Hard to tell. It was dark, and they had on hoodies, I think. One guy was big, really broad shoulders, the other smaller." She thought about it for a second. "The bigger guy just laughed and pulled the little guy away." She shook her head again. "So, dumb fuck that I am, I tell Willie. It totally freaked him out. So he dug out the gun I kept in the safe. Hell, I almost forgot I had it. I got it years ago when we used to live in a 'bad' neighborhood." She half-cackled again. "Like this is fucking Nob Hill." She flicked the butt out the window.

She was strangely calm. "That's how I found him. He had all the cleaning stuff and ammo on the table. At first, I thought he might have fallen asleep on the table. I went to lift his head. That's when I saw the blood. It was just a tiny little hole under his chin." She hhmmphed again. "I kept trying to wake him up. But no. The EMTs said it was instantaneous. He never felt a thing." She paused. "I hope they're right." The tears started again.

Chapter 73

Dr. Anari-Kopek glanced around the settling throng in the gymnasium. A bit subdued for high school, but actually pretty good considering the situation. She turned to Principal Dale.

"I believe that keeping this assembly was the wisest course."

He nodded and smiled as he looked around, doing his best "everything's fine" impression for the staff and students.

"If you say so," he agreed, hoping she was right.

At the far end of the gymnasium, the temporary stands were pulled all the way out, exposing the platform that allowed for the setting of a podium and microphone. Hanging above it were several banners. The center banner had a picture of Willie along with the words "We will miss you" in bold italics. To its left was one listing 'Iron Conference Champs,' 'Region V Champs,' and, much to the chagrin of Coach Wolf, 'State Runner-Up.' To the right hung a banner containing the pictures and names of the four individual state champions.

Many parents had been invited and were attending, as this was ostensibly a reward and recognition assembly. The inclusion of a 'celebration' of Willie's life had been hastily superimposed by the powers that be in an attempt to counteract the negative impact of a 'suicide' on the student population and to try to assuage the threats of lawsuits from Willie's mother, who insisted that his death was accidental.

Seated behind and around the podium were school and district administration, as well as the wrestling coaches. Jake Alder, representing the team, sat stoically, staring vacantly ahead. The student body settled into their seats, many of the wrestlers having cleared and saved a spot for family and friends. Heather sat alone on the end of one of the bleachers that surrounded the entry to the trainer's room. On the second row, with a few empty spaces around her, she, like Jake, stared vacantly ahead, waiting for the assembly to begin.

She looked up, startled, as someone slid in next to her.

"Hi," the person whispered into Heather's ear as she slipped an arm around her shoulders and gave her a big hug.

"Hey, Mom," Heather added in surprise. "What are you doing here?" Realizing the harshness of her greeting, she added, "I mean, I'm not getting any awards or recognition; just gotta be here. School and all." She tried to smile.

"Just wanted to see my daughter." She did her best to keep her bright smile. Sliding her arm around Heather's shoulders again, she added, "And I thought it might be a tough day for you."

A tight smile rose on Heather's face, and a few tears escaped her eyes. She wanted to say, "Don't worry, Mom, I won't kill myself," but she controlled herself and actually felt comforted by the arm around her. They sat silently for a moment as the buzz of the crowd swirled around them.

The inevitable screech of the PA system as Principal Dale adjusted the microphone got everyone's attention.

"Thank you," he said, allowing a second for the hum of the crowd to die down. "Thank you, parents, students, administration," he turned and nodded to his guests, "and to our excellent wrestlers."

A roar of a cheer exploded, and he allowed it to die of its own accord before continuing.

"We also wanted to take a moment to remember one of our own, who tragically passed away last weekend in a terrible accident," he added, just as he'd been reminded a thousand times by his guests that morning. "Willie, you will be greatly missed." Although it was already deathly silent, he added, "Please join us in a moment of silence in his memory."

Dale bowed his head and stepped slightly back from the podium. The silence was held for quite some time. Dale finally picked his head up after a cough behind him broke the stillness.

"But today is also about recognizing the success, of which Willie was an integral part, of our Scarlet Knights wrestlers." Another roar, though more subdued, rose and quickly fell. "So let's give a big welcome to our own Coach Wolf."

Dale held out a hand, turning and stepping away from the podium, glad to be leaving.

Coach Wolf deftly adjusted the mic upward (no screech) and welcomed the crowd in a subdued tone.

"We'd also like to welcome the parents and family members who have taken the time to join us today." He nodded to them in recognition. "As Principal Dale said, this is a somber day, yet also a day for recognition." He paused. "But before I begin, I'd like to take a moment to introduce one of our state champs—actually, a two-time state champion."

His eyebrows knit and he paused again as he saw Jon Martin and his father, in full state trooper uniform, enter and climb the stands. For some reason, he'd brought along a half dozen troopers with him. Coach Wolf thought to himself, *Or one of the geniuses from downtown thought we needed extra security.* He shook himself back to the mic in front of him.

"Excuse me," he coughed, many spectators thinking he was choked up over Willie, and began again.

"As I was saying, one of our captains, Jake Adler, who, by the way, has committed to State on a full wrestling scholarship." He paused and allowed a somewhat less-than-normal cheer to rise and fall. "Would like to take a few moments to represent the team."

Wolf stepped back and gestured for Jake to take the podium. As Jake stepped up, he also noticed the troopers spreading out around the room.

"A lot of things have been said, here in the halls and online, about Willie." He pulled in a deep breath to steel himself. "None of them are true." He paused again briefly, the crowd strangely hushed and attentive.

Gazing over the crowd, he began again. "Willie did not kill himself."

Principal Dale winced. *Why did he have to say it?* Dr. Anari-Kopek's brows knit. Ms. Barton seethed.

Jake continued, "And it wasn't an accident." Tears began to stream down his face. Wolf was about to go get him when Jake's bombshell froze him in his seat.

"We killed him."

An audible drawing in of breath ran through the crowd. Jake shook his head up and down, a sob joining the flowing tears.

Dale rose to move toward him and guide him away from the podium, but Jake froze him to his seat.

"No!" he screamed, pulling a 9mm pistol and putting it right up to his temple. The crowd let out a collective gasp yet surprisingly kept their seats as if fascinated by a looming trainwreck. Quietly, the troopers began to move strategically, hands-on holstered weapons, yet cautiously, not trying to inflame the situation.

Jake gazed around the shocked crowd, tears overtaken by resolve.

"It was us, his teammates," he continued. "We drove him to it. We may as well have pulled the trigger."

Now, his head went back and forth.

"We harassed him. We bullied him." Looking toward Juwann. "We even threatened his mother."

Juwann nearly rose, wanting to tell him to shut the hell up, but his mother's hand on his arm kept him still.

Jake looked out over the rapt crowd, a sniffle escaping as he pressed the gun tightly to his temple. He sighed and spoke again.

"He loved wrestling, you know. And he was really good. If it wasn't for us, he'd have been a state champ one day." His voice dropped off. "But not now."

He shook himself.

"There's a tradition here, with wrestling. I don't mean all this stuff," he waved at the banners as if dismissing them. "I mean what we do to each other. Kind of an initiation."

Half the wrestlers and both coaches wanted to leap from their chairs and wrestle Jake to the ground and shut him up, but the gun stayed with them.

Jake continued. "It's called 'checking their oil.' It sounds gross and kind of gay. I'm sorry, but I can't think of another word. It's…"

He struggled for the right words.

"It's wrong, but it was done to me. To all the new varsity wrestlers. Probably to every wrestler for the last fifty years. What happens is that a couple of us hold the new guy down, yank down his shorts, and everyone takes a turn sticking a finger in his...” He paused. “Rectum.”

Eyebrows knit, and a small murmur ran across the crowd.

“We did that to Willie.”

The wrongness of it ran through the minds of all, and a verbal rustle rose slightly, then fell.

Jake scanned the crowd again, his hand tight and shaking as he held the weapon to his skull. His eyes finally found Heather, and he mouthed, “I’m sorry,” toward her.

She continued to sit stoically, watching, seemingly unfazed. Her mother sat confused.

With a final big sigh, Jake continued his story.

“Willie was tough though. Just like the rest of us, he could have dealt with that. But this year was different.” His eyes searched for Heather’s again, but she gazed back evenly. “This year, we had a female wrestler.”

The crowd sat again, silently enthralled.

“And we meant to treat her the same way, the same initiation. But... it got out of control. Willie tried to stop it, but he was small and new, and we pushed him down and held him back. Jon Martin tried to stop us, too. It took three guys to hold him back.”

He hung his head. “But instead of ‘checking her oil,’ we did other things, and I’m the one who held her down...”

That was all Juwann and Marco could stand.

“Sit the hell down, man!” Juwann jumped up and yelled.

"What the fuck!" Marco squeaked, standing up and looking around for support. His parents pulled him back down. Two troopers moved toward Juwann, and his family quickly dragged him to his seat.

Jake just shook his head again.

"We... most of the team," he hesitated, and it came out almost as a whisper, "raped her."

A deep drawing in of breath, many eyes turning toward Heather, who was still sitting stoically, watching Jake fall apart. Her mother gasped and pulled Heather closer with her arm. Heather seemed to not react at all.

Jake seemed to be speaking directly to Heather.

"It was wrong. So wrong. And afterward, we knew it." Once again shaking his head, he went on, "But we were cowards. Instead of coming forward, we swore each other to secrecy. And when Willie wanted to do something about it, we attacked him, pushed him, bullied him, tortured him. Anything to stop our crime from coming out." He nodded up and down. "That's what killed him. Us."

Jake stared at the horrified and fascinated crowd.

"So, there's no going to State. There's no glory here. I'm guilty. We're all guilty. We deserve whatever we get." A giant sob wracked his chest. "Heather, I know you'll never forgive me. Or us. But I'm so, so sorry."

He closed his eyes. A sound of horror arose as what was coming next sank in. But just as his finger tightened to squeeze, a powerful arm forced Jake's arm into the air toward the ceiling. The gun went off with a deafening roar, and pandemonium ensued.

Huge waves of bodies swept down the bleachers, people tumbling and sprawling as they went. The gym floor flooded with panicked forms. The state police tried to create some order, to no avail. Despite there being twelve doors at the end of the gym, a huge throng swarmed against each other like a Walmart Black Friday.

Heather's mom tightened her arm around her daughter, trying to protect her as bodies swarmed past. Heather leaned into her mom, eyes closed to the chaos around her. A hand touched the protecting arm and pulled lightly.

"Come with me."

Mother and daughter turned simultaneously to see Ms. D's worried look, pleading with them to go. They quickly slid out of the bleachers and followed Ms. D as she led them through the gap between the bleachers that led to the training room door.

Meanwhile, Captain Martin jumped into the wrestling pair of Jake Adler and Coach Wolf as they struggled for the gun. He deftly grabbed and snapped back Jake's thumb, likely breaking it. Jake's scream of pain was lost amid the crowd noise as Captain Martin stood and tucked the gun in his belt, then produced a set of handcuffs. Within seconds, Jake was cuffed and subdued while Wolf sat back, winded and in shock.

Ms. Barton called from the squeaking and screeching microphone to exit in an orderly fashion and slow down, but the logjam at the door seemed to finally start to clear, and people streamed out in droves.

When they reached the trainer's door, D flipped through a large ring of keys and thrust the correct one in. They pushed through quickly, and D slammed the door shut behind them. Flipping on the lights, she quickly maneuvered past several golf carts and hit a button that started up the garage door. Heather and her mom followed closely. As the door rose, D turned to them and handed Mom a set of car keys. Pointing to a white Jeep, she quickly instructed, "Take my car but don't go through the driveway. Just jump over the curb and drive right down the entryway."

"But..." Mom started to retort.

"Yes, it's one way, but no one's going to be coming in. Just go. Don't worry about it. It's a Jeep." She gave them a gentle shove. They started to move. "And don't go home. Go someplace quiet, and I'll call you later." She grabbed the still shell-shocked Heather and gave her a quick hug. "You're gonna be okay. Just stay with your mom."

Heather actually gave her a half smile. "I know. Thanks."

D smiled back. "Now go!" She shooed them along.

Heather and her mom jumped in and fired up the Jeep. Mom was crying and on the verge of panic as she ground the gears. Heather lightly touched her arm, the very picture of calm.

"It's okay, Mom. Take a deep breath. There's no hurry."

Something in Heather's serenity flowed into her. She got it in gear and slowly went over the curb and grass, finally heading the wrong way down the school's long, curving entryway. Heather sat back in the passenger seat as Mom got it together and started driving away.

Chuckling, Heather watched the rearview mirror. In reverse, she saw the words on the school's welcome sign: "HOME OF THE SCARLET KNIGHTS." As they drove through the curve, the words disappeared, letter by letter, until they left the mirror entirely. Heather waved to the mirror when they were gone.

Mom tapped the brakes lightly as they crossed out of the entry and onto the adjoining street. She hit the gas, and they were quite a ways from the school when she finally spoke.

"Honey. I'm so sorry."

"Why? You didn't do anything."

"But… I should've. I mean, I should've been there for you."

Heather lightly tapped her arm again. "It's all right. You didn't know."

She pounded the steering wheel with both hands. "Fuck!" she screamed. "I should have stood up to your father then." She shook her head violently, then asked, "Why didn't you come to me? I could've..."

"Done what? Un-rape me? Un-pregnant me?" She laughed harshly. "The milk was already spilled." It was Heather's turn to shake her head. "And what, live with Dad's 'I told you so' and you crying because I'm 'broken'? No thanks." She turned and looked out the side window.

Mom started and stopped several times with a response. Finally, exhaling a deep sigh, she said, "You're right. That's probably how it would have gone. But," she added, pointing a finger in the air, "it doesn't have to go that way now."

"Yeah, right," Heather muttered, noticing they were entering the freeway. "Where are we going?"

"To my place."

Heather turned toward her, her knit brows asking the question.

With a lift of her shoulders and eyebrows, Mom responded, "Your dad and I are… separated."

Heather waited for an explanation.

"I was a coward," Mom said matter-of-factly. "I should never have turned my back on you." She hesitated. "I didn't even realize it at first, but after you were gone awhile, I started to see what I'd become."

Heather just sat there with knit eyebrows.

"Do you remember when I used to work at the law office?"

"Sure."

"I guess you were seven or eight, and your father got promoted to regional manager, and his raise was even more than I made." She shook her head slowly in memory. "So *we* decided it would be a good thing if I quit and stayed home full time. And… it was a good thing. I loved doing everything with you." She paused again, trying to figure out how to express how she felt. "But little by little, I started to fade away. I stopped being me, and it was like I was just 'the wife' and 'the mom.' And pretty soon, I wasn't even really thinking for myself." She hit on a thought. "It's like whenever we went on a long trip, Dad would drive, and I'd just doze off in the passenger seat until we got there. For the last few years, I've been living like that."

Heather interjected, "So, what changed?"

Mom let out a short chuckle. "Oh, just everything."

"Yeah, I guess a few things happened."

Mom smiled and looked over. "I was starting to feel it a little before you wanted to wrestle, but I couldn't quite put my finger on it. When your dad dug his heels in and refused to sign, I didn't really think about you or how this all might affect you. I just signed it to be a brat, you know, just kind of stuck my tongue out at him." She looked over again. "To be totally honest, I didn't really think you'd follow through and stick with it. I thought it was kind of a whim, maybe even just to get his attention."

It was Heather's turn to chuckle dryly. "Well, I stuck with it."

Mom nodded her head. "We started fighting from that point on. Little ticky-tack things at first, then worse and worse. I felt like I was waking up, and I think he'd become very used to 'driving,' and between the two of us... well, I think he just got more and more pissed off."

Shrugging, Heather muttered, "Poor baby," which caused a wry smile from Mom.

"So I called Paul at my old firm, hoping I could start back up as a paralegal. But I kinda lucked out." Switching lanes, she accelerated up to 80. "Ruthie, the office manager, was retiring. So he offered me the job on the spot," she said, looking over with a nod and raised eyebrows. "At three times what I used to make."

"Go, Mom."

"Thank you. So I told your father, and he hit the roof. 'No discussion! Behind his back! Was I having an affair with Paul?'" She shook her head. "So, the fight got bigger, and I walked out." She laughed a little. "Of course, when he found out, I got a deal on my condo rental because Paul is one of the investors... well…"

Heather just shook her head. "Sounds like it really hit the fan."

"Indeed it did. He even changed the locks," she chuckled. "But that's okay. By then, I'd already taken what I needed." Mom stared over toward an exit. "But we've had a few civil conversations since then." There was an awkward silence as they headed off the exit ramp and sat at the light. "I'm not sure how he's gonna handle this, though."

Shrugging her shoulders, Heather gazed out of the passenger window. She watched as they drove a few blocks and turned into a well-landscaped new development. The buildings were gracefully designed and constructed in an in-and-out pattern that made them seem less 'condo-ish' and more individualized. The buildings and lots were also angled in such a way as to create more of an air of privacy. It was a pretty nice place, she admitted to herself.

"Paul did help me a lot, though. It's an end unit that kind of backs up to the pond. It has its own side yard..." She turned down one of the intersecting lanes. "It was a model for a while. They even left some of the furniture. It's got three bedrooms." She glanced over at Heather quickly. "Mine's downstairs. The upstairs has two bedrooms, one larger one with its own bathroom and a smaller one. I'm not using it at all. So…"

Heather quickly cut her off. "Mom, stop."

Mom did. Pulling into a spot beside some colorful bushes, she turned off the car. "I'm behind that bend. Like I said, it's kind of private." They both got out and started following the walkway around the building. Putting an arm around Heather's shoulders, Mom pulled her close as they strolled. Heather did not resist.

They didn't speak as they turned the corner toward the entrance to Mom's condo. A sight caused them both to stop mid-stride.

There, standing in the middle of the cobblestone walk, was her father. They all stood and stared at one another, like gunfighters at high noon. Mom felt Heather tense as if she might bolt, but she squeezed her shoulders a bit tighter and whispered, "Wait. Let's just hear what he has to say."

He took the first step forward as the women stood frozen. Picking up the pace, he came toward them. As he grew close, Heather heard a sound she had never imagined she'd hear—a deep, guttural cry. It sounded almost painful as if it were ripping free from the bottom of his soul. She had never even seen a tear in his eye before, let alone heard this heart-rending sob.

He practically dove into them and pulled them toward him in a full embrace. Heather, in shock, couldn't resist. Mom leaned in and closed her free arm around his shoulders. The cry brought a similar release from both women. Paul Prince choked out a pitiful "I'm so sorry" between sobs. Heather melted into her family's arms.

The three—no, the four—held one another close as if they were one. And though things would be immensely different now, they were, at least, once again, a family.